Natural Selection

Elizabeth MacDougall

Suite 300 – 852 Fort Street
Victoria, BC, Canada V8W 1H8
www.friesenpress.com

Copyright © 2014 by Elizabeth MacDougall
First Edition — 2014

All rights reserved.

No part of this publication may be reproduced in any form, or by any means, electronic or mechanical, including photocopying, recording, or any information browsing, storage, or retrieval system, without permission in writing from the publisher.

This book is a work of fiction. Places, names, characters and incidences are products of the author's imagination, used fictitiously and are not to be construed as true or real. Any comparison to an actual person, event, locale, organization, etc., living or dead, is simply and entirely coincidental.

ISBN
978-1-4602-4562-0 (Hardcover)
978-1-4602-4563-7 (Paperback)
978-1-4602-4564-4 (eBook)

1. Fiction, Mystery & Detective, General

Distributed to the trade by The Ingram Book Company

DEB —
TO A WONDERFUL PERSON!
AND A GREAT MENTOR —
THANKS FOR YOUR SUPPORT!
HOPE YOU ENJOY THE BOOK!

ELIZABETH M.

This is my first novel.

To my mom, brothers and sister, and in-laws of ours; thank you for your love and support over the years.

To Naomi, my niece, for offering assistance and input on the book – much appreciated.

To my colleagues, particularly Barb & Tom; thank you for your acceptance and friendship.

To my land barons, Beth & Duncan; thank you for your friendship, a great place to live and access to two of the sweetest creatures alive; Oreo & Jacob.

To my camping pals, Marg and Nell (and in memory of their husbands Lorenzo and Wes); camping in the fall is always great and made better by your company.

Thank you all so very much!

This is my story – this is my life. *Most of this really happened. Some of the names were not changed, others are purely coincidental and a complete fabrication of my own twisted grey matter.*

Dedicated to

My Mom, Joyce
&
My Dad, Kenneth Cameron MacDougall
(1920-1998)

Only the strongest survive...right?

Natural Selection is a theory brought forth by Charles Darwin, a British scientist, who lived during the eighteen-hundreds. His basic premise was that certain species continue on because they can adapt to their environment.

Individuals that fail to adapt, regardless of strength and size, do not survive; therefore eliminating that particular species and their genetic traits.

Think of it as a group of cave people, all sitting around the fire at night. Those that have the awareness and good sense to stay by the fire are somewhat safe, continue to live and procreate. Those that choose to wander away from the protection of the light, are often struck down by some predator or suffer a fatal injury in the darkness. Thus, they no longer exist.

That is natural selection.

Maybe that's why we still like to hang out by the fire!

ONE

Ten Years Ago

Towards the northeast, the sky was turning a soft, inky hue, a sure sign the day was fading. *A very pleasing colour,* I thought to myself, as I stared blankly upwards between the looming glass and steel towers. Soon the city would be swaddled in blackness. Neon lights cast their harsh gaze upon throngs of urbanites heading home from work and others, like me, who begin their day going into the night.

    I liked living in Toronto. It was the end of April and the days were finally warm, everything sprouted and the purple finches warbled from early morn to evening time. That was the truest indication, at least in my mind, that spring had finally sprung. The city was nice in the summer too. Sometimes the heat and humidity became quite unbearable but that was periodic at best. Fall was always quite pleasant in Hogtown; Toronto, and the rest of Ontario for that matter, had three great seasons. Especially important to me for all the photography I did in my spare time. Winter, on the other hand, could be down-right brutal here. Sparse daylight would speckle through endless mounds of grey concrete. The wind whisked around building corridors so violently it would knock you on your ass. The biting cold penetrated deep down, right to your very bones. Dirty, slushy snow, along with very angry people impeded movement at every turn. The thought of it sent a shiver down my spine and into my toes, snapping me back to reality.

We had started our shift about a half an hour before, at the substation, just north of Bloor and Yonge Streets. Once all the supplies and equipment had been checked and the ambulance fuelled, I confirmed the radio status and vehicle number with dispatch. Our rig was sent to 'stand by' at Gerrard and Yonge Streets. This was a common placement location for our unit, especially at the beginning of a weekend – right smack dab in the heartbeat of the city.

Working the south region in the downtown core of Toronto was just fine with me. We always got good calls and lots of action so the time went by quickly. Now that the warmer weather was here, people-watching filled the intervals between each run.

Ambulance crews worked twelve-hour shifts. Ours presently; Friday night into Tuesday morning, then one day off, back on Wednesday and Thursday nights, then four days off. Then we switched over to days in the reverse order and hours. Start on a Tuesday morning, Wednesday and Thursday off, then back to a four-day work weekend. *Lather, rinse, and repeat.*

My crew partner was Peter Singh. We'd been paired up for the last year or so. Pete was several years younger than me. Not long out of the paramedic program, he was already hitched to a wife and father to a baby girl. He was a good looking kid; light brown skin clear to nary a fault. Almost my height – shorter at five seven but he had one-inch lifts on his heel and boot sole. He topped out at one hundred and seventy pounds; ten more than me but some was accumulating near his gut. *Home cooking will do that.* His hair; jet black, thick and styled up super-cool was what caught those second glances from the senoritas. I thought he must still have a few wild oats to sow 'cause every opportunity, work be damned, he was out chatting up the ladies. He was doing it now as a matter of fact. With him dressed in his dark-blue jump suit, utility belt laden with gear, all the girls wanted to check him out and he didn't mind a bit.

I think I knew more about Pete than most people in my life. That's the thing when working with a partner on a regular basis, you work the same hours and are off the same days so you bond, and inevitably, end up hanging out. At least we did in the beginning. We used to golf a bit in the warm months, played a little tennis together, shared a few BBQ's and some bar hopping with other crew medics. But Pete was a bit off. Hard to pin point exactly – he seemed almost angry. After that first summer, I had nipped it in the bud; no more socializing outside of work. Maybe his being married so young and hog tied to a family was the problem. It seemed to grate on his nerves and he was prone to outbursts and radical behaviour once the booze kicked in. When I started to see those red flags pop up, that was it, I had to phase him out of my off duty personal life. Probably a good thing too; you spend twelve hours a day with someone, then hang out some more after that, it would have to create friction at some point. *I'm not overly social to begin with.*

I busied myself with updating the trip log, which Pete should have been doing because I was driving this week and he was attending, but the sight of some honeys gets the better of the lad and off he goes. No matter. *It's all pension-able time,* as one of my east coast acquaintances would often say.

"You boy's behaving yourselves tonight?" The voice bellowed from back behind the driver's side of the ambulance, out of my view.

I was startled for a sec but knew right away it was Officer Donald Jacobs from 55 Division. Every so often, he'd try and spook me, sneaking around out of my eyes' reach and then whammo! Got you again Stevens! This had been going on for years. Donny's not a psycho, just warped enough for me to really like him.

He had the night beat, from 19:00 (seven p.m.) to 05:00 (five a.m.) and our paths crossed frequently as Pete and I worked the

19:00 to 07:00 hour shift. We would miss him for the most part while on day rotation, as he was on steady nights. The rookie cops, or those with a lot less seniority – they always got the shit shifts. Donny didn't seem to mind, especially in nice weather.

"Yeah, just getting started on the paperwork and waiting for the fun to begin," I said.

"I think its going to be a busy one. The weather is warm, it's going to be a full moon, and those teenage hormones are starting to rage."

"Well I hope you are wrong but wouldn't want to bet on it," and I asked about his family.

Jacobs was close to my age, twenty-six but looking like forty. Working the streets can suck the life right outta'ya. That wasn't all that withered the six-foot, two-hundred-pound structure of a man. His kid was sick. Bad sick with the big 'C' and tied to tubes at Sick Kids Hospital most of his short life.

Donny already had grey hairs in his black, close-cropped head of hair and it was even more pronounced in his well-trimmed Van Dyke around his mouth. Those soft brown eyes were blood shot most times. Poor guy didn't see his wife for more than a few hours a day as she was a perpetual bed side fixture at the hospital. Who could blame her? Their first child, not yet even two years old – sad. What a way to begin, saddled with this horrible disease. Funny how life struggles, pain, and death never seem to take a holiday. Emergency Services see it every single day of the year.

I considered Donny a professional colleague, who over the years had blossomed into a good friend. Prior to him and his wife Peg having their child, both Donny and I had howled at the moon and closed many a tavern, ending up shit faced and silly-ass in the wee hours of too many mornings. Although we both still hung out with our own professional colleagues at times, our relationship was much more cerebral. It was never all shop talk, although a good call has to be shared. It was more diverse, intellectual, to the point of being philosophical. We hadn't spent that much time together outside work lately, due to his family situation and all, but had enjoyed a few tamer get-togethers. He was a real, genuine, straight-from-the-heart kinda guy and I liked him a lot.

"How's the Indian?" he asked holding up his hand in a gesture reminiscent of an old American western.

"He's okay – still lazy and his mind is on other things as you can plainly see," I thumbed in Pete's direction, on the other side of the rig. Pete was now hugging a few of the babes and posing for pictures. *Geezez, what next?*

"Wrong kinda Indian by the way," I astutely pointed out.

Donny put his hand to his mouth signifying 'oops, my bad' as an apology for his failed political correctness.

His radio burped. I couldn't hear the call details as his ear piece was in. Donny listened intently, wrote something in his black book and replied, "Roger dispatch." Then, to me, "Got to motor, the girls are bashing the boys at the strip club!" He rolled his eyes and sported a mischievous grin.

"Stay safe," I responded as I always do when we part.

"Please! It's the Parrot Lounge – how much trouble can I get into over there?"

I added a caveat, "Never know Donny, a couple of the girls may be PMS-ing."

He waved. "See ya Nate," and hustled across Yonge Street.

The Parrot Lounge was a stone's throw from our location. *Good policing service – right on top of the scene,* I thought. Now, how long would it be before we got the call to attend that location and treat one of the ballerinas? *Or patrons, as the case may be.*

As it turned out – no request from dispatch. But ten minutes later, we got a hot call and took off. Lights, siren, speed and precision, the cars parted like the Red Sea, adrenaline flowed and the senses piqued. What a rush. *I love it!*

We had two heart calls in a row. First patient was a frail little old lady with a bit of unstable angina. She was up on the tenth floor of a high-rise building off of Wood Street. Thank goodness, the elevator not only worked but was big enough to lay the stretcher flat. We've had calls before where the lift was about a metre by a metre and a half, at best. Try doing CPR with someone angled half-upright and nowhere to even move. *Geezez!* Turns out she was swallowing her nitro instead of letting it dissolve under the tongue, thus causing the angina to be unstable. *Duh!* We treated with oxygen and some coaching on proper medication usage, and ran a base line strip of the heart rhythm along with standard vitals. Once she was stable, we packed her into the stretcher and zipped over to University and Elm, dropping the nice old bird at Toronto General Hospital ER (Emergency Room) for medical follow-up.

The second call was a bit more complicated. We found the location after a bit of fumbling around. It was a century-old brownstone, over towards the north end of the entertainment district. The residence was so well hidden, behind old-growth trees and a maze of bushes, that you would never even have known a house was tucked in there – very secluded. An older fellow, sixties, with no medical history but complaining of chest pain and shortness of breath, met us at the door. I parked his butt on the sofa immediately and we went the full nine yards on this guy. He was throwing wild, PreVentricularContractions (PVCs) on the heart monitor as soon as we hooked him up and was in substantial distress. We inserted an I.V. line running saline; oxygen, given via nasal cannula; standard vitals of blood pressure, pulse and respirations. The ER doc approved our med request over the radio and lidocaine was administered prior to transport, to counteract the PVC's. We ran hot into Toronto Western Hospital ER, over on Bathurst and Dundas Street West.

Upon arrival, Pete gave a rather terse briefing to the frantic young female nurse and just walked away, dropping a copy of the transport form on top of the patient. I just glared at him as he smiled and actually whistled while he left the room. I stayed and helped stabilize the patient until the nurse got some backup; a male orderly and a staff ER doc.

"You got this or do you need me for a bit?" I asked, as the nurse swung into action.

"I think we're okay, thanks," and her eyes really meant it.

I held her gaze for an embarrassing moment too long. *Wow... great eyes!*

I was in the ER touchdown pod updating my black book and waiting for the next call when the RN from the last patient came over to me.

"Officer Singh?" she asked.

"No, that's my partner you almost met. I'm Nate Stevens, his better half," I said, almost getting her to crack a smile.

"I'm having a bit of trouble reading the stats on the patient you brought in," she said, pointing to several areas on the form after she laid the report in front of me.

Her body pressed into mine as she peered over my shoulder. Her one arm draped across my back and she smelled of something fruity and nice. *Good grief!* I reviewed what Pete had jotted down. *Geezez! The guy was almost useless.* If I hadn't been on the call I would not have known what his notations meant. I deciphered the squiggles for her, hoping I got it right. Pete was nowhere to be seen, having weaseled off some where, to do some thing, other than his actual work.

"My apologies, my partner is a bit young, somewhat lazy, and from that last performance totally unprofessional. I'm his senior and I'll talk to him. If he continues on his wayward march, then management will definitely have a chat and get him in line."

She smiled and patted my shoulder. "Most of the medics that come in are very good – present company included. We get so overworked and short-staffed that an extra pair of hands is really crucial when a patient first arrives. Try and explain that, if he'll listen."

Again our eyes met and there was a definite connection. I felt myself flush and could feel the heat rise up into my face. Those green eyes were not of this world. "And you are?" I asked as my hand moved towards her for a 'howdy do.'

* * *

The rest of the weekend was a steady flow of calls. Saturday night started with a real ghastly punch up outside a scuzzy bar over on Dundas Street East. By the time we arrived, the fight was over, leaving two guys exhausted and covered in blood. The actual injuries weren't that bad, it's just that the face is so vascular that cuts to the head spew red stuff every which way. One combatant came with us for stitches and one went with 'Occifer' Donny to the holding tank. The ragged little puke didn't want to get into the paddy wagon so Donny helped him find his way. It was like watching an oversized guard dog whipping the crap out of a plush chew toy. Donny could not control the grin on his face or the joy in his heart. *He lived for this shit!*

We knocked off a quick stabbing call, down in the entertainment district. Young kid was in for some real pain as he had three good knife jabs to the gut. He was still running his mouth when we snagged him, probably explains how he'd gotten into this predicament in the first place. This call was a 'fast load and rush' delivery; surgery was what was called for. We doused him with a full complement of oxygen, placed multiple abdominal (abdo) pads on the wounds with pressure, then ran hot into Toronto Western ER.

A few early morning car wrecks, known as motor vehicle collisions/accidents (MVCs/MVAs), had us tied up from about 02:00 to 05:00 hours. Can't take chances with rollovers, T-bones and such as the spine might get compromised, so we wrap them up in a cervical collar and KED (Kendrick Extrication Device), then secure on a spine board. I am often amazed at how much the body can get smashed and bounced all over the place and yet remain quite intact on the outside. Problem being, the inside can be all jumbled up. Always gotta watch out for things like busted bones, ruptured organs like the spleen, internal bleeds, brain and spinal damage issues. Sure is fun. *I like puzzles.*

We got tagged for the Sunday night special; a little old lady feeling lonely and complaining she's not very well. A frequent ploy we see near the end of a weekend for someone to get a bit of attention and TLC, in an otherwise vacant life. Funny how they always have their bags packed and are all dressed up when we arrive. Part of the job and we always make sure that's all it is. *Complacency will come back and bite you in the ass.*

There is never a shortage of inebriated regulars, vehicle smash ups, domestic squabbles, psych calls, medical emergencies, stabbings or shootings and of course, a few dead bodies.

Those DBs are actually quite easy for the most part. We confirm the patient meets the Prime Directive (eyes fixed and dilated, no pulse, no respirations. The body, depending on the length of time it has been idle, will be mottled purple and reddish in colour). And, if the body has been idle for more than a few days, then the smell factor will hang with you for the rest of the shift. It's a very definite odour to be sure and certainly one that is never forgotten.

We had a hot call last December; directed to respond to a house over on Cecil Street for a possible heart attack. Yeah right, some heart attack. Apparently an older gent had invited his kids over for Christmas dinner – no big deal right? Problem was his wife had died about four days before that. He had left her on the floor in the bedroom, covered with several blankets, and the heat was cranked to the max to keep her warm. You could smell it out on the street for goodness sake. Poor old gal's body was actually blackening and degrading something awful. That was gruesome! The kids were a bit shook up. *Go figure!*

Anyway, at that point, we wait for the police to close off the scene, they take our names and just like shit through a goose, we're outta there.

I used to count the number of DBs I came across. Once I reached a hundred, there didn't seem to be any point in continuing.

Can't even remember why I started counting in the first place. Perhaps as a mile marker; measuring experience. The public never hears about ninety-nine percent of what goes on in emergency services work – probably a good thing too. No matter how you try to avoid it, you become a bit cynical and develop a rather twisted sense of humour.

I always had a sick sense of life's absurdities, seeing as I have been blessed with some unusual circumstances and personal conundrums. My little secret, kept bottled up tight since childhood, has affected me in a negative manner and ruined any sense of normalcy. *I'm a perfect fit for this job.*

★ ★ ★

On Monday night, about 22:30 hours, Pete and I hovered over an expired male. The guy was probably in his fifties, although it can be hard to tell sometimes. He was lying half-naked on a severely soiled bed at the back of a squalid rooming house. Supine, mouth open, eyes open, pupils fixed and non-reactive, no signs of life… he met the Prime Directive, so we started our notification process.

"Probably a day or so, look at the mottled appearance and the pooling of blood in the lower portions, his scrotum is engorged too."

Pete nodded and I thought about the cause of death. Esophageal varices came to mind; bleed in the throat caused by heavy and prolonged drinking.

Maybe. Not our job to figure out why they die. Certainly enough empty alcohol bottles strewn about. No signs of trauma. Guy was skinny; like no meat what so ever – typical of an alcoholic. Inside the mouth was rotted away, seriously nasty-like. Could be a crackhead too, which would add more damage to the oral passageway. Didn't notice any drug paraphernalia in the room though, so maybe just super-bad dental hygiene. Toronto had hundreds of these types of rooming houses and many a resident ended up exactly like this, or worse, if you can imagine such a fate.

We could hear Donny call out to us as he and another cop bounced down the hall, their combined weight causing the fatigued floor boards to stress with an audible squeak.

"At least it's not a stinker," Donny's partner opined when they entered the small quarters.

They had a look-see at the body, scanned the room, made some funny faces and logged our names and badge numbers. Neither Donny nor his partner touched the body. I don't think they liked doing that. I find it amusing; the reaction of certain people around an expired body – how they conduct themselves around death. A lot of things come into play like religion, upbringing and experience. A person's internal fortitude and intestinal constitution is tested and some of that ends up on the floor occasionally.

"Whaddaya think, Nate?" Donny inquired. "Longer than a day?"

"Barely, if that. Looks like a serious boozehound though; probably had a snoot-full on the weekend too. Coroner can do a body temp and tell you for sure. Want us to stick around some?"

"No, looks straight forward enough. You are clear to go."

"Have fun lads, we'll see you on the next one. Stay safe."

★ ★ ★

The nice thing about this job and about shift work in general, is that you get time off when most others are working and therefore get to conduct your personal business and hobbies with little or no people interference.

On Tuesday morning, my day off after the shift ended, I was still wired and not even close to being sleepy. The day had turned out to be spectacular and I wasn't about to waste it lolling in bed.

By 09:00 hours I was at High Park and caught the early blooms of the cherry blossoms. The ambient light was good and I had the place to myself – hardly a half dozen people around. I grabbed some good landscape pics, playing around with the exposure settings and angles.

After humping a circuit through the trails to the northwest, grabbing photos of various ducks and getting a few artistic shots of trees with sunlight beaming through, I wound around back to about centre of the park. Just southwest of the large parking area of the local restaurant, I landed for a rest, enjoying the view overlooking Lake Ontario. The squirrels and chipmunks were happy to see me, as always, and they received copious amounts of peanuts in the shell. The babies were not out yet, perhaps mid-May and I'd have to come back for sure. They are so perfect when they are young. And it's hilarious to watch them with their first peanut too. I blasted off dozens of shots, catching my furry friends in all sorts of positions. They knew me well and I could touch them easily. I sat for a spell, my family around me, just enjoying the peace and quiet. The fragrance of the blossoms wafted throughout the park, it was awesome. *I come here a lot.*

Using my pump action 100-400mm lens I shot some cedar waxwings. They rested in the holly bush before moving northward for the approaching summer. Such a pretty bird too, their feathery coats so smooth and really waxy looking. Missed a purple martin, he was too fast, or I was too slow for the capture. Sure would have liked to add that guy to my collection.

Decided on an early lunch at that park eatery, the Garden Spot, which is usually quite good. It offers a stellar, southwest view of the park, having windows that wrap around the dining area. I was pondering my next move as I inhaled a BLT and fries. Still wasn't sleepy, might have had something to do with the six large coffees I'd downed during my last shift.

Sometimes, when I had a day off through the week, I would go out to the Toronto islands. A great ferry ride, no crowds and you really felt like you were away from the city. Toronto has an excellent skyline to shoot, both in the daytime and at night. The CN

Tower and Sky Dome are in the backdrop, along with all the new condo buildings and financial district towers, making it seem in a dynamic flux. It was too early in the season to venture out to the islands though, no flower gardens would be planted yet and most of the restaurants and facilities would still be shuttered. I opted for the Queen streetcar back east towards the core of the city, hopping off at Nathan Phillips Square, and walking for a bit.

That afternoon, I was clicking away down near the financial district at King and Bay Streets, making a foray into architectural photography. Toronto is rife with potential. From the interface of old and new at the BCE tower on Bay Street, just north of Front, to many one-hundred-plus-year-old buildings in the downtown core that have been saved and refurbished to their original stature. Most people are in such a hurry that they fail to notice all the detail in, and on, these wonderful structures. Some of the art deco and masonry is certainly unmatched today. From the gargoyles at Old City Hall, the dozens of weird faces carved into the City TV building on Queen West, to the old western scenes at the Post Office down on lower Bay Street. Inside some century-old banks, domed recesses with inlaid tile tapestry form all sorts of patterns and icons. Sometimes you have to pull off the shot inside real quick, as security will get after you. Maybe they think you're gonna use the photo to plan a robbery – who knows? They really are anal about it.

All throughout the lofty financial area, a myriad of art displays are tucked away in various alcoves, nooks and crannies. Everything from a family of elephants to cows, porpoises and abstract sculpture permeate the area. Very cool stuff indeed. That's what I was focusing in on when a voice behind me squeaked.

"Officer Stevens?"

As I turned, my eyes met hers and I knew the nurse from Toronto Western ER was standing right beside me.

She overwhelmed me for a moment as I took in her simple beauty. Gone were the scrubs and tied back blond hair. Her face was at ease and unlined by stress from the profession. A slim, five-foot-eight, one hundred and ten-pound goddess was smiling at me. She wore faded jeans and a simple, pale-olive tee, with a light-cream sweater draped over one arm, and a rather expensive Coach purse slung to one side. And those jade-green eyes; sparkling, magical, my goodness! I stumbled with my words.

"Janet...Janet McSorely from the Toronto Western ER," she quickly reminded me.

"Yes, I remember. I have to say you have the most beautiful eyes I have ever seen in my life."

She blushed a bit. I like that, a girl who doesn't really know just how beautiful and sexy she is and remains grounded, not letting her head swell up. We exchanged the usual pleasantries, asking about work and such. Since both of us had some time, we decided to go for a drink and chat some more.

There was a small bistro two blocks away on the north side of King Street East and I suggested that. I told her it was known for great burgers and lots of eclectic beers on tap. She said it was her kind of place. Five minutes later we were seated at a secluded table, inside the Taps 18, like new lovers on an illicit tryst.

I was awestruck on how we got along. Janet was single and no kids, as was I. She lived for her job, as did I. She liked the outdoors and simple things. Golly gee so do I. She did go out periodically to some bars with friends. *My goodness, as do I! Peas, pod, ayup!* An hour flew by and before we knew it the place was rammed with the after-work crowd. Didn't even notice them come in. *Wow!*

Janet looked at her watch and said she had to go. She needed to get some grocery shopping done for the week, and have an early night, as she started the six a.m. shift at the hospital.

As we were leaving, I stumbled again and tried to get some words out. She took the lead and asked if I would like to come over for dinner one night when she was off. I agreed and told her I looked forward to spending more time with her. Although, when

I spoke, the words came out kinda funny. *Who am I…Cary Grant? My, my…I think Cupid just shot an arrow in my ass!*

We exchanged numbers and addresses. She lived off Eglinton, about three blocks west of Yonge, and I told her I could find it. She would call and square the date and time with me later. She touched my shoulder, turned and left. My jaw dropped a bit as I watched. *Golly do I hate to see you go, but love to watch you walk away.* This had disaster written all over it, again!

★ ★ ★

Wednesday and Thursday were working nights. Pete was acting like Pete and we did our thing. I did have a talk with him about his behaviour and he promised to be better. And he was, for a few hours. I wasn't about to harp on the guy – one mention, one suggestion was all. Pete would have to decide who he wanted to be and how he wanted to act.

This profession takes a certain individual fortitude and personality that many just don't possess. I had my doubts about Pete. I felt he was more dialled-in to the image of a medic than to the job at hand. Time tells all I guess. Besides, who was I to sit in judgement of others? I was just a field grunt. *Stones and glass houses, eh.*

Donny Jacobs came across our path on some calls. We chatted and he told me his kid was stable and might come home for a short stay. I thought that was great news but for some unknown reason, Donny was not as optimistic. Maybe he'd learned not to get his hopes up after all the setbacks. I told him I had a tentative dinner date and he said that it was about time. Not sure what he meant by that. Had I cut myself off from others to a point it was noticeable? I did wonder at times.

★ ★ ★

By 08:00 hours Friday morning, after the last night shift, I reached my home. Well, it wasn't my home per se, as the people upstairs owned the place. I was in the basement apartment. Comfy little place on Rusholme, south of Bloor, in a very nice neighbourhood. Not fancy-shmancy, richy-rich but homes built over one hundred years ago, kept up, and improved upon. Friends of mine owned it. They wanted a good tenant and I wanted a clean, quiet place to reside in. It had worked out very well.

From the backdoor entrance you turned left, headed down split use stairs and entered into a huge kitchen totally upgraded with new cupboards and a double sink. There was an office slash laundry room to the right, a small but functional living room moving forward from the kitchen, and one small bedroom off to the right of that. The washroom had access between the office and bedroom, either way. Shower only. Ceramic tiles covered the floor throughout. For one flat fee I got a washer and dryer inside, heat and hydro, free cable, and the use of a really nice backyard. There was no driveway, street permit-parking only but that didn't matter as I had sold my car quite some time ago – too expensive to operate a vehicle in the city anyway and the Toronto Transit Commission (TTC) got me where I needed to be.

I was just a tad soggy from the rain but glad to be home and have the weekend free. Booker T and the MGs were playing in the background, the land baron's new dogs were visiting, and I was giving them way too many treats as I am prone to do.

One pup, Oreo, was a Border Collie-cross with black on white (she was my little cookie monster) and the other, Jacob, or Jakester as I called him, was a beagle and lab mix; pure black and quite a bit smaller of the two. They were only months old and full of piss and vinegar, the both of 'em. We were wrestling and I was spinning them around on the ceramic tile. They couldn't get a grip – great fun. Having other people's dogs is like having their kids for awhile, you get to do all the fun stuff, then give them back. *Perfect.*

My cell phone rang and as I turned down the music a tad (*can't cut out Booker all together*) the dogs ears perked up.

"Well," I said to Oreo and Jakester, "who could this be?" To the phone I said, "Nate speaking."

"Hi Nate. It's Janet."

"Hello Janet, I was hoping to hear from you. How are things?" My heart went into palpitations and sweat started to form on my brow. *Geezez buddy, calm down.*

She was fine but tired and I briefly thought she might cancel.

"I have the weekend off. If you're still interested I was thinking Saturday, maybe about seven or so."

"Yeah, absolutely, I can do that."

"I don't know what you like to eat. How does pasta and some wine sound?"

"My favourite combination," I replied.

"Great! Got my address?"

"Sure do. No problem."

"Okay, I'll see you then. Bye."

The conversation was short and to the point – my kinda girl. I was really looking forward to this. Then I thought of all the things that usually went wrong. Sweat dripped from my brow and my heart bounded wildly. "What the hell is wrong with me?" The dogs didn't know but wagged their tails and got a biscuit for participating.

I had most of Friday and Saturday to figure out what to wear. Hummed and hawed over the wardrobe. Let's see, home-cooked meal – keep it casual; faded jeans, light-teal tee under a smart grey designer pullover with a V neck to accent the colour and bring out my blue eyes. *That only took an hour ... Geezez.*

I played on the computer and used a photo-processing program to refine some shots. Painted the cherry blossoms in water colour, turned a few of the art deco shots into black and white, worked on a few bird shots from the park visit, along with some older camping shots, then dumped the ones I would never use. Always saved the original photos and the ones I would continue to work on, by creating a back-up on memory. I still didn't trust my computer. Didn't really trust digital cameras yet neither but it was sure growing on me.

Shot my mini crossbow at six or seven metres away, from the living room, through the pass-way and into the kitchen. I had a metre by metre target hanging at the apartment door entrance and I was hitting the bulls-eye near every time. Of course the dogs were not in the apartment and I had backing behind the target so as not to shoot into the wood door itself. *I may be a bit nutty but I'm not stupid.*

Years ago, I had gone with a colleague, on a lark really, to a gun club out in Mississauga and tried rifles, pistols and such. I had always wanted to know how to shoot and handle a weapon like a handgun. Just for knowledge. We saw some archers and tried the old bow and arrow stuff but I was terrible at it. Then I tried a crossbow and was hooked immediately. I used a few free passes to attend the club again, gained some experience and wisdom, but didn't join, as it was a bit 'red neck' for my tastes. Too much testosterone mixed in with misogynistic tendencies and hillbilly behaviours – no thank you.

I did buy my own bow unit at that time and now had two crossbows. One was a larger pro kit; a Harrier, compound cross, one-fifty-five-pound draw, in carbon black with a great 3X32 Hawkeye scope. That was strictly for outdoors and held twenty-two inch arrows. Plus, I had a mini; a Lobo-80, which fired shorter field point arrows. I think it was the control, holding a line, and the measured breathing that attracted me to the weapons. It was like trying to take a handheld photo of an object. It was like each hobby, each discipline, helped improve the other. I also found it very relaxing. Your attention gets dialled in, no outward thoughts or distractions, focused down to a tiny pinpoint moment in time when the release is triggered and the arrow flies.

I don't hunt with them. I love animals too much and would never hurt one unless certain situations called for food, like starving in the woods. And before I even dared shoot inside, I had practiced for years outside. This property was narrow and long, particularly in the back yard, with a stop in the form of a neighbours' brick garage wall. This is where I shot the big Harrier bow at times. Twenty metres away and I could hit centre mass every time. What an awesome 'thwack' sound as the serrated tip of the bolt dug through the target and into the dense hay bale backing. And man alive, does that carbon fibre sliver ever dig in deep!

Once bored with the bow, I played a computer game of solitaire and then a game of speed chess. *I beat the computer, I swear.* Time for bed, at least a brief nap, so as I worked on getting my sleep patterns in sync for day shift starting on Tuesday.

★ ★ ★

Saturday, I slept way too late and blew any chance of getting out early to shoot photos. After amusing myself on the computer for a titch, I watched a movie, shared a sandwich with the puppies, then had an afternoon siesta. The alarm clock shocked me out of a deep coma at 16:30 hours – time to get ready.

Indulging in a long shower, and using up most of the hot water, I dried off and started messing with my hair. Dirty-brown, blond hair, fine but full, had now become my nemesis and would not behave. "Great!" I gelled it, combed it, scrunched it up, shook it out and started again. Finally, after thirty minutes of torture, I ran my fingers through my mane. I was good to go. While getting dressed I caught a few holes of golf on the tube, slathered on some Aramis, brushed my pearly whites and damn near choked on the mouthwash. At 18:00 hours I was headed for the subway.

From my place to Janet's was a fair distance, but on the TTC subway it's a snap. A ten-minute walk to Ossington Station, less if I didn't feed the squirrels, and down through the Delaware entrance. Hop on the eastbound subway train to Yonge and Bloor. Wait for the northbound train, then straight up to Eglinton Station.

She was three blocks west of that and I had twenty-five minutes to spare. I strolled slowly and found the place in fifteen. Hmmm… about ten minutes early. I began to feel the beads of perspiration form again on my brow and my heart was doing that thing again.

"What the hell is wrong with me?" slipped out and I looked around to see if anyone had heard that.

I dawdled for five, mumbled, "Screw it," to myself and bounced up the landing of an eighties-looking, three-storey, beige brick building. Looked like a square block, four apartments per floor, no balconies. Once inside the front door, I was stumped for a sec, *Hmm…twelve units and twelve buzzers… What was the last name…? Mc something…? Ah, McSorely, #304… Ta da!* I rang.

"Nate?"

"At your service, madam." She buzzed me up.

Two flights of stairs; her unit was at the back, with a southeastern exposure. She peeked out of the doorway.

"Hello."

"Hello back," I said.

I walked in and kicked off my hiking boots. Thank goodness I'd remembered to wear socks with no holes in them this time. *Jeepers, that can be embarrassing!*

Janet's place was outstanding. The living room had pale, mint-green walls with white trim, darker wood-laminate floors, and beautiful area rugs along with simple furniture; well built and comfy. She had several high-end prints on the wall and I recognized a Trish Romance immediately. Some other photos of friends and family, I assumed, were well positioned throughout the space. A few personal knickknacks dotted the area – not too many in my humble estimation. Some plants; a pathos and ficus, I think, filled in the room with a few others of which I had no idea what they were. No sign of any pets. Neat and tidy – I could live here. *That's always the litmus test, isn't it?*

Booker T and the MG's were funkin' it up on the CD player. *How interesting.*

"Are you real hungry?" she asked.

"I could wait a bit, no rush."

"Glad to hear that because I'm running a bit behind. Make yourself at home and look around. Feel free to change the music."

I told her that when she'd called me the other day, I'd had the same music on myself.

"Really? I love the old stuff too."

Janet came over and handed me a glass of white wine. "I hope you like chardonnay. I decided to go with Alfredo pasta and cooked some chicken to mix in, that's why I'm a bit tardy."

"Hey, one of my favourite meals and worth waiting for, so don't rush on my account."

I followed her into the small kitchen. Again, neat and tidy – everything had a place. I think she was a clean freak. *Nurses… go figure.*

"I must say your apartment is gorgeous. Have you been here long?"

"About two years now. I used to live down by the hospital, in Little Portugal, but the old house I was in was being sold. So I had to move and just by luck, another nurse was moving out of here and I grabbed it."

We went back to the living room, sat and talked for a bit. Finished the first glass of wine a little too fast – nerves, at least on my part, and poured another. I asked why I hadn't seen her in the ER before.

"Oh, I just transferred down a few weeks ago from the surgery unit. I was there for almost three years and did some floor work, fill-in mostly, in different sections. I've worked ICU and OB too, just trying to increase my knowledge and experience."

I kept the conversation mostly on her. Out of habit I stayed away from personal info, particularly about myself. Self-Defence 101. The wine was hitting me and for some bizarre reason I was tensing up. *I'm an enigma to be sure.*

It was now close to 20:00 hours. "Once I start the pasta and sauce it'll be about fifteen minutes. Okay for me to get going?" she asked.

"Go for it. You want me to do anything – set the table or rip out some flowers from the garden downstairs?"

"Just sit back, relax, and I'll radio you when it's ready Medic Boy."

I did what I was told. This was a great place and Janet was a gem. Booker and the boys were playing "Green Onions."

The meal was tasty. We talked all through it. I told her of my passion for photography and going camping most every September in Algonquin Park. She didn't own a camera and had only camped in smaller parks like the Pinery. Janet thought the whole idea of driving for hours, just to sit in dirt, a little rough for her tastes. *Fair enough*.

She loved movies, simple walks, and bouncing around town when the special events are on in the summer months. She was a perennial at the Pride Parade and loved the area down along Church Street. I found that exceedingly interesting.

We did the dishes together and had a coffee; brewed, not instant. Hugged at the door and I was headed back home by 00:45 hours…still time to catch the subway. What a stellar night. No harm done.

★ ★ ★

Sunday was a bust for taking pictures. Spitting rain and very windy. *Coronation Street* was on tap for the morning. I always tape it and have been watching this British serial forever.

I made my requisite call to the folks; every other Sunday – same old stuff with minor updates and occasionally hearing what my other brothers and sister are doing. We are not a close family. Not an estrangement really, just standard operating procedure. Always been like that. *I was never hugged as a child, that's why I'm this way! Yeah, right.*

Golf was slated in for the late afternoon. Final round on the boob tube, Tiger Woods was tearing up the course, again. This kid had turned out to be a real record-setting golfer. He was sure fun to watch, explosive shots and not afraid to take chances – the exuberance of youth, eh?

★ ★ ★

Monday looked like a promising day, according to the weather channel, so I headed out early. Subway eastbound all the way to Kennedy Station and then a long bus ride, direct to the Toronto Zoo. It was quite a trek, about two hours in all, but worth it. Not many people as usual, no line-ups, free rein. I headed for the tigers first.

Crisp early morning and they should be moving about. I was not disappointed. It was a challenge to shoot through the wire fencing but that is the beauty of digital cameras, you can blast hundreds of shots and then review on site and dump the bad ones. As far as I was concerned, DSLR was a total game-changer over film, especially for this particular application in photography. I got super lucky and nailed the big male cat yawning, his humungous fangs in full view. *I so wanted to go and scratch his belly, beautiful creature.*

Through and out the far side of the African pavilion, I lucked out – cranes with really spiked up crowns wandered about in an outside enclosure and I got them good; full body and close-up head shots. Over towards the penguins and giraffes, then down towards the Canadian exhibit. Pulled some good photos along the way, particularly of the lynx and grizzly bear, then back up the sweeping incline and over towards the polar bears. Always a favourite, especially if they were out playing in the water. Sure wished there were some younger ones.

Nailed some peacocks with their tails spread in full array, they just wander all over the zoo area. Failed to get any shots of the otters – they never slow down, swimming furiously and constantly in their pond…very frustrating. My 100-400 mm lens was good to capture the coyotes. They had a fenced-in, elevated expanse to wander through and would circle the area in packs of three or four.

A snack and drink, then through the Asia area and pavilions. After six hours I was exhausted, my back ached, and I dreaded the two-hour commute back home. Once I got the photos loaded on the computer then I'd know if I really got some good stuff. I had started making my own greeting cards, pasting my photos, usually in a four-by-six size, on card stock, then adding all sorts of words and captions. Sold hundreds of them too! I found the zoo shots could serve numerous purposes, especially for birthdays and what not. I was excited to see the fruits of my labour.

★ ★ ★

Tuesday, 07:00 hours; the start of two weeks on day shift and it would fly by like a trek to the North Pole…slow and arduous. Patient transfers and non-emergent calls filled the days, with only a handful of hot calls. True grunt work and I was beat at the end of every shift.

I had spoken to Janet once on the phone, thanking her for a great night, and we'd arranged to meet for an evening meal on my day off. Neither of us could stay out late, which worked out well as I was always nervous about any relationship getting too serious. They always ended in disaster, yet I crave companionship and closeness just like anyone else. This caused me so much anxiety and stress I could hardly bear it at times.

Day shift meant I missed seeing my one and only friend, Donny, although he did call once to check in on the success of my dinner date from the weekend before. His kid, Andy, was home and doing well. I was grateful. Both that Donny sounded upbeat, and that his boy might finally beat that horrible illness. It was the kid's birthday in about a week too. *I made a wish.*

Pete was behaving in a very distant manner, snarky and curt when he did share any conversation at all. I think his home life was imploding around him. Like a trapped animal, he was lashing out at anyone that came near him. Pete's attitude towards people was not good. I let him drive the entire time, keeping him up front for the whole two weeks. This spared the day-time transfer patients from his wrath. They didn't need any other hardship in their lives, as most were quite ill, getting shuffled back and forth for very uncomfortable tests. Many of these poor souls we cared for were often in the late stages of some nasty disease and just counting down the remaining moments.

★ ★ ★

I made it down to High Park a few times and lucked out, baby squirrels abounded. They are so much fun to watch as they explore and learn about their environment. I sat for hours, totally engrossed, as they bounced around like zany balls of fur. The photos turned out great.

★ ★ ★

Late May, Pete and I were on night rotation again. He was getting worse, the unprincipled behaviour had morphed into utter disdain, not only for the job, but for anyone or thing around him. This was way beyond my pay grade and something for the upper echelon to deal with. He had been surly and downright mean to several patients, staff at two different hospitals, and me. That was just in the last night! This had to go on paper. The guy was stressing me out big time and I had made my mind up that this was the last straw. I planned to phone the night supervisor later, set up an appointment to meet on my day off, then ask for a new partner. Failing that, if the supervisor didn't grant it and had to know why, well, I'd have to file a written report. Didn't want to be that guy but couldn't continue on this way.

* * *

Saturday night, we cruised north along the Yonge Street strip, checking out the action while making our way back to the substation for supplies. We had just handled two MVAs. Both vehicles in each crash had been occupied by high school students celebrating summer's onset, drinking to excess and believing they were invincible. Every year it happens, countless times. Doesn't seem to matter how many educational seminars you do at the high schools, never fails, what a shame. Serious head injuries on one and luckily, minor bone snappage and bumps for the others. When the call went out to the family from the hospital, the parents were going to freak out. *You got some 'xplaining to do Lucy.* I'll say, and good luck getting the car keys again – at least for a few years. The police hadn't laid charges yet, but that was hanging over their heads as well.

At the substation, we filled the ambulance with the prescribed numbers of basic this-and-that stuff, like triangle bandages, abdo pads and Kling wrap. Grabbed a spare femur splint, an extra spine board and KED, changed out the small oxygen cylinder in the Flynn kit and loaded a fully-charged, torpedo-sized main tank of oxygen under the bunk seat. Snatched an assortment of cervical collars and loaded a few more sand bags for bracing the head. Did a fast brush out and straighten up in the back. Gave the vehicle a hose down on the outside, along with a quick wipe off so the rig would look fresh and clean. Ready to rock and roll.

I radioed dispatch and low and behold, "Stand by at Gerrard and Yonge 2810. Notify when 10-7, 23:45 hours."

"Roger, dispatch, 2810 is 10-8."

* * *

It was just past midnight when I swung the vehicle up over the curb and onto a concrete pad. It was a convenient spot just off the roadway that we always used, just meters west of Yonge on Gerrard, across from the Delta Hotel. The nose of the ambulance was facing the street and slightly angled towards Yonge, for optimal viewing of the wildlife. We never knew how long we'd be stuck here so might as well take advantage of the scenery.

I notified dispatch: "2810 10-7 Gerrard and Yonge."

"Hold location 2810, double 0:12 hours."

"Roger."

We waited for the next call, not talking. *Probably a good thing*, I thought, as Pete was not in my good books. I started to people-watch. Downtown was beginning to sizzle with activity, bars going full tilt, buskers and hustlers plying their trade. I spotted a pair of hookers trolling, hoping for a nibble. There's a tough gig. Nothing against the girls, or boys for that matter, that sell what they were given. It's the animals that feel compelled to beat, rape, and rob them that stick in my craw. You can argue all you want as to whether prostitution should be legal or not, the fact remains there will always be a demand for it. *Why do you think they call it the oldest profession?*

The radio had been dead quiet for more than fifteen minutes straight – an ominous sign to be sure. Bar fights and stabbings would break out pretty soon, never failed, especially in the entertainment district. Copious amounts of booze, the ingestion of recreational pharmaceuticals, and inflated egos just don't mix. Cops would be out in force along King Street West and the side streets. The problem had gotten so bad that a moratorium on liquor licences was in place for the whole neighbourhood. No more clubs – period. Even the police horses would be lined up, ready for crowd control. That's how bad it was getting on Saturday nights.

Recently, guns had started to make an appearance downtown. Some clubs countered with metal detectors or security searches. Video surveillance was iffy at best, in and around the district. Many would stash their weapon of choice in the area, close by, so that when the trash talk started inside, they'd just wait outside. Then the gunshots would zip by or the walk-up stabbing would occur. Scary shit, particularly when most of these little hoodlums were only nineteen or twenty years old. Do TV and movies put these images and ideas of behaviour in their heads? Who acts like that? What happened to a bit of self-control? *What the fuck is wrong with the youth of today?*

I watched a steady stream of strange, ugly, beautiful, inane, comical, neurotic and psychotic pass us by. Toronto will give you every look, if you just wait and watch. What a city. Twenty-four hours a day. All freaks and outsiders are welcome in the Big Smoke. *We have no where else to go.*

Some fool was walking by. This kid was wearing his pants halfway down his ass, as was the style of late. His hands and arms were fully occupied, carrying a big whack of take out food. As he walked along, his pants dropped farther and farther down. Now the pants were around his knees and falling fast – what a predicament. He couldn't pull them up 'cause his hands were wholly engaged, and he couldn't walk any farther because he was half-naked and about to trip up. He actually stopped and stood there for what seemed like a minute, thinking on what to do. I was awe struck. *He's gonna be late for his Mensa meeting.*

It was a great night, clear as a bell, warm and not too much of a nasty odour. You get that sometimes in Toronto, depending on the area and businesses surrounding it. And which days are for garbage pickup. My mind wandered; I stared at nothing but saw everything.

"2810 call dispatch." Pete was attending, sitting in the passenger side seat and he snatched the radio before I could.

"2810 go."

"2810, code four, gunshot, John Street at Richmond West, police officer down, police on scene, use caution. Double 0:44 hours."

"Roger dispatch, 2810 is 10-8."

As soon as I heard dispatch relay a code four, the rig was fired up. Given the general location, I floored the ambulance and hit the wigwags and siren. Simplest route, straight south, down Yonge to Richmond, and then Richmond was one-way heading west. Four lanes on Richmond would give me lots of room and I could fly. It would intersect with John Street about two blocks past University Avenue. A vague itch hung in my mind's shadow and I got a shiver as I peeled away.

When driving an emergency vehicle, you still have to obey the rules of the road, meaning that at stoplights and stop signs, you actually have to stop and only proceed when it is safe to do so.

Inside the ambulance is a little round card, changed out daily, from a little round clock device that is attached to the dashboard. It records all the functions of the vehicle; speed, stop and start, lights activated, siren activated; every minute of activity in the rig. I told Pete to pull the 'tach' card and I broke the rules. A cop is a brother or sister to all members of emergency services and they deserved our best effort.

We roared into the Gerrard and Yonge intersection, people scattering like cockroaches, afraid of being squashed. Pete put the siren through all its permutations and a few mutations. Thankfully, most traffic behaved by pulling to the right and stopping. I was totally amped up! Using two feet, one to control the accelerator and one for the brake, I beat the crap out of the rig on this one. I forced cars off to the side and punched the gas. Approaching the Dundas intersection, I'm looking left and Pete is checking right. As soon as I hear my partner yell "Clear!" we blow the light and I hit ninety clicks in seconds. We screamed past the Eaton Centre, the noise from the siren echoing off the closed in cavernous street. It was deafening. Bottle neck ahead – cars blocked my lanes so I pulled into oncoming traffic and forced them over. The ambulance's alternating headlights shone on the faces of the drivers, illuminating their shock and sheer panic at the sight of us coming at them full tilt. *Probably wondering what 'ECNALUBMA' means!*

South of Queen, I braked hard with my left foot and swung westbound onto Richmond, punching the gas with my right foot, and bringing the speed up as fast as I could. I hit a hundred and ten clicks on the flat, anticipating the movements of other cars, traffic lights and pedestrians out in front of me. It was a super-fast boxing match – me against them, I bobbed and weaved and slid under a possible hit. Jammed up intersection ahead, no worries – just pop up on the sidewalk and punched it past the blockage, around parked vehicles – what a ride. We made our destination unscathed and arrived in less than four minutes. The 'tach' card magically slipped back into place.

I notified dispatch: "2810 10-7 John and Richmond, will advise, over."

"Roger 2810, time double 0:47 hours."

The street cop flagged us into a spot in front of a non-descript dance club. *Black brick, black doors, no signage – go figure.* Two police cars had already blocked an area off and a crowd was forming. I killed the lights and grabbed the portable radio from its charger, looping it through my belt clip. Pete and I got out and grabbed all our gear from the back of the rig, loaded up the stretcher and started to move in thirty seconds flat.

The cop hollered, "Inside, first floor at the back, follow me!"

This was serious and that bad-ass itchy irritation tagged along with me. Pete and I hoisted the stretcher and equipment, scaling the half-dozen stairs in front. We trailed the cop, joined by another holding the door open. We rammed through the security area and into the club. The laser lights and strobes made all physical body movement seem stuttered and surreal.

The place was packed. *Where do all these people come from, geezez!* The music was off the charts loud. The uniforms in front, leading the way, were yelling at the kids to "Back the fuck off," and "Clear the way assholes!" One cop even pushed some rubbernecker so hard he fell on his arse. *This was really serious.*

Two more officers were at the entrance to the men's washroom and cleared a path while frantically pointing inside, in a hurry-up motion.

I could smell the urine and acrid stench of the shithole as soon as we entered. There was a small group huddled around a body at the back, just outside a toilet cubicle. A lot of smeared blood was on the floor and dark-red paper towels littered the area.

Pete moved in to have a look and find out what was what. I broke out the equipment from the cases. My mind raced. Think! Ambu-bag, laryngoscope and blade selection, intubation tubes for breathing, monitor, saline solution and lines, Flynn primed and ready with suction and O2, abdo pads to plug the holes. Okay, good start.

"Pete what's happening? What do you need?" I yelled over the monotonous thumping music.

Pete got up from the jumbled mass and came over to me, all casual-like. He put his arm around my shoulder and got close to my ear. "Nate, this guy, a cop they say, has two in the chest – no vitals, man. It's been like over ten minutes and nobody really seemed to be doing CPR. He'll probably be brain dead anyway."

I looked at him, a bit stunned, and barked back, "Bullshit! It's a cop and we work on him regardless. Now let's go! What do you need?"

"Look!" He postured up. "I'm attending and this is my call and I say he meets the Prime Directive and we end it."

I just about flipped out. "You little prick! I'm the senior here! Now *I'm* attending and you will help me or I swear I'll beat your ass to death! Now move!"

I yelled at the cops surrounding the body, "Get outta my way!" and moved in to assess the patient. As soon as I looked down at the cop's bloody face I knew it was Donny, "Oh, Christ, no!" But he wasn't in uniform? No vest!

I checked for breathing and a pulse simultaneously. I was unsure, my own heart and pulse was bounding like mad, I couldn't really tell. I listened to his chest through the stethoscope but the noise in the club was making it damn near impossible to hear anything.

"Pete! I want a number-seven intubation kit, greased and air checked with the large blade attached to the laryngoscope. Now damn it!"

At any other time, I would have used the portable demand valve ventilator in the Flynn kit to start getting oxygen into someone. But this was Donny and I planted my mouth right on him and started in with some forceful breaths. I could taste the blood in his mouth, coppery and sickly sweet. I started compressions. I looked around the dank room. Pete was still screwing about with the scope and blade. I desperately needed bodies that I could count on to help me, right now!

"Get me a line into his vein and run saline wide, fire up the monitor and toss me some of those pads." I was a machine, all the training kicked in and controlled me now.

"Who here knows CPR and has done it on a real body before?"

An older cop stepped up and it looked like I could trust him. "Listen and watch me!" I said. "I want one inch or so compressions at a super-fast rate. Do not break his ribs or you could cause worse damage. I know it's not how you were trained but this is what I want. Every fifteen or so, give him a couple of breaths until I can intubate him. Got it?"

He didn't hesitate and showed he had experience.

"You, take these scissors and cut his shirt off ... do it!"

"You!" A cop I've seen before with a grim look on his face. "Hold these pads over the wounds, tight to his chest."

Pointing to a young female officer, "Go out to the ambulance and bring in a spine board, they're in a sliding compartment by the bench seat ... go now!"

I pried Donny's throat open with the laryngoscope and slid the tube into place. Grabbed the ambu-bag, pumped once to verify it held volume and hooked it onto the tube connector. "Stop compressions for a sec." I pumped in a few breaths.

"You! Hold this bag and when I tell you, squeeze down fully and quickly with both hands and release."

I got my stethoscope positioned and told the cop to squeeze. "Again!" Good breath sounds on the left side. I moved to the right side where Donny had been shot and the two bullets had entered. "Again … again." The tube was in place but I could hear gurgling on the right side a bit. *Fuck it. Good enough.* I inflated the inner balloon with the outer plunger at the side, to hold it in place inside Donny's throat, and locked off the valve. "Start compressions again, go!"

As I did a fast butterfly loop around the tube and Donny's mouth to tape it down, I said, "Now, every break in compressions you squeeze that bag and release at least twice… Got it!"

Pete had a line in and another officer held the bag elevated.

"Let's get that monitor on him, get the leads positioned and snapped into place and see what we got!"

The female office returned with the spine board.

"Where do you want this?"

"Hold it for a minute." I checked Donny's eyes – there was good pupil response. *Pete probably didn't even check, the little prick!*

The monitor came to life but the electronic line stayed flat when the leads connected.

"Paddles and charge to 300. When I say clear everyone goes hands off or you will get a shock. Got it!"

I applied the sticky pads fast, centre chest high and to the left side, lower. We waited for the system to charge. It was only seconds but felt like long, drawn-out minutes.

Green light. "Clear!" All hands left Donny and I applied the charge. Nothing. "Damn it! Charge to 300, let's hit him again. Keep squeezing the bag, Officer and keep chest compressions going too."

I was soaked with sweat already. My back and knees ached from being bent over in an awkward position.

Green light. "Clear!" We left Donny and I zapped him again. Nothing. "Mother fucker! C'mon Donny! Charge to full, all the way to 360!"

Life was tenuous at the best of times and now held in limbo – roll the dice. Craps or a win? Green light. "Clear!" I stared at the screen while activating the paddles and sending the juice through. The charge caused Donny to twitch something fierce. Bingo! A squiggly line, a rhythm of sorts, and it was continuous. *Better than nothing.*

"Pete, run a tape and have a closer look."

I turned to the officers helping me. "Okay, stop chest compressions but you keep bagging. Are you okay?"

The young cop appeared scared; his colour was washed out completely but he nodded he was okay to continue to breathe for Donny. I hooked up the portable oxygen to the ambu-bag and set flow for five litres. "Okay, now every five seconds or so, you breath for Donny. Okay?"

The young officer nodded and went to it.

"Who found him?"

The older cop who was doing compressions said he was first on scene. "I saw him partly in the toilet stall, all twisted and bent up on the floor, so I pulled him out flat and into the open."

I sent another cop for sand bags and a large cervical collar, just in case, telling him which cabinet to grab from and to check under the bunk seat for the bags.

"Now listen up. I need to tilt Donny on his side, see what's leaking behind him and how much damage is back there. This is how we are going to do it."

I had the cop bagging Donny stay put and continue breathing for him. I had the female cop go to the right side with the spine board. Donny had been hit in the right chest. That meant his heart should be okay if we could get it pumping good. I wanted to roll him to the left side, check for holes and spinal damage, plug it up, and slide the spine board under him. I had the older cop grip Donny's head and we rolled him as a single unit.

One hole, well away from the spine! The rest felt intact. *Good stuff!* Some relief flooded my body and energized me. I started to feel that Donny could turn the corner on this one. From the gurgling sounds in his chest, one bullet had hit the lung on the right side. I plugged the back area with abdo pads, slid two joined triangular broad bandages around his chest for pressure, and we positioned him on the spine board. The other bullet was still inside and could have ricocheted anywhere. I suddenly noticed I didn't have any gloves on. After the initial shock at my stupidity, I realized I'd be okay; this was Donny, not some unknown puke off the street.

"Pete! How's our boy?" I shouted as I positioned the collar around Donny's neck, the sand bags going tight to his head.

"It's a fucked rhythm – got over a hundred and ten beat. He's lost a whack of blood and I started another bag of saline. Probably won't make any difference anyhow."

"You stow that shit Pete, right now! Get a BP on him and watch that monitor for any arrhythmias. I want to know immediately. You hear me!"

I could hear mutterings from some cops. The blue line doesn't like quitters.

"Lets cool down a bit and everybody take thirty seconds to relax before we move him." I had a cop on each side hold the spine board elevated at one end for a sec as I looped tape around and clamped Donny's head in place.

I glanced up at all the cops in the washroom. There were at least a dozen; all of them staring squarely at me. I grabbed the portable radio and keyed the unit. "Dispatch call 2810."

They were waiting and answered immediately. "Go ahead 2810."

"Dispatch, we have a male, mid-twenties, shot times two in right chest, one exit wound in back right, significant blood loss, was VSA (Vital Signs Absent) at scene, shocked times three, unstable heart rhythm, unconscious, heart rate now above one-ten, right lung damage, hemo-pneumo thorax. BP... Pete?"

He shook his head.

"BP not attainable, running second bag of saline wide open, we'll be coming in hot once we load, advise which ER, we'll need hands out front and should advise surgery unit ... over."

"Roger 2810. We will have your info when you go 10-8."

I was spent. My back ached and my knees felt bruised. "Okay, we need to load Donny and do this in a smooth, orderly fashion." I leaned over and gripped both sides of the stretcher, pulled the side release, dropping the bed low to the ground.

Everyone was in position. Using the spine board, we moved Donny onto the stretcher and flipped the rack over him to set the monitor on it. The portable oxygen cylinder went into the basket behind the head of the gurney. One cop held the bag of saline. I said to the cop bagging Donny, "You okay to travel with us?" He nodded yes.

We loosely covered Donny's half-naked body with a sheet and then a blanket, and strapped him in for a little ride. We raised the bed height up slightly to make travelling easier.

I got some of the other cops to pick up equipment and we started to move out of the crapper. I hadn't noticed until now but the music was off in the club and the lights were brighter. *Some cop must've really told them to 'grab a cup of shut the fuck up!'*

As we exited the washroom, the crowd parted and seemed subdued. Funny how things seem to appear in slow motion but in reality, go very fast. We had two cops on either side of the stretcher and took the stairs with ease. Out in the street, the whole place was awash with red flashing lights. An epileptic's nightmare – quite a scene! The night air felt great and I gulped it in like I had almost been drowned.

Pete and I straddled the stretcher, dropped the bed flat and heaved Donny up and into the back of the ambulance, locking it in place. My back was screaming at me! Once the gurney was loaded, I had the cop sit in the jump seat at Donny's head, so he could continue bagging. Saline pack got hung from a hook on the wall. I told Pete to drive but not to leave just yet until I could check vitals and we had our hospital ER destination from dispatch. Equipment got tossed in through the side door of the rig. Another cop tapped on the panel of the ambulance. "You need an escort?"

"Talk to my partner up front. When he has the hospital location, you guys can blaze the trail."

I could feel a faint pulse in Donny's wrist. It was weak and thready, definitely something though. This was a good sign. We had some pressure in his vascular system. I ran a tape on the heart monitor, marking the time on it and squinting to read it. The tape printout looked ... okay? Christ, I couldn't focus my eyes. Using the portable unit, I checked the BP as I made other adjustments and got another nod that the cop was still okay to keep breathing for Donny.

The heart rate shown on the monitor was still rapid, getting above one-ten now but that didn't worry me as long as his heart kept pumping. Breath sounds in the chest were good, at least on the left side; oxygen was getting in to the right spot. The BP came up on the screen ... eighty over fifty. I smiled. "Got you now, baby!"

Pete had a destination; Toronto Western ER and all hands were on deck. I told him it was okay to start his run but to keep it smooth.

Sweat poured off my face – my shirt was soaked completely through. The pain in my back was shooting into my head. My knees felt brittle and weak. A few more minutes and I could take a breather.

As we rolled hot towards the hospital, I checked the wounds and they still gushed a bit of blood. Donny's pupil reaction was fast when I scanned his eyes, using my flashlight. Excellent responses so far, hopefully he didn't have any residual brain impairment due to a lack of oxygen. "Hang in there Donny, I got you." I could hear the dispatcher call out the time, 01:34 hours. *That was the toughest 45 minutes of my life.*

From John and Richmond, it was straight west across Richmond to Bathurst and north on Bathurst to Toronto Western Hospital. In minutes, the back doors swung open. As I hopped out of the rig, throwing the saline bag on top of Donny, Pete came around the side. We pulled Donny out and dropped the under carriage of the stretcher with the side release. Just as the wheels slammed into the ground hard, my back cracked under the three hundred and fifty pounds of weight and gave out. I made some kind of high pitched shriek and almost passed out, falling to one side and curling up into a foetal position on the oily pavement.

I screamed, "Someone please take over bagging the patient," and a nurse jumped into the fray. A crowd surrounded Donny and whisked him into the ER.

Still coming in hot, police cars littered the parking area in no time, stopping anywhere a cruiser could fit. One of their own was down – that was personal and hit home. All I could hear, as I lay on the ground, was the cacophony of metal pings from the overheated engines trying to cool down in the early morning air.

The young officer in back of the ambulance, sitting on the jump seat, looked dead. He was staring at me, unblinking, mouth agape and not moving. From the pavement I looked at him and gave a 'thumbs up' sign. He smiled. *Not quite dead.*

The ER team was already through the doors with Donny before I got upright. I shuffled gingerly after them. *I think I hurt myself.*

Going through to the back rooms of the ER, it didn't take but a second to know where they landed. Surgical room A and I knew it well. A crowd of cops hovered and ER staff seemed to be moving at a frenetic pace. But I knew it was all well-oiled, controlled, and precise activity.

The charge nurse saw me struggling to come closer and said, "No you don't, we have all the info we need and you are not looking so good, so come right here and sit down before you fall over."

I did as I was told but watched over my friend's treatment like a fierce hawk protecting her young.

The ER team quickly grabbed chest x-rays and stuck Donny with all sorts of tubes and gadgets. As they wheeled him out and up to surgery, I had one brief, last look at my friend. I didn't see Janet in the group but everyone moved so fast she could have been on shift and in the mix.

Two male cops came over to me and knelt down to my left and right. "That was some amazing shit you pulled off. Nice work!" the one said.

I looked at them and said, "Just part of the service boys," and smiled faintly. Christ, my head was pounding and my back ached like nothing before. I felt sick, like I'd been kicked repeatedly in the guts. I was ready to puke. *Perhaps,* I thought, *this is why working the streets rapidly ages you.*

"Listen, some detectives are investigating at the scene right now and will need to speak with you and your partner as soon as they get here. Do you guys hang around for a bit or are you going to take off soon?"

I knew a supervisor or other manager was going to show up soon and I also knew I was done for the day...night? *Morning?* "Its okay, my back is wrecked. I'll call dispatch on the phone here and tell them we're off service. We'll be around for quite a while yet."

They asked some other questions and took notes. I asked what Donny had been doing at the night club. They didn't know. I guess he could have just been out on the town. Had he walked in and stumbled upon something? I couldn't think straight. It made no sense.

When the nausea passed, I called in and explained the situation. Dispatch advised that Winston Berry was on his way down. Winston was night supervisor and a twenty-year veteran of this type of work. He was a good guy and a friend.

I hung up the red phone at the touchdown pod, and just sat there and stared, unblinking. Running the call through my head, I just felt sick, then became furious. Pete walked by, headed back to the rig with some of our equipment, giving me a look somewhere between a fiendish Mr. Hyde and a comical Mr. Lewis.

You little rat fuck, I thought. The twig snapped in my pea-sized brain. Something welled up in me and I literally saw red and stormed after him. I corralled him in the hall and stood right in his face. "What was that out there at the scene!?"

"Whadda ya mean, bro?"

"Don't you fucking bro me, you lazy shit! Callin' Donny dead, walking away like he is just some poor schmuck and it don't matter!"

"Hey, I didn't know it was your friend. Besides, I call 'em as I see 'em."

I don't think I had ever felt that kind of rage before. It became surreal. I felt myself leave myself. I put everything I had into an over the right hook and contacted Pete's jaw square. He spun against the wall and the equipment fell from his hands, crashing down. His eyes rolled back as he dropped like a sack of gerbils. His body went rigid, splayed out on the floor.

I moved in for the kill, ready to stomp this little bastard into the great beyond when big John grabbed me from behind. He quietly said, "That's it. He's down. Back off."

If you are ever at Toronto Western Hospital ER in the wee hours of the morning and start acting a little stupid, you're gonna meet Big John, the ER orderly. He is six foot-eight, two hundred and fifty pounds of solid muscle, and the best investment this place ever made when it comes to keeping the peace.

I calmed down and did as he said. Winston Berry had just shown up and he asked, "What's going on here? Why is Pete on the floor?"

Big John went about seeing to Pete. I didn't care and slumped back against the wall and slid my ass onto the cold, polished floor.

Winston stood over me. Looking down at me, shaking his head, "Rough call?" he asked.

I looked up at him and barely nodded.

"You don't look so hot, what's up?"

"My back is out."

"Okay, I'll take you off service. This is OHS/Workers comp now, so you get checked by the doc and don't go anywhere until I get the report. Got it?"

I held up my hands and surrendered. I was ready to pass out anyway.

★ ★ ★

I must have dozed for a spell because I was lying on a gurney and didn't recall how I got there. The curtains were drawn and the light was low. I thought for a minute. Had I heard Pete and Winston yelling at each other before? I guess the prick was still alive. I vaguely remembered wanting to kill him. I stared at the ceiling and started counting the little dots on the tile above me. *Strange habit I appear to have.*

Just then, I heard someone familiar ask, "You okay?"

I turned my head in their direction but couldn't make out who it was. "Not sure."

Warm hands touched mine. It was Janet. "You're freezing. I'll get you a warm blanket."

Before I could say, 'don't bother' she was gone. Seconds later, I felt the warmth of the preheated cover go over me. It felt good.

She said, "Everyone's talking about what you did. Saving that cop's life!"

I looked at her in earnest, "Donny's okay?"

"Yup! I thought you would want to know so I checked. He's in the ICU. He's stable. Luckily there wasn't all that much damaged inside; mainly a tear in the lung. Surgery was fast and went well."

Tears welled up and dribbled across my face. She wiped them away.

"What about his cognitive abilities? He may have suffered brain damage. It might have been way longer than four minutes without oxygen."

"Don't know any of that yet. All signs are pointing to a positive outcome. We'll know more a bit later when he's off the ventilator."

I was blubbering like a grade school kid after a first fight.

Janet blotted my face some more, trying to keep up with the water works. "You're a bit emotional Medic Boy." She kissed me lightly on the forehead. "I'll be back later. The doc wants to speak to you about your back and your boss is still out there."

"Winston. Is Pete still here?"

"Oh yeah!" She chuckled.

My heart bounced. I closed my eyes. Christ, I must've hurt him bad.

Janet could see the worry on my face and calmly stated, "Don't fret. He's upstairs in a room for precautionary measures only. You turned his lights out. Once he came around, your boss Winston told him to take a night's rest in our hotel. Possible concussion and all – you know the drill."

I smiled. No second-degree murder rap. I started to doze off.

★ ★ ★

"Nate?"

My eyes opened. I was peering up at a face that I knew well, hovering over me. "Doctor Livingston I presume." His name was actually Dr. Livingston – Guy Livingston.

"The one and only," he said. He scanned my chart. Made some verbal mumbles and scribbled something. "Look, Nate, they tell me you may have hurt your back on that last call. I'm sending you for x-rays. Are you in much pain?"

I thought for a moment. "No, I feel okay now."

"Good. We'll get the ball rolling, so you just relax and leave the driving to us."

"You're the boss. By the way Doc, what time is it?"

He looked at his watch. "Just a few ticks before seven, it's a splendid day out too."

I thought to myself, *Wow, where did five hours go? I was totally out of it.*

Doc Livingston could see what I was thinking and added as he left, "We gave you a shot, to relax you and let you sleep a bit, after that kerfuffle in the hallway."

"Ah." So I did.

* * *

The next four hours were spent being poked and prodded, scanned and tested. I felt used. I got the okay to dress and was directed to take two weeks rest. They would call me and let me know my results when the doctor reviewed the file. I got a script filled for codeine; 30 mg, one hundred tabs. Oh joy! Free, clean pharmacy meds and all perfectly legal. Things were looking up, yes indeedy.

I was still a little stupid from the shot and had trouble tying my shoes but managed to get dressed and work my way out of the ER, in a slow, elderly fashion.

Winston Berry was still there in the waiting room, talking to Larry Carmichael, the day shift supervisor. I went up to them. They asked how I was.

I shrugged. "Not too bad right now."

Winston looked really tired and a bit angry. He and Larry already knew I was on two weeks rest and Winston said he'd square the paperwork for me.

"I guess I'm just gonna head home now."

They both stared at me ... and neither one had a happy face.

"What?"

Winston nodded to Larry and took the lead. "We've got a problem."

"What, somebody steal the ambulance?"

They did not find that funny – not funny at all.

The chat took a serious turn as we sat in a corner. I was gobsmacked. Apparently, my decking Pete was a serious breach in professional etiquette. *Yeah, I have to agree with that.* Furthermore, Pete was gonna "…sue my ass and the departments ass" and wanted me fired, "or else." In addition, expensive equipment had been ruined when it fell from Pete's grip.

Nothing was resolved during the one-sided conversation but Winston told me it would have to go to the top and that I should expect disciplinary action, at the very least. He advised me to contact my union rep forthwith, first thing on Monday.

My, my, I smirked… *forthwith and all that, eh!* I knew they were only doing their job and following protocol. I didn't hold it against either of them. I took a cab home.

★ ★ ★

It was 13:30 hours by the time I slowly crab-walked through my apartment door. Sunday I think. Maybe that's why everything seemed quiet and subdued on the street as I rode home in the taxi.

I could hear the dogs running across the floor above and in a flash they were beside me, asking how my day was. "Hello my little babies! How are you two?" I fed them a few treats then had a few of my own, eagerly gulping down a handful of codeine, which I chased with a cold beer. *Not really the prescribed method. Is it, Doctor Stevens?*

I shooed the dogs out after a bit, closed the door, then parked myself under a hot shower for twenty minutes. Put on sweats and a tee and crawled into bed. "Good night Nate," I mumbled to myself. *Bad night Nate…* I thought in my mind's eye.

★ ★ ★

I woke up several times during the night. Bad dreams as usual, more of those demons nipping at my heels, so to speak. I popped more pills than I should have and chased them down with more beer, passing out again. Codeine binds up your intestinal system. Did you know that? I probably won't poop for a week. *Jeepers!*

★ ★ ★

The radio clock beside the TV, across from my bed, stared at me, unblinking. It showed eleven and the little red dot beside the numbers told me it was in the morning. I didn't really want to get up but did.

I hurt something awful, not just my back but my whole body was rebelling against me. Talk about delayed onset. More pills? No. Ease off those. Be smarter than last night's behaviour.

My bones creaked when I stood up and I quivered on weak legs. Unsteady, waddling along to the bathroom, I had a pee and after, looked in the mirror. "Ouch!" Enough of that and I slowly wandered out to the kitchen and heated some water on the stove.

As I stirred my instant coffee, I thought what was needed might be a bit more petrol in the old gas tank. I poured two fingers of Cardhu, a lovely single malt whisky from Scotland, and chugged it. *One more and I'll behave.* I just sat there, for goodness knows how long.

Forthwith … it reverberated in my head. I looked for a union letter to get the office phone number from it.

Grabbed my cell phone and looked at the screen; six missed calls and four messages waiting. I didn't want to deal with either, especially since I was feeling truly miserable at this point. I shuffled back to the bathroom like an old geezer, stripped and got into the shower, just letting the hot water scald me.

★ ★ ★

It was now 14:00 hours. Union people should be back from lunch and I had to make the call. I knew I was in trouble and I knew I shouldn't have hit Pete. Spilled milk. *Now ya gotta clean it up.*

"CUPE 79, this is Linda. How may I help you?"

"Hi, this is Nate Stevens calling. My supervisor, Winston Berry, suggested I phone you…"

She cut me off and said they were expecting my call and that the chief steward was waiting to speak with me. The chief steward… nobody goes directly to the chief steward… did I just poop my pants? *Maybe codeine doesn't bind up your system that much after all.*

After speaking with David Angelo, the chief steward, I had an appointment to go to their offices at 10:30 hours, on Thursday of that week. He wanted me to have a few days' rest. By his tone, I needed to heed his advice and relax because I thought I was gonna need it.

I scrolled through my calls on the cell. Hit voicemail and started the first one.

"Hi Nate … its Janet. Hope your okay, just a quick update on Officer Donald Jacobs – improving and off the ventilator. Motor skills and cognitive reflexes are good, no real impairment. Call me if you need anything."

I sighed with relief. *Good*, I thought. *Start out on a positive note.* Not so painful –mood better.

"Nate. It's Winston. The union is expecting your call on Monday. Here's the number and don't put this off. Hope you're okay. Bye."

And down I go a bit.

"This is Detective Martin of the Toronto Police Service. I'm investigating the shooting last Sunday morning, involving Officer Jacobs, and I need to get a statement from you. Please call me directly at 416-808-2222, extension fifty-five. And by the way, we're all damn proud of what you did for our officer. It won't be forgotten. Call soon. Thanks."

And back up a bit.

"Officer Stevens this is Conrad Breton, manager of EMS-South Region, I have been briefed on the events of early Sunday morning last, and need you to contact the union immediately. A meeting is being arranged that will be attended by me, Supervisor Berry, and others. This is a priority and we fully expect this to be done forthwith. I'm sorry to hear you were injured on the job. Please follow up and I hope you are okay. Bye"

And back down again! *I'm becoming manic-depressive.*

★ ★ ★

I behaved badly over the next few days, popping pills like they were bits of candy. Swilled copious amounts of Cardhu, pounded back beer, and failed to eat much of anything. I didn't poop either.

I did manage to call Detective Martin and give him my synopsis. He asked a bunch of questions. He could not, or would not, tell me what Donny had been doing at the dance club.

★ ★ ★

At 06:00 hours on Thursday, I was up, showered, and actually had a poop. *Zippity-do-da!* Clean clothes for a meeting I was not looking forward to. Black cargo pants and a white-on-black golf shirt were good enough. Grabbed a spring jacket, just in case, laced up my hiker boots and took off for a real breakfast. The pain was minimal but that could have been due to all the residual booze and meds.

I wanted to stop by and see Donny before the meeting, so I headed towards the Bathurst and Dundas area. There wasn't a good diner open at this time near the hospital so I cut down Rusholme to College, walking east for two blocks, to a neat little place called Cracked, located on the south side of the street. If you didn't know it was there you would walk right past it – just a hole-in-the-wall breakfast place with a small door and even smaller front window. I knew it from past night shifts when we got hungry. They opened at 05:00 hours. I had the 'Big Breakfast' from the menu and finished every little crumb. *Ready for battle, I am, I am.*

Used my TTC Metro Pass to hop on the College streetcar and headed east to Bathurst. Toronto Western was just two blocks south of that so I hoofed it. I was at the hospital well before typical visiting hours but took a chance and went straight up to the ICU.

I rang the buzzer. It didn't buzz because it doesn't. It sends a quiet signal to the nursing station and someone came along smartly. The door opened.

"Hi, my name is…"

The nurse, whom I didn't know, just grabbed my arm and pulled me through the entryway. "We all know who you are, Nate. Janet calls you Medic Boy, isn't that cute? You'll be anxious to see Officer Jacobs and he really wants to see you!"

"He's awake?"

"Oh yes, and bright as a sunny day too!"

And up again, I thought, as she guided me along.

She led me over to a corner in the large, open room. Curtains, not walls, separated all the beds and patients. This allowed for easy access and the movement of large medical devices like portable x-ray machines and such.

I peeked into Donny's area, not sure what to expect. He was lying supine, partially upright, facing me. It was him but he did not look good; pale and washed out, no colour – kinda like he was dead. My heart sank as I saw all the crap he was attached to. Tubes were coming out of his chest. *Bright as a sunny day; Geezez lady, where do you live, in a bat cave?*

Donny opened his eyes and I jumped a bit inside my skin. He looked straight at me. I looked straight back at him. He smiled that silly grin of his then half-waved with his left hand.

And back up again. *Jeepers! How many more of these emotional swings do I get this week?*

I moved slowly, like sneaking up on a small, injured animal, nearing the bed to his good side. He reached up with his left hand

and I reached out. He grabbed my hand hard ... harder than I thought he would have strength for. I couldn't hear what he was trying to say and inched in closer.

"Thaan yoo... Thaan yoo for savinmy life."

Christ! My eyes started to leak and I thought I was gonna lose it. Thankfully a nurse and doctor came in and I backed away, wiping wetness from my face. *When the hell did I become so emotional?*

"Officer Jacobs. I'm Doctor Meadoway. Do you remember me from yesterday?"

"Yeeesh."

"I was the surgeon that operated on you, Sunday morning."

"Yeeesh. Thaan yoo."

"Oh, you're quite welcome. Need some water? Nurse, give Officer Jacobs a sip or two, his mouth is dry. You're doing very well. Do you have any pain?"

"Noo."

"Very good. Now we're going to do a few things around you with the equipment; take some readings and such. You just relax now, nothing for you to fret about."

I stepped back closer to Donny, touched his arm, and told him I'd be back later when they we're done with the tests.

"Thaan yoo."

I spun away, unable to stop the tears. I couldn't wait to get out of that place. My heart just ached. Then I heard it.

"Nice work, Medic Boy!"

I turned back around and Doctor Meadoway was grinning at me. His whole body was jiggling with internal laughter.

I started to say something but he just held up a hand and said, "Relax Nate. I was asked to say it as a joke. But seriously, nice job out there in bringing one of our finest back."

I gave a quick nod of appreciation to him and took my leave. *Right after my meeting at the union office, I'm gonna find Janet and strangle her a bit ... just as a joke mind you.*

★ ★ ★

I had lots of time and strolled eastward, over towards the union office on St. Patrick, just north of Queen West. Fed some squirrels along the way, as I often do. *Don't get me started – it's a long story.*

It was 10:15 hours when I arrived and I had some time to ponder. My mind was a blank slate. Staring up at the crystal-clear blue sky, I didn't know what to make of my situation. Play stupid and keep my mouth shut, came to mind. *I have a plan.*

I walked inside the building and took the elevator to the second floor. I guessed that was Linda sitting at the reception desk. "Hi … Linda?"

"Yes, how can I help you?"

"My name is Nate Stevens and I have a ten-thirty with the chief steward."

"Yes, just have a seat for a bit. They are setting up the big conference room for you."

Oh boy, a whole conference room for me! Seeing as there is just me, there must be a lot of other people coming, if they needed the 'big' conference room.

And down again!

I was just sitting there looking at the floor. The place was worse than a doctor's office, not even a two-year-old magazine for goodness sake.

"Nate Stevens?"

I stood up and faced a short, stout man, probably-early fifties. He sported thick glasses and was balding. He had a Mr. Magoo quality about him. Casual dress pants, shirt and tie. He was not quite a suit, but no longer a field grunt neither.

"Yes." I took his proffered hand and shook it.

"David Angelo. I'm your chief steward at the union."

"Nice to meet you," came out of my mouth, but in retrospect, I would surely have postponed any such meet or greet for an indefinite period of time.

He led me down a narrow hall and as we walked I asked, "So how much trouble am I in?"

"That's what we're going to find out today," he said, pointing into a large double doorway.

I walked into the big conference room, expecting to see a dozen faces peering back at me but it was empty.

He offered me a seat and brought me up to speed.

"The others are not here yet because I told them to come at eleven. I need to have a private chat with you first. I'm not going to lie to you Nate, you're actually in big trouble."

And down I go some more!

Chief Steward David Angelo could paint a pretty picture. I had several problems, according to his analysis of the situation. *Geezez, if he really knew me that would be an understatement.* He read straight from his notes.

"Firstly, striking an officer is a serious occurrence."

I silently agreed with him – a big bad thing to do. Yet, in truth, I felt the prick deserved that smack in the chops, along with numerous kicks to the groin too.

"That offence alone could very well have you fired outright. But…" he conceded, "there are extenuating circumstances, mostly relating to information I have garnered over the past few days, in conversations with supervisory personnel and others, that could be considered."

I'll bet there was, a whole bunch. I listened as he continued.

"Secondly, there could be assault charges laid by police."

I thought about that and highly doubted it. There wasn't a cop in Toronto that would lay that bad boy on me.

"Third, your partner Peter Singh could sue, not only you, but EMS as well."

Apparently, he thought that would be pushing the envelope a tad, but still, within the realm of possibility. A legal opinion was being sought from the city attorney since the threat of legal action had been made, repeatedly. "Also, there was over fifteen thousand dollars in damaged equipment from the fight, although insurance will probably pay for replacement stock."

He explained there would be disciplinary action, at the very least. Suspension most definitely, without pay probably, for maybe a month, to longer terms. There could be a probationary period before full reinstatement. "Any questions so far?" he asked as he turned to look at me.

I shook my head. Quite a summation on his part I thought. I pondered an insanity plea. My mind wandered, I looked up and low and behold, started counting them.

We waited for the others to arrive without talking anymore. Chief Steward Angelo was making copious notes. Kinda 'cover your ass' scribbles, if you will.

★ ★ ★

EMS people are always on time. Have you noticed that? I've noticed that. Precisely at 11:00 hours, a steady little stream of managers; Conrad Breton, and another pair I didn't recognize, came in, followed by supervisors; Winston Berry and Larry Carmichael, then a whack of others, union people I think, and finally Peter Singh. They all looked at me when entering, stern faces on the lot of them.

I guess we do need the big conference room after all. I had to look downward to stifle the grin on my face. Pete sat as far away from me as was geographically possible in this room. *Nice*, I thought, *the little fuck stain hates me.*

Conrad Breton, looking ever-so-dashing in a double-breasted suit, which matched nicely with his ever-so-slightly greying hair, spoke first. He laid out the ground rules and reminded everyone this was an informal, in-camera session to see if we can work a few things out in a fair and equitable manner. How tactful and politically savvy he was. *Fucking suits!*

David Angelo spoke: "Since all the information has not yet been filed formally at the union, any and all comments herein basically do not exist and if anyone objects to that then the meeting is over."

It appeared the union was in a pickle as well. Two unionized employees, two protected unionized employees…what were they to do? I wondered.

Pete spoke up. "I just have one thing to say and I'll make it perfectly clear. Nate goes! He doesn't work for Toronto EMS anymore. If he gets off with a shitty little suspension, I'll sue all of you. I'll put in a grievance every day if I have to and fuck this system and all of you for the rest of my days!"

I have to hand it to Pete – that was pretty darn clear.

"Before you get carried away, Pete," Winston chimed in, "you may want to consider a few things."

Pete was indignant and in no mood to listen to anything.

Winston continued, "Nate took over that call when you apparently wanted to bail on the cop that was shot. My phone, and that of other supervisors and managers, has been ringing constantly for the last few days and people have been telling me exactly what went down at last Sunday's shooting scene."

Pete slunk down a tad in his seat and turned away slightly, feeling the shame and all eyes upon him no doubt.

"They all had the same story so I'm inclined to cut Nate some slack here."

"Pete, I'm David Angelo, the chief steward of the union local that represents both of you."

Pete half-nodded at him.

"If you aren't able to find it in you to let this go and move on, well, I'm afraid everything from this point onward goes on the record and becomes totally official."

Pete glared at the whole room and screamed, "He goes or I fuck you all right up the ass and that's final!" He ended his mini-rant by banging hard on the table with his closed fists.

I was taken aback by that outburst. And quite glad I wasn't sitting anywhere near him, neither.

Nobody said a single word. They just stared at Pete and then each other, for what seemed like several minutes.

I saw one woman, who'd come in with Breton, look at Winston, then Larry, then at Conrad and the other manager. They all nodded.

She looked directly at David Angelo and said, "We're done here."

Ah! She's the lawyer for the city.

Conrad Breton stood and formally ended the meeting by saying, "You will all be notified in writing of any future proceedings."

With that, we were free to go. Pete stormed out in a pissy huff. The others strolled away slowly, talking in muted voices and looking back at me. I sat in the big conference room by myself, looked up and started counting.

About five minutes later I quietly left the union office, heading back west along Queen to find a convenience store and grab a juice. Popped a couple of pills I had with me and wandered slowly back to Toronto Western ICU, to see Donny. It was a magnificent day out, sunny and warm, no need for the jacket I'd brought.

I started to think of the personal demons I was dealing with. I had been talking with psychologists and psychiatrists for over three years now and going to group therapy. These stressors in life brought my issues to the forefront and I was really having trouble coping. A sick feeling came over me. Cold sweat dripped from my brow and armpits. Tension snaked through my whole body creating a constant ache and my hands trembled uncontrollably. Those demons gnawed at the edges of my sanity – more and more. How much longer could I hang on? The options given to me were little more than fantasy. To cure myself I would have to change so radically that death actually seemed like a viable alternative. No one really knew me. Not the real me and what I felt inside. This is why I keep people at a distance and shut them out of my life. No one could accept me. I suddenly became overwhelmed, feeling totally alone in a city of millions. *How curious and strange. How sickening and unbearable.*

★ ★ ★

Donny was awake, had some colour in his face, and was speaking a bit clearer when I saw him again that afternoon. I fussed over him like a mother hen. Was he too cold? "No." Did he want a drink? "No." Did he want me to go? "No." Do you want to be shot with a gun? "No." I sat with him for another twenty minutes until his wife came in to his area of the ICU.

"Hello," she said brightly and smiling.

I got up and shook her hand. "I'm Nate Stevens, a friend of Donny's. We met briefly once, do you remember? It was a few years ago."

She just looked at me with tearful eyes, gave me a big bear hug, and damn near broke my back.

"Oh my... you're much more than a friend to Donny. I know what you did for him! Everybody knows what you did. Thank you so much for not giving up!"

"Glad I could help," was the only thing I could choke out.

I spoke to her a bit more while she tended to Donny, plumping his pillows and washing his face. I did not ask about their child, as they didn't need anything else on their mind to worry about.

I finally said good bye to Donny and Peg, turned and headed out to give them their privacy when Donny's wife said, "Thanks again Medic Boy!" and I heard Donny let out a subdued cackle.

The comment caused a brief stutter-step but I didn't even look back, just shook my head and kept walking. Finally relieved, a weight off my shoulders, I knew then that everything was going to be okay for my good friend.

As I headed down the elevator, I couldn't wait to get my hands on Janet. I hunted her for a bit but she was no where to be found, lucky girl.

★ ★ ★

The weekend was a blur. I was too exhausted to go out and take pictures and, with my sore back couldn't carry the cameras and equipment anyway. I edited photos with the computer to the point I could do no more, except start printing shots, and I didn't want to go downtown on a weekend to process them. Grocery shopping, at the Dufferin Mall around the corner, used up some time and got me out of the apartment for a spell. Using a bundle buggy to haul my groceries and limit the strain, I fed squirrels on the way there and back. I bought crap food; microwave shit and snacks, what a diet.

I couldn't lie in bed all day and night because my demons crept in too easily. It seemed that drinking alcohol and popping pills was the only sane way to deaden the pain and scare off the banshees. I had half a bottle of Cardhu left, about fifty codeine pills, some beer and a stack of DVDs. "What the hell," I said to the dogs. Movies while drunk and high seemed appropriate. The puppies and I cocooned for days. The monotonous lure of the two-dimensional people was broken only by sporadic pee breaks and snarfing down food when needed. Janet called with updates and kept pushing me to come over. I kept putting her off.

★ ★ ★

Monday morning was not pleasant at all. The hangover was one part nausea, two parts headache, and a jigger of guilt. Somehow, I had wound up with puppy fur in my mouth. I thought of 'hair of the dog' but that would only be short-lived at best. I knew this because for the last few days, that had been my solution. I didn't grin but I did bear it. After numerous coffees and some toast, I had the energy to check my cell. One voice mail from the hospital, I called.

Apparently, Doctor Livingston wanted to see me about my test results and have a consult, could I come in this afternoon about 14:30 hours? I could and would, letting the office assistant know.

This would work out well. Go see Doc Livingston, then visit Donny, and then strangle Janet. *Three birds… one stone. Ayup!*

★ ★ ★

I was at Toronto Western by 14:15 hours and went to the intake desk. The admin person advised me, "Dr. Livingston is just finishing some paper work and will see you shortly. Please take a seat."

Sitting on a rock-hard chair, I blurted out, "Great, two-year old magazines, my favourite!" No one found my insightful gibe funny. I ignored them. Not busy in the ER at this time – I watched a few of the suffering and their antics for entertainment while pretending to leaf through a shitty magazine. Ten minutes later, Doc Livingston came out and got me, leading me back to an office area.

I don't think it was his private office but more a generic one, which several doctors used and worked out of. It was sparse. No personal knick-knacks; sterile. No emotion, just 'matter of fact' discussions took place here like; you're better, you're worse, you're dying, take this.

I sat down on the only chair, other than the one at the desk, as he flopped into that one. Doc Livingston just stared at me then said, "Now, how are you feeling, Medic Boy?"

I heard a laughing screech outside the half-open door and I knew right away it was Janet.

"Damn it!" I got up and went through to the hall only to see her and a few other nurses running down the corridor in fits. I came back into the office and Doc Livingston was grinning ear to ear.

"Sorry, she made me do it."

"You know this could scar me for life, Doc."

He just shook his head and opened the file. "You know Nate, that there girl is a real fine nurse and she is crazy about you."

I looked him dead square in the eyes and said, "I know what you're trying to do and you shouldn't. It would never work out."

He was puzzled. Then the proverbial light bulb went off, "Oh god Nate, I'm sorry. I never know who's gay or straight. Really I'm sorry and so insensitive."

"Its way more complicated than that and just for the record, I'm not gay. But that might make things easier."

He was truly perplexed and I know he wanted to discuss this further but thankfully he let it go.

"Okay, let us get down to it. Nate ... I got some bad news. Your spine is a serious mess."

Well don't sugar-coat it Doc, give it to me straight. "What's the problem?"

"Basically," he said, "bone loss has caused deterioration in the spine and you have two areas of weak discs, in the lumbar and thoracic sections. They are twisted up bad, full of scar tissue, and obviously degrading and getting worse over time."

A silly, crooked smile crossed my face. *Weightlifting patients will do that.*

"The x-rays show previous surgery on your spine, in the lumbar region. What happened there?"

I explained that as a young kid, about thirteen years old, I'd had trouble walking and was in a terrible amount of pain. It started out as periodic episodes, then I spent more than a year in and out of hospital – they couldn't figure out what the problem was, even after numerous tests and such. After lying in bed month after month, in agony mind you, they decided it might not just be 'all in my head', so surgery was opted for. They removed the spinal tips in the lumbar section, and repaired a bunch of ganglia and some other stuff that was of concern. I was fine after that. I was just happy to be pain-free and able to walk half-ways normal, even if the rest of me was ruined forever.

"Well, you need to go see a specialist for a consult and other tests, plus rehab. Start on some calcium builders and other helpful drugs, to stop the bone deterioration and maybe get the discs and other areas improved. You may need more surgery."

"I guess sports and such are out of the question?"

Doc Livingston said it looked like a seventy-year-old's spine. I could not go back to doing the ambulance work or it would be disastrous and put me in a wheelchair, or worse, for the rest of my life. To do any sports like golf or tennis or skiing could also be a risk, I should avoid anything that caused torque, twisting or hard compression of the back and spine.

He gave me a script for a muscle-relaxing med and two hundred more codeine. He also had to forward a copy of the report to EMS, since it was an OHS/WCB claim and he was legally bound to. Before I left his office, Doc Livingston gave me a copy of the report so I could digest it at my own pace. The office would call with the referral info. He was truly sorry.

After filling the script at the hospital, I wandered over to a liquor store, picked up two more bottles of Cardhu along with several six-packs of imported beer, for appetizers, and headed home. I didn't go visit Donny and didn't bother with Janet.

★ ★ ★

I was sitting in my swivel-rocker lounge chair, bouncing to the tunes of Dire Straits with the dogs at my feet. The Cardhu was evaporating, right in front of my eyes. I was ripped, from the booze and drugs. This shit from Doc Livingston was topnotch. One must savour these brief opportunities of being paid to not work. My life was changing in monumental leaps and bounds. *I'm coping well.* Time had little meaning I thought, drifting by, unconcerned with me, like a little seedling blowing in the wind… *Whoa, I guess that's why they call it dope. Smarten up.*

I remained slug-like for days. Even the dogs seemed concerned. At least until they had cookies and belly scratches, then all was right with their world. Periodic updates from Peg regarding Donny's progress. He was asking for me. Try and stop by soon.

★ ★ ★

On Friday, a voicemail left me feeling apprehensive. Conrad had phoned and a meeting was set for Monday at the union office for just me, him, Winston, David, and a city attorney. Pete was not invited. Be there at 10:00. Remain off work. Click.

★ ★ ★

I toyed with my mini crossbow while totally buzzed, then foolishly decided to shoot some targets. The first one hit wide left, about a foot off bulls-eye but still on the protective backing board. I overcompensated as the next carved a groove off the side of my kitchen counter end gable and lodged deep into the entryway door jamb.

"Oops!" I felt a chunk of change drop from my security deposit and quit. Perhaps my judgement was impaired.

I invented reasons to go out and walk for a bit, just to get out and walk for a bit. The walls were closing in and I felt like a trapped bug. At least the weather was nice. Early June and I hadn't taken a picture in what seemed like weeks. This was making me even more crazy and frustrated.

I finally caved and met Janet for a quick lunch on Sunday, over at the hospital. She was pressing me for more time together and I could see where this was headed. Same place it always went and I just couldn't face it again. I almost told her what was going on – I should have. I hate even the illusion of being untruthful. Half of me wanted her friendship and warmth desperately. The other half cringed at the thought of another cycle of frustration and internal anguish.

I popped up and saw Donny. He was much improved; getting up now and glad he could actually go to the bathroom, in a real bathroom. Funny how we miss those simple things in everyday life, once they are taken away. He would be going home in a week if all went well. The recovery was excellent – no infections or complications. He could get nursing at the house for a spell. Light duty at work, maybe, in another few weeks after that. He was looking forward to watching TV and hanging out with his kid more.

★ ★ ★

I got ready for the meeting and was out the door about 09:00 hours on Monday, with a jacket and umbrella 'cause rain was threatening from the east.

I had five minutes to spare as I entered the union building and was greeted by Linda at the second floor reception. She ushered me right in to the big conference room where everyone else was present and looked like they had been for awhile. Papers were strewn all over the table, along with open computer laptops and legal pads.

Winston stood, welcomed me in and closed the door. I sat and waited for the bad news. *Play stupid, speak not.* It was my only defence.

Conrad took the lead, introduced the city lawyer and said they had a number of things to discuss with me.

A simple nod was all I could muster.

"Nate, we have received the medical documents and report from a Doctor Livingston at Toronto Western Hospital. Your injury and back issues are going to keep you off work, probably for good."

He let me chew on that for a moment. He was setting me up for the offer.

He continued, "You have done some great work while on the job, Nate. I couldn't be more proud of how you handled that last call."

Have done some great work – the past tense...Uh oh, here it comes. I squirmed in the seat, preferring a fast and hard hit, as opposed to a slow and agonizing drag across the keel.

"We have a mixed solution that we want you to consider. It solves a number of issues and is fair to everyone, in our opinion."

The master at work, I thought, *giving me silent breaks in between each course he feeds me.* Now, just a tad longer, so the concept permeates my brain. What a perfect set up and delivery on Conrad's part.

"This is what we propose."

My mood was flat. I just started walking, with no direction or destination in mind. It was raining lightly. I didn't take any notice. I had left the umbrella back at the union office.

I found a sprawling elm tree near the Osgoode courts on Queen West, stood underneath it, fished out some peanuts, and tossed them to my friends. The squirrels sat close and enjoyed their morsels. I got some comfort from their presence. "Now what am I to do?" I said to them but they didn't answer me. *That would be weird if they did though.* I half giggled to myself.

The content and outcome of the meeting percolated through my mind. I had to admit, the offer was good, even though I was out of EMS. That was made clear and was final. Not so much because I decked Pete … I think both Conrad and Winston felt that was justified. "Just too bad it wasn't done outside of work," they had whispered to me. I was actually quite relieved they didn't offer me desk work, dispatch duty, or any other menial position. Perhaps they couldn't, due to their fear of, and the threat of, a law suit.

On the plus side, worker's comp for the injury, rehab, and retraining would be provided, as would all benefits. Certainly much more than even I would have expected. Somehow that just seemed too good. *It was too good.* Maybe higher forces had intervened. The 'blue line' was not to be trifled with. It would have taken one call and a two-minute conversation. They obviously had my back, so to speak.

The real downside ... I lose a job I love, although I wouldn't be able to do it anymore with the serious back problems, so why fret over spilled milk, eh? Why indeed. Because EMS was my life and I couldn't see into the future without it. *That's why, Einstein!* I'd buried myself in that job just to retain my sanity, staying focused on other people's problems instead of my own. I'd been hanging on by a thread at best, and now this!

I bounced a peanut off a squirrel's head, not intentionally mind you, just happens sometimes when you toss one at them. "Sorry!" He got an extra one for the indignity.

I thought to myself ... with the other issues in my life ... a fresh start? Could it work? Was this the time to go for broke? They'd given me a week to think it over. They would tell Pete I was out. That would satisfy him and he didn't need to know any other details – period.

The rain came down harder and I was totally bummed out. Didn't even go and see Donny.

★ ★ ★

Handed another week of being paid not to work, except on making a decision. Some people could get used to this, I mused.

The days passed and I floated in a fog. I never left the house. Janet called and wanted to come over but I pushed her away, nicely. Peg called to give me an update on Donny but I didn't go and see him. The upstairs land barons dropped by with some food to cheer me up and made sure the dogs kept me company. I think they knew something was seriously wrong but I couldn't talk to them about it, not yet anyway. One bottle of Cardhu was punished repeatedly. I always added some pills as garnish to my drinks and pounded back beer in between sips. I had asked Oreo and Jakester their opinion of the whole mess but they sat mute. Smart dogs! They knew which side their biscuits were buttered.

★ ★ ★

I was sitting in silence. It wasn't just an offer. It was what I was getting. There were no 'ifs' or 'buts'. This was my package deal and I'd better get used to it. I just kept rolling it over and over. By the weekend, it came to me like a flash bulb going off in a cartoon.

I knew what my decision was. I had no choice. I couldn't wait any more! My heart started to flutter and beads of sweat formed on my brow and I knew now what I was going to do about those demons in my life. What was the worst that could happen to me? I could die, so what? That would be better than living like this. Because living like this was just more of the same; more pain, more grief, more depression and frustration, never allowing anyone into my world because I always feared they would hate me and despise me, and then I lost everyone. A vicious cycle – never ending! I was a fish swimming upstream, like those salmon returning to their spawning grounds, but I was always swimming up stream. It never ended! Either I would make it, or die trying. I set my mind right … then I threw up. But it was only booze and some half dissolved pills.

★ ★ ★

I called Conrad on Monday morning, first thing, and agreed to the deal. He would start the paperwork, which I thought was probably already done. They knew I had to take it. I gave him the combination to my locker and said anything they could use, keep. The rest was garbage. *Cut the cord quick*, I thought.

I would have to go in to the admin office for document sign-off and such, the WCB would contact me. Dr. Livingston and

EMS would notify anyone else that had to have any info and make referrals for me.

And just like that, I closed out a brief, seven-year career as Medic Boy! *Now,* I painfully thought, *time for the tough stuff.*

The sweats came first. Then a dash of nausea and an all-over body ache, extremity shakes rounded out my symptoms of dread.

★ ★ ★

Other than a few doctors and some group therapy individuals, what no one knew, or if they suspected never spoke of, was that I suffered from Gender Dysphoria. And when I say suffered, I mean suffered. My very core was disrupted, perpetually. It's a nasty disorder that affects about 1 in 300,000 people. Actually that ratio may be incorrect – I believe there are many more.

As a young child, I knew there was something amiss. I had no understanding of what that was. There were no words I knew of to put it into some sort of context. Into my early teens, I realized that I wasn't gay; my sexual orientation was definitely towards women. This was super weird. The one thing I knew for sure was not to share my feelings with anyone. No one could grasp this. No one, not even a doctor, could understand this. Any mention of gender or of being gay, in general conversation, was hit with cruel and unrelenting hatred and ultra-vile comments and jokes. From everyone around me; family, school peers, medical people – didn't matter. That was my reality. I was totally alone. I buried all feelings inside. The stress was enormous. Some days I actually prayed for a quick death.

I started to hear about men and women trapped inside the opposite gender's body. Hard to believe and yet it was happening to me. As I grew to adulthood, there was continued private cross-dressing and experimentation. Was I just a transvestite? Was it just a fetish? This is quite common in straight men, I had learned. The stress only increased as I aged. Available information on the subject was limited and seemed almost infantile in nature. I was truly trapped in an invisible cell, with no way out.

After a life of agony and suffering in silence, I started to make inquiries, see psychologists and psychiatrists, and attending group sessions with other sad souls with similar afflictions at the Clarke Institute on College Street. I was not alone but I was by myself, as it was all new to me. Of course, during work as a medic in downtown Toronto, I came across a few gender benders. I had to remain distant and professional. This though, was the first time in my life that I had actually met and interacted with other people in various degrees of transition from one gender to the other. *Not always a pretty sight!*

The stressors in my life seemed to bring on bouts of depression and the realization I was screwed. I was a man. I looked like a man. I was not a passable woman, even when I tried to dress like one. There was no way out, I was doomed, as was every relationship I'd ever had. I was not afraid of death, that's one thing I knew for sure. It could not come soon enough. Imagine that! Maybe that explains my behaviour at times; the chances taken, abuse of drugs and booze, no fear. It explains why I dreaded making friends or getting close in a relationship with a woman. How do you explain this? How do you explain your frustration and anger at times; what you are feeling and why? Being close to a woman makes you really aware that you are not one too. Quite frankly, anyone that doesn't suffer from this disorder can never know just how debilitating it really is. And anyone that doesn't suffer from a gender identity syndrome isn't about to give it much thought. Simply because it is so alien and mind-numbingly freaky that it causes discomfort just pondering the idea.

The other thing I knew for sure was that make-up does not do what it shows in those stupid commercials on television. I should write the manufacturer of those products and tell them if you really want to show your product is remarkable, try it on me and show how dramatic the results are. *Yeah right!*

My life was such a mess and I was so tired of the torment, trying to be something I was definitely not that I made the decision. To take this opportunity and find out, even if it killed me, whether I could make the changes necessary and find some kind of internal peace and be able to live with myself for once. I was totally scared and freaked-out, and yet somehow a liberating feeling was washing over me. *Maybe that's just the booze and pills.*

I drank Cardhu until I passed out.

Two

The Last Ten Years

The last decade of my life has been surreal, to say the least. A whirlwind of self-discovery, personal growth, and physical evolution transpired.

Since leaving EMS, every waking moment of the first two years was spent getting to the point where I could start feeling 'not so obvious' in public while presenting in the female role. You need a strong mind and tough skin, baby! I put the blinkers on, stared straight ahead, and with a total conviction set forth on what seemed like an impossible journey.

Of course, the workers comp people didn't like this very much. To them I was no longer disabled, as gender dysphoria and the changing of one's gender was not considered part of my injury claim. Therefore, my benefits were cut, since I was not actively engaged in pursuing work or training all of the time. What could I do but carry on and deplete all my savings and assets, while in pursuit of my goal.

In Ontario, we have a no-fault system in place called Worker's Compensation. They assist injured workers, or so one might think.

The Workers Compensation Board, known as the WCB, decided to change its name to the Workplace Safety and Insurance Board, now known as the WSIB. They were going to focus more on safety and on ensuring workers didn't get injured in the first place, or so one might think. They built a brand-new, twenty-something storey building in the heart of Toronto, right downtown on real expensive property, to serve the injured workers, or so one might think. What a racket! If you have never been through the discomfort and humiliation of dealing with these boobs, avoid it at all costs. However, I'm a true believer in karma; what goes around comes around kinda thing. *I pity the fools!*

★ ★ ★

Changing your gender (transsexual) is no easy task. The learning curve is steep, particularly for a male-to-female, heterosexual, transgender person. I say this because homosexual transgender persons (men and women who are gay and also suffer from gender identity issues), may actually have had more exposure to situations and information than not. This doesn't always make it easier; it is just an observation.

The first order of business – finding a doctor that is even willing to start treatment and hormone therapy. A trial and error exercise at best, but it can be done. My approach was simple, be straightforward and explain as best I could. I went to several physicians and finally landed on a very helpful young man in an office not far from home. He first wanted to verify my resolve and check with the Clarke gender clinic on the veracity of my claim. Easy enough and proven, the relationship between doctor and patient, both of us learning as we went, was a good one. Once the requisite pros and cons of hormone therapy were discussed, I started on female hormones. The first were actual birth control pills, then a med called Premarin. I was moving forward at last. Hope finally made a brief appearance, peeking through the curtain, spurring me onward.

Next step, electrolysis of the facial hair, the only way it can be done. No small matter, it is a long drawn-out, agonizingly painful necessity, which takes years and costs a fortune. Again, by my being straight forward and explaining what I was planning, it was easily arranged. The owner of the personal service business discussed it with her staff and ensured that whoever took me on as a client was as committed as I. She was aware of individuals who had requested such treatment before and was not only sympathetic to my needs but seemed really motivated to provide excellent service. This is one step that often precludes male to female individuals from pursuing a full gender change, or at least slows them down. The time and cost are prohibitive, to say the least, not to mention the pain involved. I am not ashamed to tell you, I shed a lot of tears. In two years, going twice a week every week for two hours each visit, I had finally removed enough growth of facial hair to think about the next step.

Now you have to decide on an unambiguous female name. No way do they (the gender clinic gate-keepers), allow for 'Jamie', or 'Laurie', or 'Brook', no way. And go ahead, try and do it. Just for fun, choose a name and try and live with it. Then change all those documents, which still have that big fat M for male on it as a designation of gender. That is, until the surgery is completed and they (the government agencies) have a surgeon's letter as proof you are now female in the biblical sense. So after months of people suggesting names, I landed on a typical Scottish derivative; Elizabeth Anne Stevens. Now off to a lawyer to change the initial documents. Finally a process that was inexpensive, pain-free and easily accomplished. Although, I didn't account for my dad's twisted mind whilst choosing this new moniker, as he started calling me '*EASy*'.

I had a new name and the documents to prove it. My hair was longer – time for a good cut, style and highlights. Pierce the ears? Surely, might as well while I'm here at the salon. Change bank documents – give proof. Change drivers licence – give proof. Change social insurance number – must have proof. The list was endless. Funny how that one box on virtually every form we fill out countless times throughout life has such powerful ramifications; a domino effect. I eventually knocked every single one of them down.

★ ★ ★

In year three; continue as per with the electrolysis, hormones starting to add curves to the right places, and the daunting task of dressing more to the female persuasion was upon me. You've probably seen a drag queen or two slinking around, be it at a Pride event or even Halloween (a very good time to indulge those desires in public, as many gay and straight men will attest to, if honest) but I wasn't after that "flaming" look. As in nature, the female often appears drab and colourless, and blends in for obvious reasons of survival. I think most heterosexual male-to-female transgender fall into that category. They don't want to sparkle too much on a daily basis. I wanted to fade into the crowd, be unnoticed, non-intrusive; basically 'pass' without too much scrutiny. In Toronto, almost anything goes but there are still pockets of people – (red necks is a polite enough term), that may want to hurt you – just because. Do they feel threatened? Do they find it exquisitely excruciating to their own sensibilities? Does it go against their God? I have often heard "You're a freak of nature!" This makes no sense to me, since nature is full of instances of hermaphrodites and gender-switching. Nevertheless, I chose the path of least resistance, opting for semi-casual, non-descript, asexual attire, for the most part.

Confidence can be fleeting at best. Just think back to your formative teenage years, when you first started to become aware of yourself, concerned with all those little things. Well for me, everything was new. You had to learn – hone your skills and mistakes could rattle your very core. Christ, just going into a female washroom made me feel like an intruder; a fraud. *Something as basic as that, having to pee – go figure.* Funny how we are segregated at birth, male and female and never the 'twixt shall mix thereafter. It is changing though, slowly, but for me at this time, or for anyone, it is a new experience and takes time to become normalized.

Normal. What is that? Depends on who you ask, I suppose. Does normal mean the most common; the average? I surely don't aspire to be either. In any other realm, no one looks for the most common or average person, they want someone outstanding; ahead of the curve; a leader. Weird, you bet. What I've found is that everything is on a continuum, a scale so to speak, where anyone or anything can be more or less of something else too. That's normal, that's diversity, that's real life. Ask any ecologist, biologist, financier, urban planner or reasonably-educated person and they will tell you that a strong habitat, ecosystem, portfolio, or city, is one that is diversified; full of variation. I rest my case, Your Honour.

But I digress. I surely would not try and change your belief system or point of view. Everyone is entitled to his or hers. Of course opinions are like assholes, everyone has one and some bring theirs to bear more than others. It just seems a shame to go through life and not experience it in full. Not that you have to change your gender to experience life in full. People often fail to learn about and enjoy the differences in someone; their culture; their food, due to archaic stereotypic beliefs imposed on them by truly ignorant folk. If you don't push the boat out, how will you know? Maybe the world is flat after all, or maybe some people really can't handle the truth. *You tell 'em Jack!*

It had been a fairly lonely existence up to this point. Something I had been used to all my life. I kept up with photography, basically walking everywhere I went, due to a lack of money. No trips, no vacations – every dollar going to the cause. I would drift in and out of relationships, friendly ones only, depending on what was going on at the time. Hang out with some 'group therapy' people every now and then – misery loves company, don't ya know. Brief but regular contact with family and only a few of the people I knew from before I began my transition, like Janet and Donny. Only those that really knew me, and liked the person inside, stayed with me for the long haul, overlooking the superficial changes. One could consider him or herself blessed if they had one good friend in their life. I had several. For others, not sure of what my outcome would be like, they kept their distance, not wanting to add to their own overloaded plate with such a strange twist of a person. *Oh well, such is life.*

★ ★ ★

Year four, I'm down to my last GICs and RRSPs – time for a few upgrades and then get back to working life. I was feeling much stronger, walking everywhere, and finally had the codeine intake down to ten or so a day. I had been volunteering at the Daily Bread food bank, partly to occupy my time, to contribute in a meaningful manner, and also to log bona fide time in the female role, which is a requirement of the gender clinic. They will not recommend surgery until a client has lived in the chosen role for at least two years, either by working, volunteering or going to school. The "Real Life Test," as it is known. For good reason too, as many think, feel or believe, that by changing one's gender all of life's difficulties will simply go away. Not true. You must actually prove that you are totally engaged in society, at some level, so you know and feel what you will be truly experiencing. Let's face it, if all you are going to do is sit at home and never go anywhere, you've got bigger problems. Further, this is a rather permanent surgery, not to be undertaken lightly or without full forethought.

I did feel that some facial alteration would be beneficial. However, you want cosmetic surgery to look more feminine, pay me – that's if you can find a surgeon that even wants to get involved with you and you have any money left. But it can be done. Many of the surgeons I approached only wanted to do shitty non-invasive procedures. That would not cut it, in my case. The gender clinic was helpful in that they gave me a name of a doctor who would try and correct some areas.

The facial structure and skin of a man is quite different than a biological female's, in that acne and pores and such need to be refined and smoothed out. My skin was terrible. From the year spent in hospital as a young teen, the acne was severe. As a young adult, I had gone to many doctors and dermatologists afterwards, each one just said, 'I can't help you,' and I hav'ta tell you, that was tough. You will never know the horror and haunting effects of that disadvantage unless you suffer from it. I was crushed. It had devastated my whole life.

Nevertheless, I'd made it this far and wasn't about to stop. Ever had dermabrasion? I did it twice. A bit of lipo under the chin and around the abdomen, scraping of the Adams apple and some implants on cheeks and chin to contour the face. A 'brow lift' – sure Doctor B., lets do that. Total cost for electrolysis, meds, and cosmetic surgery to date – over fifty thousand dollars. I was broke, time to get back to a real paying job. But what?

★ ★ ★

I was fortunate because I found a lawyer who saw my case as a rarity that had no simple answers or outcome and took pity on me. I went for aptitude-testing and landed on many possibilities, including government inspections. That led to a talk with a Ryerson University advisor. In turn, I applied to Ryerson for the Environmental Health program, majoring in Public Health. Two days after submitting previous educational records and applying, I received a letter for Offer of Admission, to start in one week, for September classes. My lawyer had all my WSIB benefits reinstated. She was a very good attorney. Thanks Lisa!

★ ★ ★

After that, I threw myself into school work. It was tough, seeing as I hadn't been in an academic setting for well over ten years. I was overwhelmed at first, but kept plugging away. I didn't approach anyone, just 'hi and bye,' to classmates and profs. I'd go from home to school, school to home, and study every waking moment. That was my routine. The first semester I achieved honours and my dad was super proud. Nearing the end of my second semester, he died. I was thankful he had known me as I truly am.

The first summer, between semesters, I was getting harassed by the WSIB. If I wasn't going to school or working, then they were going to cut my benefits. It was disheartening, to say the least. I received phone call after phone call, ongoing threats and harassment, from the nameless freaks of the WSIB Gestapo. One of their favourite ploys was to ask for Mr. Stevens and call me 'sir' on the phone and in written letters.

The second year of school was tougher academically but easier in that many of my classmates started to engage me. The bonds of friendship were being developed. It was a great group of kids that made me feel welcome and valued. I had continued to press the gender clinic, wanting the approval for reassignment surgery, since I had easily fulfilled the 'Real Life Test'. People could go elsewhere for surgery; Montreal, the United States, even parts of Asia. That is, if you had the money. I was more interested in getting the approval from a long-standing clinic, partly for my own sanity and partly because they had the best surgeon.

So, halfway done my degree, at the end of term in May, I got approval from the gender clinic for sex reassignment surgery. One of the last ones in Ontario to get the funding for reassignment surgery too, since the Ontario Government cut that benefit as part of downsizing budgets and such. *Nice going guys!* Further and more importantly, after contacting the surgeon's office, I had an appointment and date set for the ultimate snip.

Now, the WSIB wanted to cut my benefits since I was going out of the country for a month, and according to them was not entitled to do so. The attorney had to set them straight. I was entitled to a vacation and some sick leave. The WSIB is persistent though – they kept threatening with phone calls, to the point I told the one nameless psycho that I hoped she got run over by a truck! Well, they flipped out and said I was making death threats to their staff. My attorney pointed out that I didn't drive a truck so it was not a direct threat from me as they had so viciously complained. That useless cockroach was pulled from handling my file and I finally got a semi-caring individual and few if any problems after that. Thanks again Lisa!

Regardless, I hopped on a jet and flew to London, England. Mister D. (they call their surgeons Mister) performed the surgery. It went well. No complications. I would be in bed, in the hospital, for at least two weeks post-op and not allowed to get up. And yes my darlings, it hurt!

My mom called several times. Spoke to the surgeon and was assured I was okay. She had actually gone and got her passport just in case something went screwy and she had to fly over. Good ol' mom, she even tucked a ten pound note in a card for me to have real English fish and chips meal. *And I did.*

Not much sightseeing though. I stayed an extra week in London, recuperating at a hotel. My daily walks consisted of touring once around Russell Square and then back to bed. Most all my meals were at the hotel. I just couldn't walk very far or sit for long, in any degree of comfort.

I took a cab to the airport and found out the flight home was overbooked. I explained that I had to leave and could not hang around for another ten hours for the next one. Maybe I should have, as the flight was uncomfortable to say the least, over seven hours squished between two burly men, right in the centre row. *Ugh!*

★ ★ ★

My family, although never that close, had come to accept my new changes. Some people lose everyone. They can't, or don't want to understand this issue and think its just plain sicko. I was very fortunate. I kept family, kept Donny and Peg, kept Janet (although only as a good friend) and my land barons were fine with it, so I didn't have to move. I stayed in my little grotto and still had the dogs as good company. Everyone around me felt closer, more connected, simply because I felt more complete and happy.

But at the outset of this journey, explaining to everyone was not an easy task. I certainly experienced the full gamut of fear and tears. It can be accomplished and it has to be done, if only for your own personal growth and well-being. You need to know where people around you stand on this issue. You need to rid yourself of those persons who do not support you. It is a cruel and harsh reality. Never, ever, let someone stand in your way of what it is you want in life, your life!

Unfortunately some people never make it this far, never find peace, lose all hope and eventually end it. Kill themselves, and why? Society, family, so-called friends, and peers beat them down and spit them out as worthless trash. Shame! How sad is it to lose all hope, feel there are no other options left to explore. How do people in good conscience ever allow that to happen? Why would they ever want that to happen? Because gender identity disorders, like several other maladies, are so misunderstood and maligned in many societies of today. Oddly enough, many cultures within and outside of North America have a history of celebrating persons of my persuasion. Look it up if you don't believe me. Check 'berdache', for one. *Told ya so!*

I blame religion, a lot, for the plethora of miseries people are subjected to. *Don't get me started!* Try not to misunderstand me. I have nothing against someone believing in, and following, the credo of a so-called higher power. Whatever form you choose – whatever floats your boat. If it gives you comfort, it is fine by me. And I have nothing against organized religion; people getting together, loving everyone, accepting everyone, caring for everyone.

But answer me this, why is it some 'religious folk' get away with bigotry and hate mongering? Why is it that some religious leaders and followers get to spout this ignorant out-dated garbage and demand compliance, by force, threat and possible penalty of death, if people fail to believe in and adhere to their tenets? *You call me crazy?*

Then there is the oppression of women and other marginalized sectors within their own culture because of this religious mantra. Manmade stories, where man is central to everything and women are mere chattel. *I don't think so mister!* Several religious sects literally hide and protect pedophiles, allowing this behaviour to decimate young souls in community after community, decade after decade. Another is so wealthy and opulent, turning a blind eye to the followers who suffer in hunger and pain, all the while amassing fortunes and living a fattened hog's lifestyle. The hypocrisy is outrageous.

Look, go ahead and practice something that feels good in your heart, do good deeds in a community, but don't leave your brain at the door. Do not push your beliefs on others. There are so many types of religion out there, so how is it even possible that yours is the only one, the right one? Many countries allow anyone to believe and practice their preferred doctrines freely and openly. But that's it. You do not get to force your will onto others. This is why we need separation of church and state. Countries are starting to see a shift to a more radical stance by religious zealots and they are taking steps to nip it in the bud. Good on them. It is getting out of hand, big time! As far as I'm concerned, religion has been responsible for more pain and suffering, more bigotry and hatred, more death and destruction of human lives, then any other entity in this world. *I told you, don't get me started! Amen!*

★ ★ ★

Once back in Canada, I changed the documents as fast as humanly possible and got the gold star; an F actually, right where it says 'gender'! Of course changing from male to female does not solve life problems – just your internal struggle and sanity. So in a sense, I had a chance to be free of my demons. I did not look overly feminine, I did not act that way either. It was me. Like it or not. The only thing I knew for sure was that I could live with myself, finally.

★ ★ ★

My final two years at Ryerson became easier in that I was more connected and had a great group of fellow students and professors around me for support. I had become a sort of mother hen, being older than most of my peers, and many sought me out for personal advice and academic assistance. Later, I finished the degree, a BASc from Ryerson University, majoring in Environmental Health. It was an honours degree, requiring six more units than your average basic degree, plus I completed the certificate in Occupational Health and Safety, concurrently. My final GPA was 3.39. Respectable, considering all the adversity I faced. I even managed to be awarded the 3M scholarship for highest academic performance in Infection Control. I gave the money back to Ryerson so they could buy a microscope and give some cash to a student service.

I was fitting in and gaining confidence in my new skin, as it were. Some of my classmates had made comments during my last year that solidified everything. "You are so normal and fun to hang out with." Normal. I guess that was the icing on the cake. Had I achieved self-actualization, the pinnacle of a hierarchy of human needs? Almost, I thought. *Maslow would be proud.*

★ ★ ★

Now what? During my added night courses for OHS credits, I had met another graduate student who was a year ahead of me and she urged me to apply to Toronto's Public Health unit, where she had just started. In order to become certified as a Public Health Inspector in Canada, you first had to complete a mandatory practicum at a health unit, then sit the oral board exam once you passed all the pre-requisites. So I did.

I found it kinda comical, in a sense, that I had no plan of action after university, as to where I would go to ply my trade. The thought had not really entered my mind. Of course, I could not go to a small urban centre. Even with positive strides made in 'rights' of those persons marginalized by various disadvantages, they were, and probably still are, not overly receptive to hiring someone like me. But Toronto, you betchya! I'll give them this, the health unit, and city for that matter, prides itself on diversity of their workforce. Was I hired simply because of my differences? Possibly, but all things considered, I think I earned that advantage. What was even more outrageous, after six months on the job, getting certified in the process, I was hired permanent full-time.

As I think back over the last ten years, it felt impossible in the beginning, yet now seemed relatively easy and straightforward. Everyone close to me; friends, family, colleagues, and school chums, could only see the remarkable change and how happy I was. There were never any real nasty confrontations. That in itself was a blessing. I guess I was really lucky. Most people I knew had no understanding of why this path was chosen or what this disorder was all about – it was just accepted. Matter-of-fact – no judgement; it was what it was. It is part of who I am, but not totally what I am.

I am now, and have been for the last two years, a full time PHI (Public Health Inspector) and POO (Provincial Offences Officer), working for the City of Toronto, Toronto Public Health, in of all places...*drum roll please*...South Region. Can you spell full circle?

Geezez I'm exhausted.

THREE

Present Day

Donny and I have met every year on the date of that fateful call that changed both our lives forever. May 25th, was etched into our brains, never to be forgotten.

This night was our tenth anniversary of that early-morning nightmare. I was pumped. The dogs were equally charged up and got a reward simply for their enthusiasm. Every year, on that day, I thought about what happened to both of us. Funnily enough, turns out the reason Donny was in that nightclub … he had to use a washroom real bad and that's all.

He had been kicked out of the house that night by Peg and ordered to go do something with some friends, to release some stress, on both their parts. Earlier that day, after his shift had ended, he and some guys he worked with had gone out for a huge breakfast. Some of the lads had invited him out to watch the fights and have a few beers that night. He had declined initially. So once Peg kicked him to the curb, he went downtown and did exactly that; joined his colleagues at a bar.

Heading home late, he had walked for a bit then was struck with the uncontrollable, sweat inducing, gut wrenching, violent urge to go… Diarrhoea! Caught short and not wanting to delay a second, he badged his way through a line and ended up in the last toilet stall of a dance club. After about twenty-five minutes of agony, he felt better and opened the door, finding two white guys standing right in front of him. One was a tall, skinny puke, with long, greasy, black hair, black leather coat, dark pants and was holding out a big baggie of what looked to be crystal meth. The other, shorter dude, buzz cut, jeans and a light top, was scooping out some of the drug into a smaller bag.

Donny thinks he made a move with his right hand to his gun, which wasn't there 'cause he was off-duty. The tall dude, all squirrelly from the ice, pulled out a small, snub-nosed revolver with the speed of a professional, Old West gunslinger and shot Donny twice; point blank. That was it. Donny remembers a flash and hot pressure on his chest.

So far no leads, no shell casings, no video, no perpetrator, and that's how it continued to stand. The detectives left out the part about uncontrollable diarrhoea from the reports. Donny is still a bit touchy on the subject. Now there you go people, poor food handling almost killed a cop. *Wash your hands properly and cook the shit outta stuff!*

★ ★ ★

If the 25th falls through the work-week, I always take the day off and the following day as well, so I can get ready and survive the night in style, without having to worry about working with a hangover the next day. *I'm a planner to be sure.*

We usually drink a bit, just before the meal, after the meal and well, long into the night. Tonight fell on a Thursday. It'll be a nice long weekend now.

I had awoken from a midday nap so I was fresh and could last the marathon. Had a longer than usual shower and I double-scrubbed all the important parts. One look in the mirror and I was okay with the reflection. "You ain't that great looking on the outside kid, but not to worry, it's what's on the inside that counts most of all." *The things I tell myself.*

New outfit already bought for tonight, lying on my bed – simple yet elegant. Black pin-stripe slacks with matching jacket over a subdued, embossed white cotton blouse. Sensible shoes of course, black, low heel (I am almost five foot nine) and some simple, sparse, silver doodads with turquoise that complemented my eyes and the outfit. Done.

Work on the hair, nails simple – clear polish (never anything else, or nothing). Done. Spritz with something fresh and lemony… CK One. Nice. Dress in the new clothes. Done.

Grab a small, square-shaped, black satchel purse thingy, not too feminine, but not that butch either. Contents; gloss lippy, gum and mints, hard leather badge flip with credit cards and ID inside, small bottle of CK One for you know … real money … $200 outta do it. *Although Donny always insists on paying… he feels thankful still, silly boy.*

No make-up because I rarely use it. *And I'm still pissed with the advertisers and manufacturers of said products.*

Tissues and other little girlie things … take an umbrella just in case? No, this evening will be clear as a bell.

I'm out the door headed for the subway. Peanuts in the shell, in hand, ready for the squirrels I saw along the way.

I stood underground at the Ossington Station platform, waiting for the eastbound train. Other riders came in through the stairwell at the Delaware access and went down past me. Sometimes I would get a double-take. It didn't really bother me anymore, I knew how I looked and accepted my limitations. Did I wish I looked gorgeous? You bet – who doesn't? And if this was Europe and if I had accessed treatment before my teenage years, then maybe I would look better. But life is full of 'ifs' along with lots of woulda, coulda, and shoulda. This was my situation; my lot in life, the cards have been dealt. *Move on.*

My voice was still husky at best. That's the one thing that can't be changed once puberty hits and your voice drops. I try to speak softly and with a bit higher pitch but it usually rings overly fake and falsetto. If I'm mad or stressed, then watch out, I swear like a trooper and growl like a bear. Scares the shit outta people though, nobody fucks with me. Operators of the premises that I inspect don't know what to think. *It's great!*

My dad, before he died, always said, "Don't worry about it," when I was transitioning into the female role. "Lots of women have a deep voice," he would pronounce. Yeah, right dad, a seventy-year-old, two-pack a day smoker, with one bad lung would. *Thanks for the morale boost pops!*

The train came in and I headed east towards Yonge. At Bathurst, the announcement came over the speaker that a fire had stopped service beyond Bay station. I got off at the next stop, Spadina, be-bopped up a flight of stairs and took the streetcar out of the tunnel, heading south towards downtown. Had a seat by the window but just closed my eyes for a bit and thought about what I might eat tonight at the restaurant.

We always met at Cyrano's. It was a funky place off King Street East, down a little side street, that had turned into a bit of a cop bar at the front and great dining at the back. I actually inspect the place now so I have confidence in the kitchen and food.

Yum! I knew what I was going to have; shrimp cocktail to start and a little side salad, followed by a nice thick steak, fillet mignon should do the trick, with a glass or two of red, maybe share a side of toasted something and top it off with liquored coffee afterwards. Then, once wide-awake from the coffee, we'd get into the hard stuff for the rest of the night. *I had a plan.*

My nose filled with a vile, putrescent odour, which could only mean I was passing through Chinatown and it caused me to open my eyes and grimace. Chinatown on Spadina Avenue was not a bad place, lots of deals and lots of people at all hours of the day, but fifty percent of the area seemed to be restaurants or other food premises. That translated into oodles of organic garbage. It was the particular blend of rotting vegetables, a generous dash of moisture, and the extended period of time the refuse was left outside that produced this caustic stench. It was even worse in the dead of summer. The heat would add a whole new dimension of rankness. Hungry? I've seen and smelled worse and that has never put me off food.

I was through it quickly and hit King Street West. Got off, caught the King streetcar eastbound to Yonge. I walked the rest of the way since it was only 18:20 hours and I had ten minutes to spare. It was a gorgeous evening, warm with a slight breeze and still bright out. I felt good, physically and mentally. All seemed right with the world. *Imagine that.*

I walked into Cyrano's and let my constricted sight adjust. It was packed – pay day no doubt and I felt the crowd's eyes on me. *'Cause I'm so good looking'*... I had to quell the nervousness somehow.

The dining manager, James, saw me and approached with a huge grin. "Ms. Stevens! Your guest and table await," and he led me through the swarming bar and back to the intimate dining area.

Cyrano's had two half-moon, black leather banquet seats on one side, enough for six diners each if you huddled close and didn't care much about elbow room. In front of those, two rows of three tables which seated four maximum at each. But what we always got for this special night, and where I could see Donny sitting, was an exclusive booth on the other side of the room. This was reserved for only a sacred few. It could seat four in a pinch, but it was just for us tonight.

Donny stood up as we approached. He wore a deep coloured charcoal suit, burgundy flecked tie and looked great. "Here you are madam," said James and he left us.

Donny grabbed me and hugged me tight like he hadn't seen me for eons. "Happy Anniversary Liz!"

That's what we called it on account both he and I were kinda born again that day. "Happy Anniversary Donny."

He pulled away, a foot or so, looked me up and down and commented, "You look slick. Nice outfit, my gorgeous saviour!"

As we sat I said, "I bet you say that to all the girls, you dusky dog."

His eyes just glowed.

Our server was at our side. "Good evening, my name is Daniel and I'll be your waiter tonight. May I get you folks something from the bar?"

Donny raised his eyebrows up and down. "Wanna go with the champagne like last year?"

"No I do not! Christ Donny, I barely found my house after I left here."

He chuckled. "That was a great night. Okay, Daniel?"

"Yes sir."

"I'll have a Heineken and the lady will have … what, something girlie perhaps?"

"Do you make a short Caesar?" I asked.

"One of the best in town."

"That would hit the spot, thanks"

He hustled up front to place the order at the bar.

Donny and I were like two peas in a pod. We clicked on so much. We fell into conversation so easily and never had a lack of topics to discuss. He knew I knew the streets and would bring me up to speed on his best calls.

"I have a surprise. Well, actually, two of them come to think of it."

I was intrigued. "Do tell."

He shook his head, "No way! This is for after dinner and during our fine single malt phase."

"No fair!"

"Tough titty kitty, you'll just have to wait."

I pouted. He didn't care. I stopped and we went back to our routine of updates in our lives.

His boy, Andy, was twelve years old and doing real good. It had been ten years of being cancer-free and he was a holy terror around the house. Drove Peg nuts half the time but they were both grateful. The kid hadn't had a real growth spurt and remained quite small. They were a tad concerned, especially for his upcoming teenage years. The doctors just didn't know if Andy would suddenly hit the typical milestones, or remain small for his age.

Our drinks arrived and Donny gulped half a beer.

I told him about my recent photos and how the public health job was going. Gave him a few horror stories of my own and made sure he'd avoid certain places in South Region.

"I hope this isn't one of them!" Donny said with a hint of fear in his voice.

"No. Well run." I thought about mentioning diarrhoea but let it pass, quickly.

We caught Daniel's eye after our second drink and started our orders for appetizers. Donny copied me for the shrimp and main course too, but changed the type of salad for himself. We split garlic bread with the meal, along with a bottle of their house red.

Daniel was a good waiter. He didn't pressure us and waited for the right moment to approach, not wanting to interrupt good conversation. Plus, I'm sure the manager James had directed him not to rush us since we were there for the night. This was a special table with his personal guests; meaning what ever they ask, you do.

Donny and I were not very demanding. We just wanted to hang out and chill the night away.

It was after 21:00 hours. I had just finished my liquor coffee and Donny was nursing a regular coffee in anticipation of the main event.

Once the table was cleared, James saw his opening and plunked down a new bottle of Cardhu and two very elegant tumblers. I would have never thought Donny for a single malt man but ... a duck to water. He was salivating and poured the first round. It was a teary first toast as always. Our bond would never be broken.

"News! Two things as I recall. Spill copper."

As he reached into his inside suit jacket pocket, I could see his firearm, a Glock, and thought that strange. Donny never carried his firearm off duty. He pulled out a hard leather badge flip, like the one I carry and opened it up, holding it out to me.

I took it, tentatively, and looked. "Detective!"

I got up and hurried to his side and hugged him tight. "Wow! You worked hard for this, now you got it! How did it ... when did it happen!?"

He gave me some details and kept leaving out stuff and going back and forth. I was worn out by the time he finished. Outstanding! I was so proud of him and just beamed.

"To you Detective Jacobs!" and we both had a nice long swig of our single malt.

He said in his best Dragnet imitation, "Detective Jacobs – Homicide" and we both cracked up laughing.

"You said two things. What's the other ... Peg's pregnant!?"

He held up his hands in a 'whoa' gesture and said, "No, that isn't it. The other thing, well it involves you actually."

Now I was so curious I couldn't contain myself. He poured more single malt and started to explain.

Donny had met and gotten to know a lot of people over his fourteen-year career at Toronto Police Services, some of whom were lawyers. *Go figure, crime and lawyers.*

A few months back, he'd been hanging out after a special dinner of some sort and quietly listened as these attorney types were discussing cheating spouses. The question of gathering evidence against one spouse came up ... how it could severely limit the benefit, assets, and alimony payment after divorce, if one's mate was found doing the dirty with another.

They started discussing tangible evidentiary things like phone records, credit card bills and the real prize ... photos, which are often entered into a case that gets built over time.

Donny had gotten hooked on the conversation. Just like cops building a case against a criminal or organization that's suspected of doing wrong, these kinds of cases get built over time with physical proof. This data gathered; this tangible evidence has to stand up to legal scrutiny in the courts so it has the necessary impact and outcome at trial.

Now it may seem a simple thing; you suspect your spouse is cheating so you follow him or her and snap a picture, right? Not so fast, it doesn't necessarily prove that much. Not from an independent source – perhaps not a credible source – an isolated incident or minor indiscretion taken out of context, and so on. It can be way more complicated, especially when lawyers get involved. *Got that right!*

These guys talked on and on about this. Several of them agreed that pictures are really worth a thousand words, as is video, for catching and proving people are doing what they are not supposed to be. This can apply to divorce settlements, workers compensation and insurance fraud – the list is endless, and particularly so when it comes to lawyers. At which they all laughed vigorously.

Then they started talking about private investigators. How they charge big bucks for a bunch of info that the lawyers probably know already, when sometimes, all they really want is the good-quality money shots.

Further, if they knew the location of these people and could have someone on contract that could just go out on short notice, wouldn't that be nice? Kinda like how a freelance photographer gets a call from a magazine or newspaper and they send him or her to cover the story. Piecework, as it would be infrequent, both in days and times.

Most of the lawyers Donny listened to agreed they would pay for that service. But who was beyond reproach? Who had a stand-up reputation, one hundred-percent credibility and integrity, and was a good enough photographer to do that?

I just stared at Donny. I thought that would be a great job. I was wondering who could do that as well and was waiting for him to finish the story. He just looked back at me, smiled while touching my hand, and sipped his Cardhu.

From over my left shoulder a loud voice boomed, "Hey Jacobs, congrats on getting the big D."

It was Freddy Savoy, I later learned, having never met him before. He was a slimy little fuck who was the nephew of a high-placed captain at Toronto Police and now he was hovering over our table in a rather inebriated state.

I knew of him, as did most everybody else, because of his shit behaviour out on the streets, most notably in vice and drugs. Donny had regaled me with stories over the years. And the fact that he'd made detective in less than eight years, probably because of some nepotism that ran in streaks through the department on occasion, irked many a cop.

Freddy had made some big busts though and everyone was shocked at how easily it had happened. He seemed to know who, where, and what was going on in places that just popped up with no hints or history of wrongdoing.

Everyone called him 'Junior' behind his back and he hated that with a passion.

Donny eyed him, "Evening Freddy, you okay?"

"Oh yeah! Not feeling any pain to be sure," he slurred. "And who might this pretty little la… Oh! It's you."

I half-nodded at Freddy then looked away. Christ! Was there anybody that didn't know who I was before and had become now? The night was turning sour, quickly.

"Well you don't look half bad for a…"

Donny flew at him, bumping his chest up against Freddy's, driving him back away from the table in a flash. All I heard was, "Listen Junior, you little prick!" and Donny, hunching down, had Freddy nose to nose, pushing him back to the bar area at the front of Cyrano's in a flurry. I didn't catch any of the other words that were said between them but when Donny came back a few minutes later, he was sweating a bit.

"Sorry. He won't be back."

James had seen the whole thing and put up the red velvet rope across the entrance to the dining area as a sign for no more diners. Bar food only. I'm not sure a silly little rope would stop Freddy, or any other cop, but Donny sure would. My personal bodyguard; how nice. I felt safe.

We sat for a bit longer, not really talking of much after that little incident. The bottle of Cardhu was damn near half gone and we were both hammered.

After paying the bill and leaving a huge tip, Donny hailed me a cab outside. We held each other tightly and he gave me a kiss on the cheek then assured me he would hop in the next available taxi. His car was at home anyhow. *Good boy!*

"Stay safe and thanks for a great night, Donny." I fell into the back seat of the taxi, pleasantly numb.

The cab ride home was fast. I slid from side to side as the driver took corners at speed. I was totally blitzed. Maybe he saw that, hurrying the ride, not wanting me to puke in his car.

I stumbled into the back entrance of the house, took the stairs down to my apartment door, and found the locks had been changed. "Did I forget to pay my rent?" Nope, just drunk as a skunk and unable to get the key in da wittle hole. *Whaala!*

I wobbled through the door, stripped, brushed my teeth and sank into the bed. "Good night Lizzy," I faintly said to myself. It was and I slept a good sleep. No more demons.

★ ★ ★

Donny called on the weekend to check on me. They were headed out, taking off for a bit of a mini-holiday to visit the folks, both sides, so the grandparents could see Andy mostly.

One set of parents was near Niagara Falls and the little squirt was super-excited to see the sights. The other set was in the Leamington area, tomato farmers. They were going to drive along Lake Erie, after a few days at one in-law's and then stop there at the other. He would see me when he got back, probably a week. "Peg sends her best, think about what we talked about. Love ya!" Click.

What we talked about? *I had no idea.*

★ ★ ★

The public generally doesn't know what an inspector for the Toronto Public Health Department does on a daily basis. Since Toronto is so big, and has a higher than normal density of almost everything, the health department is broken up into divisions that deal with specific areas. For example, my division, which is called Healthy Environments, has the Health Hazard focus which deals with almost anything not food-related, out in the environment; and the Food Safety focus deals with anything relating to food, food premises, etc. The overall health department has an infection-control group, disease surveillance group, TB group, healthy babies group, nursing groups, sexually '*trans-smitten*' diseases group (*ha*) ... jeepers, the list seems endless. The inspectors in our division only number about one hundred and fifty in total. We have five offices throughout the city, which was amalgamated recently. Business is non-stop.

For the food safety focus, Toronto has a fairly good system in place called 'Dine Safe' which includes a colour-coded posting that each food premises was subject to. Green Pass of course tells the patron most all areas are meeting the minimum standard during the last inspection and enjoy your meal. Yellow Conditional

Pass, means caution, problems have been found of a significant or crucial nature and the operator is misbehavin,' so maybe move on. And Red is for Closed. This means that the premise is so bad that it is unfit to eat in, usually from an infestation (cockroaches, mice, rats). Or any other situation that is deemed a health hazard, like sewage overflowing, gross unsanitary conditions from rotting foods, no water or hydro, etc.

There is also a website that people can check to see how their favourite haunt is doing and get the history for the last two years or so. The Toronto system has been copied, to one degree or another, in many jurisdictions surrounding Toronto and throughout North America and other countries. It works.

Most of the public health inspectors working in the downtown office don't use cars for travelling to a location; we use the TTC. I hadn't owned a car for over ten years. Parking, if you can find it, costs a fortune as do all the other expenses. The city pays for the Metro pass, which saves me a whack of money, which I get to spend on cameras and assorted goodies. Plus, I try and do my part to save the environment by lowering my carbon footprint.

My map areas that I am responsible for at present are compact. Situated near our office on Victoria Street, they run from the east side of Yonge to the west side of Sherbourne, then south of Adelaide East and down to the waterfront at Queens Quay East. Know as S2810 and S2812. Similarities in life, eh! *They follow you around.*

For the most part we set our own day. It's a great job. Not quite the pace of ambulance work but pretty cool nonetheless. You prioritize calls that come in from the public or other agencies and divisions, called 'demand calls' and then continue with the mandated routine inspections, day in and day out, meat 'n potato grunt work. You never catch up. There is always more work. The day passes quickly. That's the other thing, straight weekdays like in Monday to Friday, 08:30 to 16:30 hours. No shift work.

Overtime is available on occasion for night calls and special events, if you want it. Good money, benefits, and pension. I Love it! Photography, unfortunately, has mostly been limited to weekends, holidays and vacation time only though. Always too many people where ever you go; a big drawback.

If I have lieu time built up, I'll sometimes take a day through the week and head to the Toronto Zoo, early spring and late fall are best as the animals are more active. Or, High Park is always a great place for birding and other animal photography. You have to go early though. They do great flower displays as well. I've been using my macro lens, capturing some really cool shots, which look great on the cards I produce. Other lieu time goes in my bank for the annual holiday to Algonquin Park in September. Never too many people up there, at least in the fall, thank goodness for that.

★ ★ ★

The week went by quickly and I hadn't heard from Donny, so Sunday morning I called Janet. We agreed to meet at Wellesley Station around 12:30 hours and go cruise Church Street for a lunch spot. I always remind myself how lucky I was to keep her as a good friend.

"Hey Medic Girl!"

Very funny, I thought. I turned to see Janet exiting the subway turnstile. The woman doesn't age, doesn't gain weight and still looks like a hot high school senior. It was a real passionate hug and quick kiss on the lips. My heart bounced.

We landed at a nice secluded patio near Wood and Church and caught up while drinking wine. Janet had stuck with ER nursing and was top of the food chain now. She was shift supervisor, had her degree, and was working on a Masters through U of T. She'd be done before Christmas and probably defend her thesis in the early new year. She would jump up the pay scale too, probably hit over one hundred thousand. I just stared at her and was awestruck. She was perfect. Why someone hadn't snapped her up yet was beyond me. The heart wants what the heart wants and I was totally hung up on this gorgeous creature. I fell into those vibrant green eyes and was lost.

"Are you listening to me?" Janet queried.

I snapped back from my trance, "Yes! Every word! I hang on them like molasses."

She flipped me off and excused herself. I could only imagine the goofy look on my face. I ordered more drinks and some appetizers before she got back, hoping to appease the goddess.

On her return, Janet sat down with a disgusted plop, folding her arms and staring at me, "I didn't realize I was so boring."

"You're not! You are the most interesting person I know. I totally love you. Please forgive me."

More drinks came. The food arrived. Apparently that was a good start in getting back to her good books. I dared not tell her what was really going through my mind.

She had the weekend off for the upcoming Pride festivities which take place at the end of the month. It will be a long weekend and Janet was looking forward to coming down, getting trashed and dancing the nights away. She had also spoken with Donny, and not only convinced him to attend but Peg and little Andy were gonna try and make the big parade on the Sunday. I was expected to be there with them. Correction, I was ordered to be there.

We had a great afternoon, lots to talk about, especially at the hospital and the funny anecdotal events that often occur. Janet kept me amused. It was well after 16:00 hours when we finally stumbled away to our respective abodes.

★ ★ ★

June was great for bouncing around town, doing calls. The weather, pleasant most days, was not overly hot or humid, only a light jacket in the morning sometimes. Most everything was going well. *It makes me nervous, not used to it yet.*

Donny called me at work on Wednesday and filled me in on his trip. He apologized for disappearing for an extra week but police stuff gets in the way of a personal life. This next week was shot due to the work load too but he really wanted to see me the week after. He said he needed to finalize our conversation from the 25th so a dinner was set for next Thursday night, after work.

I still couldn't remember what we'd talked about. *Do I have a drinking problem? Seems my mind wandered and I can't stay focused either.*

★ ★ ★

I made it down to High Park on the weekend and this time finally got Janet to come with me, although I had to bribe her with the promise of fun and a free meal. We walked a circuit of the park, from the entrance at Bloor, down through the small zoo, over to another small pond, and then back across to the Grenadier pond. I added some good quality bird shots and of course more squirrel and chipmunk pics. When Janet asked when the fun was supposed to start, I pulled out a whack of peanuts and introduced her to my friends. She couldn't believe the way they came right up and took the food. I was snapping pictures as she was giggling at the prospect of a chipmunk running all over her. *Lucky chipmunk!* Birds landed on her hand and took bits of peanut. Her face was beaming.

As promised, I bought her lunch at the restaurant. She was having a great day and couldn't believe that she had never come here before. Afterwards, we strolled around the gardens and soaked up the sun and quiet. We parted at my subway stop. *I think I'm making inroads with this girl!*

★ ★ ★

Around 17:30 hours on Thursday, I was waiting for Donny, sitting on the patio at Taps 18 on King Street East. The tables ran down a corridor between other buildings, very secluded. Each seating area had its own umbrella but there wasn't any sun to block.

While I sipped on a Grolsch, he snuck up behind me and scared the crap outta me. Beer spurted out my nose and mouth. After that gaffe, he sat across the table and ordered a Heineken, all the while just grinning at me, simply because he got me again.

"What a day!"

"Busy?" I enquired, still wiping little bombs of beer foam from my face and the table.

"The shit never stops in this crazy city," Donny said, then asking, "so, how you doin' Liz?"

We gave each other our updates. I was surprised he'd agreed to go to Pride. He reminded me that not all flatfoots were ignorant rednecks and that he had developed a deeper understanding of life and all its diversity over the years. Donny then winked at me. Further, tons of cops loved working the event and it was about time he saw what all the fuss was about. They were all coming down a week Sunday for the parade.

I was never so proud.

"Now, let's you and me get down to business!"

We ordered more imported beers and some appetizers, followed by one of their funky burgers and we split some fries.

As we noshed, he reminded me of the lawyers ... the dinner he'd been at ... taking pictures ... It came back to me slowly, I musta been really trashed.

"Look. I've set something up for you with these guys. You don't have to accept but I hope you will. It could turn a pretty penny and I know you could handle it."

Donny gave me some more details and it sounded kinda cool. Bouncing around town, snapping some pics and getting paid for it. I started to think of all the new gadgets I could soon afford. Before we were done our meal, Donny gave me a business card from one of the lawyer firms, reminding me to call, soon.

He squeezed me tight after dinner and fled back the way he came to grab his car. I headed for the subway entrance, full of food and beer, excited at the prospect of my new gig.

★ ★ ★

I was at High Park on Sunday, early, before the crowds. Wandered from the Queen Street side entrance at Colborne Lodge, through the woods and ended up by Grenadier Pond in the centre. Snagged a few good shots of the swans and some cormorants sunning themselves, and took a few landscape photos.

I sat on a bench and fed the chippies and squirrels with a bag of peanuts in the shell. I always had peanuts with me. Have I told you why? This is really sappy by the way – feel free to skip it. I'll give you the short version so as not to bore.

It started when I was about fifteen, just out of the hospital where I had spent the last year due to back problems. I had missed school all that time and wouldn't start for at least four more months, in September. I was weak, about eighty pounds, no friends and left alone at home all day. Fortunately, we had a big yard with lots of walnut trees and gardens, which attracted numerous animals, including squirrels. They were my friends. I fed them, tamed them, played with them and, well, talked to them. They listened to all my problems and worries, never said a harsh word to me and thus, became indelibly ingrained within me. That's it. I am nutty! My colleague at work, Nick, who is an excellent photographer in his own right, often chides me for taking so many pictures of squirrels and chippies. *He just doesn't get it. No one could, unless they lived through it.*

Looking at the business card Donny gave me, I thought it was high-end expensive. Off-white textured stock, three-colour printing with raised letters in a slick font. Power and money were behind this, I'd best act accordingly.

Did it conflict with my job? No, at least not that I could figure. Did I want to sacrifice time off doing this? Well, it was taking pictures and video, I had the gear and I could find all sorts of other neat things to shoot while pursuing some goofy fraudster for their purposes. I let the idea filter around in my head.

The squirrels and chipmunks were not getting along. This was normal, but when they were fighting each other while atop me … time to move. As I strolled up the incline, towards the restaurant for a bite to eat, I snapped off a few shots of the waterfall running down the slope, cascading over rocks and forming small pools.

Scarfing down some grilled chicken on a Caesar salad, I decided. Sure, why not go talk to them? As Donny said, I could always decline.

The flowers were out all over the park. The staff did an excellent job; eclectic mixed displays abounded. I set up my tripod and had the macro lens attached. Some little tricks of the trade, I had a small spray bottle filled with water to give a misting and have drops form on the petals of certain shots. Also, small scissors and tweezers on hand, for removing little flaws and doing trim work around the flower, for a cleaner shot. I had a halo light attached to the macro lens, which could be increased or decreased in intensity, or increase light to one side. This helped decrease shadows and better illuminate the details. I used a shutter release cable to take the shot, once I manually focussed and set DoF (Depth of Field). Always shoot at 100 ISO and the largest format. Most people have no idea of what goes into the perfect shot – getting the perfect shot.

After two hours, I was soaked in sweat and ready to head home for a shower and nap. My back ached, but it was worth it.

★ ★ ★

Once back at my office on Monday morning, after coffee and a scan of the paper, I fiddled with work stuff until it was just after 09:00 hours, then made the call to the lawyer.

"Blakley, Delahunt and McCoy, this is Angela, how may I help you?"

Wouldn't it be funny if they were called 'Dewey, Screwum and Howe'?

"Hello?"

My mind snapped back. "Hi. My name is Elizabeth Stevens and I was directed to call."

"Oh, yes Ms. Stevens, Mr. Delahunt advised me to make an appointment, at your convenience, for a brief meeting. I was led to understand that you work during the day so we could arrange something after that, if it suits you?"

We settled on Wednesday at 16:30 hours. Their office was located in the Sherman Tower, just east of the Royal York Hotel on Front Street, the sixty-first floor. Their building location was on very expensive real estate indeed. I started to feel inadequate; my brow was moist and my heart experienced a few hiccups.

★ ★ ★

On Wednesday after work, I found the building easily, rode the stylish elevator up, and as my ears popped, I found myself walking into a moneyed foyer. The view from the seating area was spectacular.

While I waited for the lawyer, I just stood and admired the panoramic scene, looking southwest over the Toronto islands. I knew why the admin person at the desk, Angela, had her chair facing the other way. Who could concentrate on work while looking out over this picture postcard landscape? I watched small planes take off and land at the busy Island Airport and followed an armada of sailboats as they raced around the inner bay. I need to bring my camera up here one day and shoot this scene. *I wondered who I would hav'ta bribe to get out on the roof of the building.*

"Mr. Delahunt will see you now," and I followed Angela through double oak doors to a large open room filled with heavy, rich furniture. As soon as I entered the cavernous space, I definitely felt under-dressed for the occasion.

Books lined an entire wall from floor to ceiling and these weren't paperback novels. A plain, but solid looking rectangular table was in front of the legal library, about a dozen swivel chairs neatly positioned around it. Delahunt's dark oak desk, the size of my bed, was angled in front of huge windows to the right. My eyes followed the marble floor over to the other side. There were six high wingback leather chairs in one corner with a centre table and matching side cabinets. Reading lamps adorned them, elegant gold plate with really expensive looking fluted green glass shades.

Four chairs were taken up with older men, dressed in expensive tailored suits, all looking straight at me. One of the gents was puffing on a cigar. *Apparently smoking bylaws don't apply here.*

Another man, wearing a light grey three-piece suit, mid-fifties, full salt and pepper hair, a bit shorter and slimmer than Donny, was coming at me with a welcoming smile. "Ms. Stevens, I'm Raymond Delahunt."

I shook his hand and he thanked Angela for showing me in. As she left, the solid double doors closed with a secure clunk. My mouth had dried up and I had trouble swallowing.

"Please, come and have a seat." Delahunt introduced the other gentlemen and breezed through their names so fast I couldn't remember any of them. They did not rise or offer a hand for a 'howdy do,' they just eyeballed me. I sat in my assigned chair, bolt upright and very uncomfortable. My heart was bouncing and I could feel sweat forming in all sorts of awkward places.

Delahunt was obviously speaking for the group and began, "Ms. Stevens, I want you to know this is just a get-acquainted type of meeting, so please relax."

These guys could spot a nervous character from a hundred metres, I thought. Inside my brain and body, the innards were squirming and I could barely control my anxiety.

"Also, we pretty much know everything about you, your work history and pedigree, life changes … "

He let that comment hang out in mid-air, giving it a few seconds to sink in. They had the research done well ahead of any meeting and didn't need any 'acquainting' with me. *Okay, let the games begin.*

His explanation was simple and to the point. This group was representing several law firms. The job, should I chose to accept this mission … *dum dum Dum!,* was to get notified of a target and location, find the target and shoot pictures and video of whatever was going on there at that time. I may have to follow a subject for a bit, using my discretion, intuition and initiative.

I explained to Delahunt that I had no vehicle.

"Don't worry about that … minor detail."

I reminded them I had a full-time day job.

Again, I was told not to worry. The assignments, for the most part, would probably work around that.

As it turned out, they had thought this through to a T and had all the answers. I was to get a cell phone with email and web access. The work would come across to me on the device from Mr. Delahunt only. All data would go only to Mr. Delahunt.

I would have a membership in various Toronto car programs where you just go to a site in most neighbourhoods, grab a car for whatever time you need it, and drop it back off.

Delahunt asked about my camera gear.

"I have two high-end DSLR cameras capable of straight shots and video. Several lenses including an 18-55 kit lens, 20-70mm, 100mm macro, 75-200 and 100-400mm pump zoom, image stabilized of course, which could handle most shooting situations. Various filters, tripods, backup batteries and flash cards, along with a computer program for editing either photos or videos."

I noticed a nod from Cigar Guy. Their resident photog gave silent assent, therefore agreed to by the board.

Other details would follow and any issues would have a solution. Money, power, and knowing the right people can get most things done, I thought. These guys covered the bases on all three, plus a lot more, I suspected.

"We want you to think about this for a bit," Delahunt said, as he rose to his feet, indicating the meeting was over, at least for now. This probably meant they had to think about it for a while.

Oddly enough, the other men rose and each shook my hand. Maybe this was their way of saying I'd been accepted by them, and now it was up to me to decide. For lawyers they didn't talk much. *Kind of an oxymoron don't ya know.*

Delahunt walked me to the double oak doors and paused before opening them. "There are a couple of other items. First and foremost, this work is confidential. Detective Jacobs has assured us you can keep material classified."

I nodded, "I understand completely."

"Second, we don't want any heroics. Just walk away if trouble starts."

"No picture is worth getting hurt over, I got it."

He said, "Why don't we meet next Wednesday, say at the same time? If you accept the work, we'll hammer out any other concerns during our next conversation. Take the weekend, enjoy the Pride celebrations with your friends and I'll see you next week."

I waved goodbye to the other men as I left the room and wished Angela to have a great day. Descending fast inside the elevator, I felt really vulnerable. Jeepers, they really did have all the research and info on me. They seemed to know Donny quite well too. Donny must be in tight with these dudes, I thought. How else could they know all this shit, including my plans for the weekend? *Jeepers? More like creepers!*

★ ★ ★

On Thursday morning the urgent request circled the office like a bad smell. The food safety team for the Pride special event was short an inspector. I had done it before, but no way could I do it this year. Janet would kill me. I had to decline. I'd be there, but not working. The years before, when I first started, I had participated with the team at the event. It was a seriously long day and long weekend of work. By the time you clocked off around 17:00 hours there was no way you could stay and party. The manager stuck it with a new inspector, seniority rules, gotta love a union shop. *My luck was holding.*

★ ★ ★

Friday, I snuck out a tad early from work and headed home for a short cat nap before the Pride festivities really took off that weekend.

Janet was going to meet me around 19:00 hours at Church and Wellesley. We'd scratch out a few nibbles somewhere and scout the area for the best party location. We had agreed beforehand, an early night tonight, maybe end around 24:00 hours and then Saturday night we could start earlier and stay longer. The weather, as always, was slated for clear skies and hot. It never rains at Pride, least not that I've ever seen.

★ ★ ★

By 18:50 hours, I was waiting for her at Wellesley and Church, just watching the activity heat up. Church Street was closed off now for the rest of the weekend but Wellesley would stay open until 06:00 hours Saturday, to allow for traffic and TTC buses to keep moving.

She snuck up behind me and grabbed around my waist yelling, "Happy Pride!" finishing me off with a longer than usual embrace. I think Janet knew I was totally hung up on her. She had always maintained, "I'm straight, I like men," from the very beginning. I had made it clear I had been a straight man, once, and my sexual orientation had always been towards women.

What funny little conversations we had about this. How can a straight guy be transgender and want to change to female? And not be gay? The only explanation I had was that if gender identity and sexual orientation were permanently and inextricably linked to one another, then all gay men would want to be female and all gay women would want to be male. This just isn't the case. Ergo, one does not depend on the other and they are totally separate issues. *I guess like apples and oranges but in the same fruit basket.*

We walked the Church Street strip south, down to Carlton and back again, settled on the annual 519 Community Centre beer garden bash and ate some barbeque sausages there as well. They always had the best music and lots of room to roam outside in the park, which was fenced in specifically for this event.

I was snapping pics of Janet letting loose. She got 'cruised' by several amorous girls. I nailed those shots of her, as she giggled and blushed, playing along coyly in the heat of the moment. As we wandered through the crowds, I took some great shots of body tattoos on both guys and gals. Everyone was happy, having a good time, enjoying the flamboyant meat market. There were certainly more women here than men. Boobs, boobs, and more boobs. Unfortunately Janet kept hers to herself, covered. *Spoil-sport.*

Janet and I had to force ourselves to leave early, it was just too much fun but we knew tomorrow was going to be even better. A good night's sleep and not being too hung over was the sensible thing to do. After making our way to the subway at Wellesley Station, we rode to Bloor and Yonge together. She stayed on and continued north and I grabbed the westbound train home.

★ ★ ★

For Saturday, the plan was to meet around 15:00 hours at Carlton and Yonge, we would catch the end of the Dyke Parade. Janet was at the corner, talking to some cops. I sidled up behind her, wrapped my arms around her waist and whispered, "Wanna get lucky lady?" The timing was perfect, as the 'dykes on bikes' roared past signalling the rest of the march was just minutes away.

After the parade passed us and continued south, Janet and I, along with a couple of thousand other folks, headed back towards Church Street. We rounded the corner near the old Maple Leaf Gardens and could see the hordes of partiers moving into the area. It was going to be a busy event.

"Hungry?" I asked as we passed by some street food vendors.

"No, not right now, can you wait 'til later?"

"No worries. Probably need a nibble after some beers though."

The drag show was in full swing at the small parking lot behind Lincoln's, one of the gay bars that had been around forever. The line-up to get into the area was at least a hundred people. I spotted the security guy at the gate, Manny something, caught his eye and held up two fingers. Manny nodded back and we bypassed the line and slid right through the gate, into the crushing crowd.

Janet was confused as to how we got in so quick. "That was a neat trick. You know him?"

"You bet. It pays to be hanging with a well-known and somewhat respected snivil servant."

She circled my neck with her arms and gave me a long kiss right smack dab on the lips. Wow! My knees went weak.

"I'll buy the beers since you got us in," and off she toddled to the outside bar.

I think I was in shock. Now that was a kiss! My heart was racing a mile a minute. *Ain't life swell!*

The music was getting louder. We pounded back two beers each while watching three performers; a Cher, Madonna and Marilyn Monroe look alike. All really good acts, nice lip-sync and slick moves. The pictures I got were definitely X-rated.

My body was vibrating as the music travelled right through me. My ears started to hurt – just too loud. Janet obviously felt the same and thumbed towards the exit. We thanked Manny on the way out.

The walk north on Church was slow. Crowds formed and blocked street areas when someone started doing something wild and raunchy, which was often, so we took our time.

The drag queens were easy to spot. Most were over six feet tall, wobbling atop scary ass heels. Flamboyant as all get-out, donning feathery boas, formal dresses, and spiked-up hair, they sashayed about revelling in the attention. They do love to pose for photos and Janet was totally into it. *I hope this isn't how she sees me.*

Janet got cozy with some hot, buff, male dancers, who were promoting a condom company brand. I snapped off at least ten shots of her in compromising positions. Oh the things I could do with photos like that but I would never.

We made it back to the 519 Beer Garden, just north of Wellesley, and couldn't believe this line-up. It stretched from the back entrance to the street and then did a serpentine between long barricades twice over. Once the Dyke Parade ended, it would have been rammed with partiers. When people get into this venue, rarely do they leave, which explains the unending queue.

"Screw this, c'mon," and I dragged Janet to the exit gate. I badged us through security, "She is with me." They knew better than to argue. Not too ethical, using it when not working, but with a Provincial Offences Officer shield, membership has its privileges. *Maybe another earned kiss too, so there, that justifies that!*

Besides, I knew most of the operators in the area, through routine inspections and doing the special event with the food safety team when I'd first started with Public Health. I could very well have been on the lookout for violations. *That's right Lizzy – rationalize your behaviour.*

"I could eat one of those sausages on a bun again," Janet pined.

"Me too, you grab those and I'll snag us some drinks, meet back here."

I found a concrete planter that we could halfway sit on and we wolfed down our food. I kept thinking of that kiss and wanted it to happen again but thought better of it. It was probably a one-off, why spoil the night and complicate matters? Just enjoy the moment.

What a blast! We danced and peopled-watched the whole night. Janet and I wandered out of there once the music got shut down after midnight. The bars were hopping, line-ups at every one.

"Feel like going in to a bar?"

Janet shook her head, "Nah, let's just walk a bit. Besides, I think I've had enough beer and noise."

As we strolled, she latched her arm in mine. I was truly a smitten kitten. This was by far one of the best nights in my life and I didn't want it to end. By 02:00 hours, we were both beat and grabbed a cab; each to our respective apartments. I almost asked Janet to come home with me but held off, telling myself it was only an impulse kiss brought on by the festivities. *I probably won't get much sleep.*

★ ★ ★

We all met up on Sunday around 14:00 hours at the corner of Gerrard and Yonge Street. *Weird, the way all these connections in life surround you.* The parade would already be starting at the north end of Church. The floats would move across Bloor East, then south on Yonge, towards our location. We had time to chat and find a good spot. Little Andy was totally into it and Peg seemed to be having a great time but Donny, he looked a bit freaked.

We all assured him he would not get molested by the leather boys, along with a few other G-rated jokes and he finally settled down. I got some great photos of Donny and his family, more with Janet whooping it up, and some great close-ups of people and the floats.

You have to love this, everyone coming together, lining the streets for the parade, one big colossal mixture. Any and every type; from young to old, male to female and everything in between – gay or straight, families, just celebrating diversity. Wow!

Halfway through the parade, Donny had a rainbow lei around his neck, with little Andy perched atop his shoulders and donning Pride beads. I banged off a succession of shots. Donny was bouncing to the beats and Andy had his arms raised up. The pictures were going to turn out great and I'd have to remember to frame those up for him.

After the parade, Janet and I walked everybody back to the subway at Dundas and Yonge. Andy was hanging between Janet and Peg while Donny and I lagged a bit behind and talked. I told him about the meeting with the lawyers and that I was scheduled to go back in on Wednesday and give them my decision.

"I hope you don't mind but I gave them a bit of background on you."

I nodded to Donny. "Kinda figured that. They knew a lot about me already and seemed to know you quite well too."

"Yeah" he said, "I've known some of these attorneys for over a decade. I also have something for you." He handed me a half-dozen standard business cards; just his name and contact numbers. "Look, if you get into trouble with cops or whatever, you give out a card and direct them to call me. My cell is on there. But only if it gets real bad, like a tight spot, understand. There are too many people out there with loose lips and that goes for police as well. Don't trust anyone and always keep the info you gather confidential."

We all hugged at the subway entrance. Andy said he wanted to come to the party next week too. Donny and Peg smiled and Janet explained it was only once a year. Andy thought that was just wrong. We all agreed.

Janet and I left arm-in-arm, went back to the festivities, and had a hoot walking around and people-watching. If you have never been to Pride in Toronto, I recommend going. There is nothing like it – there are never any problems, no one will force you to do anything weird unless, well, you know. *Trust me!*

★ ★ ★

By Tuesday I was finally feeling myself again as the weekend had taken it right outta me. I had been working on a court case coming up for next week, just a bunch of tickets that were being contested. I spent most of the day making copies of reports, prepping the court case summary for the prosecution and compiling a second copy of documents for disclosure in case the defendant wanted it. My evidence was solid. I could relax.

★ ★ ★

Wednesday was definitely hump day and I did exactly that, humped my ass all over my area, not to mention other people's areas, doing calls. I just wanted to go home and sleep but knew I had to see the lawyer. Decision day was upon me.

After work, I went through the ear pop on the elevator, meeting again with Delahunt at his office, just the two of us this time. We sat at his gigantic desk, facing each other.

"Well Ms. Stevens, what's it going to be, in or out?"

I agreed to try it, see if things worked out and to see if they liked the end result. I gave him an out. If they didn't like the relationship they could cancel, no hard feelings.

He gave me the cell phone and ran through how info would come across. There would be attachments of names and pics of the target, along with other vital information germane to the cases.

I would not be told what the reasons were for tracking and photographing each subject and quite frankly, I didn't want to know. Delahunt explained something crucial; the investigator has to be impartial, unbiased – evidence has to be beyond reproach. It cannot be skewed or shaped to fit the case. He gave me a map and line listing of the car lot locations for the membership services, and he explained how it worked. A car would be booked by the time I got notification of the job at hand. Just grab one and go.

He handed me a leather flip case. There were business cards inside and an 'Investigator Licence' warrant card attached. Delahunt had me pegged, right after our first meeting, no doubt about it. *That was fast*, I thought. No police check, no forms to fill out? Donny must have greased the wheels.

"Whatever happens, protect the info and subject matter, including any photos or video. This is hugely important. There are too many people out there that use info in an untoward manner and that includes police at times. Do not trust anyone." If I got hung up with security or cops or whatever, I was to keep quiet and give them a card from Delahunt's law firm. "Direct them to speak with us and we'll look after it."

I guess both Donny and the big wigs had my back.

"Now, one other thing, when you get to work tomorrow, your manager is going to speak with you about taking periods of time off. All you have to do is log the time away from work. It won't be often, we hope, but it has all been cleared and they won't lose any monies."

I said it again in my mind: *money and power and knowing who to talk to… it does get things done, yes indeed.*

I left feeling a bit weird. I was excited to get my first assignment but on the other hand, my heart was skipping a bit with the dread of messing up. Sweat permeated those awkward areas again. Another item bothered me too; both Delahunt and Donny kept mentioning police … protect the info even from the police. Were the police not to be trusted? *Jeepers, that's ominous.*

★ ★ ★

True to Delahunt's word the manager pulled me into his office Thursday morning and said he was aware that I may need to arrive a bit late or leave a bit early for personal reasons. All I had to do was track my time and there would be no disruption in pay. He had been directed not to ask about it and he didn't. *These guys are good.*

I pounded off calls in my area, mostly routine, a few complaints. One operator was giving me some back talk, saying I didn't have a right to come in without giving notice to him first. He became quite animated and aggressive with me. I explained the law; the Health Protection and Promotion Act (HPPA), showed him my badge and warrant card. I gave him the choice – he could obstruct me by denying me access and I would charge him, or he could shut the fuck up and let me do my job. I don't want to say it was a cultural thing but some men in some cultures think they can tell women what to do, no matter what. I find this really offensive. He was fortunate that his co-worker pulled him aside and educated him. The call and complaint were straight-forward. A Pass issued, a bit of education on some food safety stuff, and a stern warning about any future thoughts on blocking a PHI's entry. He continued to act in a pissy mood when I was done. All part of the job – I let it go. Manners and respect, I'll give it, but I also expect it. I'm not afraid to kick down doors and use harsh language, meaning, I don't balk at barriers and will tell it to you straight up. *I do have a wonderful personality, honest!*

★ ★ ★

Friday was hot out. Humidity was up for the first time this summer. I didn't feel like doing much so I hung out at the St. Lawrence Market. Had a great breakfast at the diner there and spent the day doing low and medium-risk calls. Wandered over to St. James Park on King Street East and fed my friends while admiring the stellar flower displays.

I cut out of work early. Rarely did I ever but was feeling totally fried. I needed a good sleep and wanted to do something special on the weekend.

***

Saturday and Sunday I combined hunting for DVDs and some music CDs with scouring the downtown for murals on alley walls and such, wanting to start a collection of those shots. I had a number of places already picked out. The artwork was outstanding on most. I had my light-weight Slik tripod, one camera with a kit lens, 18-55mm, 100mm macro and an 18mm lens. You had to be mindful of some of the riffraff flocking to the alleys but they usually had no interest in me. It was a good two days spent photographing and a good start for this portfolio of shots.

***

Monday I had court at Old City Hall on Queen West near the Eaton Centre. I'm usually at work by 07:15 hours and had time for coffee and a bagel, read the paper for a bit and returned some calls. I reviewed my court case files. This guy deserved his tickets, no doubt. He had been warned twice before on two counts, plus had crucial violations. He wanted a trial, so be it. I slid the file into my satchel.

About 08:30 hours, I walked from the office to the courthouse. For court you had to dress nicely, I wore pin-striped charcoal slacks and a black embossed top. Instead of going through the regular entrance at the front, I hoofed it around back and showed my badge, which allowed me to enter without being subjected to a search. Courtroom N was on the third floor, elevator up and I arrived just as the prosecutor was entering so I followed her inside. No justice on the bench, so no need to bow to the court. I identified myself and gave the prosecutor the file, taking a seat to her right, waiting for the entertainment to begin.

The room began to fill up with defendants, most looking haggard and unkempt. Several City of Toronto agency and police officers came in as well. It would be a busy morning as usual. They all checked in with the prosecutor, as did the defendants, opting in turn whether to plea out or continue the fight. Defendants sat to the left and the other officers joined me on the right. Court reporter and clerk were in position.

"All rise." The justice came in and sat. Everyone else sat

The prosecutor identified herself and took care of all the plea cases first, so those could be dealt with and fines assessed. My defendant decided to plea once he saw me in the court. That is a typical ploy for many, show up to court and hope the officer doesn't, thereby having the ticket withdrawn. Nice try, asshole. He got almost a thousand bucks in fines and had ninety days to pay. I had no other business, so off I went, bowing as I left the court room, happy as a clam.

Since I was dressed in my finest clothes, I stayed in the office and finished off the court case summary file and other paper work. No way was I going to ruin two-hundred dollar slacks out in the field. I ended the day by completing an insect identification for a walk-in client. Not a bed bug, carpet beetle only. Toronto had been experiencing a surge in bed bug issues and the media were all over it. We had developed fact sheets and had a nice little microscope for looking at critters. The scope attached to the computer as well, so I printed a photo for the client and walked through any concerns and questions.

★ ★ ★

Mid-July and still no assignment from Delahunt. I had my gear all ready to go, just in case. Work kept me busy and I was dragging my ass most days, so not having a secondary gig was just fine with me.

Other inspectors were off on holidays and the work just piled up, not to mention all the overtime on night calls and special events in the city. I was banking lieu hours like crazy, trying to get all the calls done. I never much wanted the money but to have extra holidays away from here – yippee.

It was just past 20:00 hours on Friday night. I was absolutely beat. Burnt out from all the overtime, all I wanted was to crash in my bed and sleep late. The lawyer phone rang.

"One new email, marked urgent, eh?"

I flipped through the menu and opened it up. *Ms. Stevens, sorry for the late notification, however we require you to act immediately. The target is about to have dinner now at Singles, 463 King St. West. Drives a BMW, dark grey coupe, licence MMKL257. Follow until arrives home at 709 Humphrey St. See attached photo and name. Your closest car access is at Dufferin Mall parking. Angela Re: Blakley, Delahunt & McCoy.*

No rest for the wicked I thought, while getting dressed. Black cargos, black tee, and a grey pullover top, take a light-coloured jacket, and black hiking boots laced on tight.

Cameras – grabbed one with the 75-200 and one with the 100-400mm lens. Both had huge memory cards, formatted, charged up and ready to shoot. Threw in the kit lens, 18-55mm, just in case, but I'd probably never get that close. Stashed my ID and cash in my pockets and was out the door in less than ten minutes.

The Dufferin Mall was less than five minutes away. I had scouted the area of the car service ahead of time and knew where to go. Grabbed a dark-blue, two-door compact, some Japanese make I think. I cut south, down Dufferin Street and blew a yellow through College, past Dundas and then Queen, approaching King West. I pulled a slick driving move through the Burger King parking lot on the left, out back onto King, to avoid a back log of left-turning cars, then stomped the car hard, going eastbound. I was really jacked and had to force myself to slow down. Getting pulled over now would most definitely blow the assignment. The core area was not real busy yet so I made good time regardless.

I crossed Spadina Avenue and started to check the numbers on businesses to get something close to four-fifty and lucked out as a driver was pulling away, so I cut into the parking spot. Put a couple of loonies into the machine and placed the parking tag on the dash.

My watch said 20:35. No one eats that fast so I should get my shots. I found Singles at 463 King Street West and was glad it wasn't a hoity-toity place that had a dress code.

I sat at the bar, ordered a Heineken and scanned for my target while looking at his picture on the phone screen. James Dufner was seated with company, second table in from the window against the west wall, fawning over a well-endowed, blondish woman who was dressed to the nines. *Way outta his league,* I thought. Mr. Dufner looked fairly young, maybe twenty-five, kinda urban preppy, with the open dress shirt and stylish hair held up with gel. *A metrosexual if there ever was such a thing.*

I had a good angle and pulled out my camera with the 75-200mm lens and laid it on the bar. I flipped the articulating screen so I could see the image from my sitting position and manoeuvred the camera so I got them both in the frame. Click. Too slow. Bumped the ISO up to 800 and tried again. It was okay so I turned it to movie mode and started shooting. After thirty seconds, I stopped and checked the video. Not bad, a bit grainy but you could see them clearly. I took some shots of the little tryst taking place, catching all the sweet touching and giggling moments. The sounds of the restaurant cancelled out noise from shooting. I kept the camera partially hidden by laying my coat and camera bag beside it, on top of the bar.

My beer came and I took a small swig – *can't get loaded and do this,* I thought. I set the camera back to movie mode and recorded brief, thirty-second bursts each time, every few minutes or so.

They were eating the main course now. I stopped shooting and reviewed pictures and video. Satisfactory so far, I would have to clean them up a tad, maybe lighten a tic.

I memorized the licence plate of his car and his home address, from the phone info, and sat sipping my beer. Perhaps over dessert they might feed each other or something interesting. I was feeling conspicuous so I pulled out my tiny user manual for the camera and pretended to read it.

The couple didn't have dessert; they just got the bill and paid with credit, then started to leave. I threw a ten on the bar, gathered my gear and moved with them. My car was west of the restaurant and they were walking east. If they got to his car I'd lose them. It was only 21:50 hours so I took a chance and followed on foot, maybe they would hit a club.

They crossed the intersection of King and headed north on John Street, holding hands, and I snapped a shot from behind, from the other side of the street. Too slow, bump the ISO to 1600. Click.

I lucked out again as they stood in line at a bar on Richmond Street West. Some dark, dingy place with no name, only a symbol above the door; typical yuppie scene, I thought. I snapped a photo of the crowd, making sure I got Dufner and lady in frame. It looked really familiar. *Christ, it was the same bar that Donny was shot in ten years ago.* This was not a good sign. The queue was at least twenty couples long; I would surely have ten minutes before they got inside. I figured I could nip back to the car, switch out my top, don the jacket and dump the big camera. Then move the rental car back to this area and follow my subject inside the club.

By the time I got back to the bar, they had either left or entered so I headed to the doorman and badged him. "I'm on surveillance and following a lead inside."

The guy with a tree stump for a neck and arms so thick he probably couldn't scratch his own ass just looked down at me with a jaded smile. "Got a warrant?"

"Look, I just need to see what they are doing and follow them. Okay?"

"Not on my watch. Show me a warrant and I'll call the boss and we'll be happy to verify the paper and let you in."

I thought for a moment. No sense getting in too deep, I'd just wait in the car for them to come out. "Forget it. Thanks for your help." Of course in my mind I was saying something else entirely different about the steroid sucking meathead.

I hustled back to where the car was parked and moved it around to the loading bay of a condo building. I had a good angle and clear shot to the front of the nightclub. Either I'd missed them leaving or I had a long wait ahead of me. I got comfy.

There was a tapping at the window. "You can't park here." It was security for the condo.

I badged him and said, "Surveillance."

He just put his hands up and walked away. *There ya go girl, just a bit of attitude and presto, no more problem.*

I took some test shots with the big lens to see what ISO I would need, then ran a movie clip. Not very good, but I could edit in the computer and bring up the brightness a bit without ruining the shots. Waiting, squirming in the seat of the compact car, not comfy at all, I moved the seat to every possible position. The log sheet was brought up to date with times and locations.

"Christ! This blows." My watch showed 01:10 hours, the bars didn't close until two, and my ass was numb. I got out of the car and did a little jig to loosen up my glutes and get the blood flowing again.

I was starting to think this job sucked and wasn't worth the trouble. I kept watching, feeling I had missed them and was just an idiot for sitting here. I was thinking of bailing as it encroached on 02:00 hours.

"Ca-ching baby!" There they were, all goofy and drunk and slobbering all over each other. Had my 100-400mm lens ready. Click, click, click. Okay, now to follow, thank goodness Richmond ran in the right direction.

Dufner headed west on Richmond Street, arm in arm with Ms. Boobs, cut south on a side street and into a small parking lot. I couldn't see him or his car. At the curb I idled and waited. After five minutes panic set in. Was there another exit?

I jumped out of my car, trotted over to the lot, and scanned the area. I couldn't tell the colour of any vehicle or see a licence plate but spotted the look of a Beamer and could see two heads grinding on each other. "Ah!" A little heavy necking is all and no other exits neither – still okay.

It was another ten minutes of waiting, but finally Dufner and said tartlet came rolling out and headed west on Richmond, cut south and then back east on Adelaide Street. He would be aiming for the Don Valley Parkway, which would take them north to cut across Lawrence East and hopefully home. I was exhausted.

I was no pro in tailing and too tired to really care if he suspected someone was behind him. At any rate, he was well intoxicated, as the BMW couldn't hold a lane very well so I doubted he would notice me. *I hate when people drive wasted!*

Pulling off Lawrence Avenue East, they hit an all-night convenience store for supplies. Idling in the strip mall and looking at the map, his address, in relation to where I was now, was two blocks east and down four blocks. Figured they would land there so I booted it to the house and found a good spot across the street. I quietly backed into a driveway and angled the car so I could shoot out the passenger side window. Took a test shot and adjusted for light.

It was quite a scene when they arrived. The car parking needed work as Dufner had the vehicle angled sharply in the driveway and partly up on the lawn. Neither of them could stand up very well or walk straight, so they buddied up and helped each other. Click. Click. Shot video of the slow motion dash to the front door. The night lights for the house were bright. I could make them out clearly.

Good stuff, lots of groping, kissing and fumbling. Once they were inside and the door closed, my job was done. "Good night!" I sure hope that's what Delahunt wanted me to shoot. It was after 03:00 hours, bedtime for me too.

* * *

It was after 13:00 hours on Saturday and I had had a good sleep. Made coffee and checked the weather channel. I scarfed down some toast with peanut butter and jam, loaded up on more coffee, ready for the day.

Booted up the computer, grabbed all my camera gear, and started to download the pics and video from last night. Morning? I cleaned up the video, brightening most of it and sharpened up the pics. Copied the clean shots and saved the originals.

I logged on to the server and sent Delahunt the photos and video in an attachment to my email, which included my synopsis and scanned log sheet. First assignment completed. No harm, no foul, no one died.

I was beat and could only manage being in a vegetative state all weekend, so watching golf and Coronation Street on the boob tube filled the days. My requisite phone call was made to my mom, always on Sunday, checking in and seeing how she was coping. She brought me up to speed on all the news from other family members and friends. Seems a lot of her peer group were dying, the list remaining growing ever shorter. I did try and visit at least three or four times a year as she lived about two hours away. Often I'd swing around after my annual camping trip, a bit of a drive but what's an extra two hours, especially for my dear mom. Besides, I got some home-cooked meals so that right there made it worth the effort. *She is the best cook ever!*

* * *

On Wednesday, while doing inspections, I got an email from Delahunt's office. *Good job. No further action required on this last case. Angela. Blakley, Delahunt & McCoy.*

Great, I didn't want to follow this guy any more, especially at those hours.

★ ★ ★

I had talked to Donny and Janet a few times on the phone but everyone was just too busy to hook up, myself included. I asked if Donny was interested in bringing Andy down to the air show on the long weekend in September and he was up for it. He would call in a week or so and plan out a dinner before that. Janet wasn't sure of her schedule and would have to let me know. I was getting the feeling she was avoiding me. Had I come on too strong? Was she afraid to go further, start something with me? *Great, more shit in my brain to worry about!*

★ ★ ★

August in Toronto can be beautiful, especially down by the waterfront area. Unfortunately it can also be blistering hot. Today the temperature was pushing twenty-five Celsius and it was only 07:30 hours with an expected humidex of thirty-eight Celsius by midday. Hot and shticky was the weather call, not a lot of fun unless you had an air conditioner or at least a fan.

I was sitting in the office prepping for more inspection calls when the lawyer phone rang. *Ms. Stevens. Require you at 83 Crawford St. for 16:00 hours today. Target is male, shoot activity around house. See attachment for photo and name. I assume you will need to get equipment at home so car is ready for pick up at Dufferin Mall. Angela. Blakley, Delahunt & McCoy.*

I would have to leave work by 14:00 to get home, grab the cameras, and pick up the car. I let the manager know I had to leave a bit early. No problem. I prayed the car would have air conditioning.

★ ★ ★

By the time I walked from the subway exit to my apartment, then to Dufferin Mall with all my gear, the sweat just poured off me. I grabbed a sporty, two-door red number at the car park and could tell by looking through the window it had air. Just after 15:25 hours; lots of time to get to my location. The windows up, the AC on full and I made sure to snag a few ice-cold bottles of water from a convenience store on my way.

By 15:50 hours, I was waiting across the street from 83 Crawford, still had the air on full, and had started in on the second bottle of water. The street was one-way only in this section so ample choice of locations to park. Lots of big trees lined the road and I had found shade but it barely made a difference. Opted for the far west side of the street so I could shoot out the passenger window again – good cover as the windows were slightly tinted.

The street was dotted with older, single detached homes mostly, intermixed with a few semis, well kept. Great gardens were in full display on most properties and Trinity Bellwoods Park was on the opposite side of their back yards. *Nice neighbourhood,* I thought, *I could live here.*

I looked at the target's picture. Dan Saunders was kinda gruff looking. I took several practice shots, got the speed and light dialled in, allowed for a good DoF, then waited. I was finished the second bottle of water and had to pee – great!

At 16:15 hours, a rusted-out black Ford pickup pulled into the driveway and I started my video. Saunders was unmistakable, and such a fine specimen too. Grossly overweight, beer belly hanging out over dirty ripped blue jeans; a fashionista he was not. His white T shirt wasn't all that clean and disgusting stains were visible even from my vantage point. His urban look was completed, most stylishly, with a cigarette dangling from mouth, ugly stubble and unlaced work boots. *Now I know why my sexual orientation is towards the female of the species.*

"What a pig!" Oops! That'll come through on the video, my bad.

He looked around like someone with something to hide, real slithery-like.

I slumped down in the seat, shooting video through the partially-open, passenger-side window. I was at least twenty metres away; he wouldn't notice me.

He unlatched the rear tailgate and pulled out a chain saw, gas can, and axe. He looked around again, then hefted all three and waddled towards the back yard.

"Gonna do some trim work, eh Dan?"

I locked the car and counted the houses from the corner of the street back to his house then hurried around to the parkland behind.

It wasn't hard to find his place from the back, as the chainsaw was already fired up and good ol' Danny boy was whaling away on a defenceless tree. I found a clump of bushes to use as cover and shot video of my plump little woodsman as he decimated an unwanted growth. I wished I had brought a tripod to hold the camera. I still had to pee too!

I had to adjust my position a few times as he went to work hacking up the log rounds into nice quarters for firewood. Dan paused for a beer and I salivated, wishing I had one too. He continued to Paul Bunyan away at another innocent forest dweller, I kept the video to short bursts. Figured it had to be a workers comp or insurance fraud case, so I got the most laborious poses and actions. Not supposed to do that but this dude was annoying me.

I was dripping sweat. It was 18:40 hours and Dan went inside. I figured he'd be back out after a little supper so I started to shoot some flowers and watched the dogs taking their masters for a romp in the park. Lucky dogs getting to pee anywhere they pleased. I made notes in a little book of my time lines. I couldn't hold it any longer. I found a bit of a hide, squatted down and let loose with a torrential flood. It seemed endless and overwhelmed the ground with volume, engulfing and spreading past my boots. *Jeepers!*

By 19:20 hours, Saunders was back. I could hear him belch and he was drinking more beer and smoking. I started filming. He was hefting a few of the wood chunks and carrying them towards the front of the house.

I raced back to the car and timed my move so he wouldn't see me. For the next hour-plus, he loaded all the wood and the equipment back into his truck, closed the tailgate and went back inside. All caught on video, thank you very much. I called it a night and left. Dropped the car back at the mall and hoofed it home from there.

The photos and video didn't need any corrections. Light and focus was spot on. I filed those, along with my email synopsis and scanned log, in less than two hours. Let's hope Delahunt is satisfied with that array of shots.

It was just after 23:00 hours when I got to bed. I wasn't getting enough sleep. *I'll be draggin' my ass tomorrow, no doubt.*

★ ★ ★

I had just had a shower before going into work the next morning. My little dehumidifier was working overtime, trying to keep my basement apartment cool and dry. I was already sweating – gonna be another hot one today.

The lawyer phone rang. "Christ all mighty!" I really didn't want another assignment so soon.

I opened the email. *Ms. Stevens. Could you stop by the office and speak to Mr. Delahunt at 16:30 today. Please bring hard copy of logs and all original data on memory stick. Call and confirm. Angela. Blakley, Delahunt & McCoy.*

After hunting about for a usable memory stick, I copied the raw data from the last two assignments, verified all the original photos and video were on the memory stick, and then I blanked those computer files. I let Angela know I'd be there.

★ ★ ★

My ears popped, again, as I exited the elevator on the sixty-first floor. I wondered how I could make that stop. They say to suck on a candy – that's what the airlines offer you, isn't it?

Angela showed me into the office immediately and Delahunt motioned me over to his desk. As I sat, I gave him the log sheets and the memory stick with the raw data on it.

"No more copies?" he asked.

"Nope."

"Good. We don't want you holding any data for very long and we need the originals for our files."

I nodded and looked out his window while he organized some papers.

"Now for the good stuff," he said as he handed me an envelope. "Go ahead. Open it."

I did as instructed and examined the cheque. "That's a bit generous," I said.

"Nonsense, you earned it and we like the work you did. In fact, we interviewed several people for this job. You were the only one that didn't ask about the money. We liked that, figured you were more interested in the quality of the work, not what was in it for yourself."

My, my, a full grand for little old me, I was taken aback. I started to figure this work ain't so bad, especially at that price. That there is almost a third of the cost of a new camera I was dreaming of.

"We decided to bump up the fee since you went very long on assignment. I know you don't normally stay up that late and the one request was made on short notice. You did very well. We all appreciate your efforts."

They know when I go to bed? Jeepers! I advised Raymond Delahunt that I would be taking my holidays in a few weeks. "My plan is to stop working at the end of August. I'll be in town until two days after the Labour Day long weekend since I like to shoot the air show at the CNE and it gives me a few days to pack. Then up to Algonquin Park for about ten nights and I'll be driving around after that visiting a few people and taking photos. I should be back in Toronto by the nineteenth or so but not back to my day job until the beginning of October. I'll be available for any assignments say… prior to September fourth and then after the twentieth."

Delahunt was fine with that. "Just continue on as you have been. We'll be in touch."

He stood and shook my hand, ending the meeting.

"Oh, I almost forgot." He handed me a bag of memory sticks. "Don't want you to have any unnecessary expenses. We would like each case on a separate stick, if you don't mind. Just the raw data, as I will have already received the cleaned shots and video. The hard copy of the log can be delivered periodically, along with the sticks."

"No problem." I left with my money and trinkets, happy as a clam and sporting a thousand of 'em in my pocket. Too bad it wasn't straight cash then I could avoid giving the government any part. *Honest lawyers, go figure!*

★ ★ ★

The humidity finally broke after a rain and we had a nice pattern of high pressure, fluffy white clouds and a cooling breeze downtown. Now this was more like it. I had about three more weeks of work and then off for a month. Life was good. I was in a groove, feeling that I knew my job well and had everything under control. Donny called Thursday and we agreed to meet Friday for an early dinner at Cyrano's.

★ ★ ★

When I saw Donny, he was at the bar yakking with some cops I vaguely recognized. He gave me a hug and introduced me to his colleagues. They were all very pleasant and gave me a seat at the bar, crowded around, got me a drink and brought up the night of nights as two of them had actually been there.

"Jesus Christ I almost shit myself! How do you guys do it? Sorry, girls I mean."

It was the young constable who had bagged Donny for the whole call. He was now a veteran cop. He regaled everyone with his version of events and a bunch of other cops pushed closer to hear the story. I felt like a celebrity. More drinks arrived and I was getting hammered. *I needed to eat some food.*

The stories led into others, everyone trying to one-up the last – it could go on forever. That's one thing, never a shortage of professional tales, most all perfectly true; the streets didn't require any embellishment.

Finally Donny saved me and hauled me through to the back and we sat at a table and ordered a light meal.

"Well, tell me, how's the job going with the lawyers?"

I nibbled on my salad and between bites nodded. "It's pretty good. The hours can suck but the money makes it bearable."

I gave him a general description of the two calls I'd gone on and how I blew it trying to get into the night club.

He laughed at my undercover skills. "You'll get better and start to figure out ways to get around people like that."

He told me the latest buzz with the fuzz. Apparently, several cops and at least two detectives were under investigation for ties with certain criminal elements in the city.

"I cannot name names or go into any department specifics but many will be glad if a certain 'D' gets his." He winked but I really didn't get the clue.

I told him about my upcoming holidays and when I'd be out of the city.

Donny shook his head, "I just can't see how you go into the bush, alone mind you, and then wander around for what, a week or two. I couldn't do it."

Grinning at the prospect, I told him, "If there ever was a place that I could stay forever it would be Algonquin Park. No matter what is happening in the world, this place is my refuge. Everything

I would ever need is there." I told him where I drive to, how I enter into the Algonquin system from the highway, and about the portage to gain access to the deeper areas of the park and all the wildlife. As we ate our roast beef sandwiches I described the food I eat while camping and he really wanted no part of that menu.

"How can you eat that shit!? Why don't you take canned goods and normal food with you?"

"Well, my fine, friendly, flat-footed urbanite, who's gonna carry all that weight, my personal Sherpa?"

"Point noted," he remarked sheepishly.

We firmed up when and where we'd meet for the air show, Peg was unable to make it and Janet had not yet confirmed. We chatted about city politics for a while, budget restraints, and why we deserved a pay raise. Then, ironically, we argued over who would flip for the bill. I finally won out and paid, Donny all the while putting up a reluctant fuss. We left Cyrano's and Donny walked me over to the subway entrance – big bear hug to say good bye and he headed back to his car.

★ ★ ★

Two more weeks of work and then I would be outta here. The thought brought a smile to my face – everything was going really good. I was being too nice to my operators during inspections but they really didn't have any serious infractions. I was tying up my area, getting ahead so as not to leave work for my colleagues, just counting down the days.

I banged off some night calls and built up more lieu time. Several high-end restaurants were completed and thankfully no real issues. One place on Wellington East, which was in a line of older buildings all interconnected, had a mouse issue. Droppings were noted in several non-food areas, mostly basement utility sections of the premises, so I cut them a break. Directed them on how to clean it up safely, to get pest control in and trap the area, fill in some access points inside on walls and clear up possible harbourage sites. The owner was lucky I was in a good mood, plus he took my advice seriously, so I knew he would comply and quickly.

★ ★ ★

The manager grabbed me late on Wednesday and pleaded with me to do a health hazard call over on Carlton Street. He was stuck – no staff available. Even though I was in the food safety focus, I had ample experience in this program so I went. It was a city councillor's complaint, so it was top priority, at least in his mind. Unsanitary conditions regarding a spa at an all-male premise was all the report stated. *Geezez! That could sure mean a lot of things.* I would inspect the premises and do the whirlpool spa inspection as well. There were a lot of these places popping up; bar and hang-out type spaces with showers and a whirlpool for relaxing. It was usually an interesting call.

I hit the premises about 15:00 hours. The name on the front of the building said 'Sprinkles' and that brought all sorts of images to mind. Spoke to the staff on site and advised them why I was there. Toured the bar, lounge, private rooms – all were clean and neat. They practiced good sanitation and used the correct disinfecting products. Every wall had at least one big screen TV showing porn, and not the soft stuff neither. Wherever I went, so did a humungous penis, bobbing and weaving, telling a story and meeting other penises. I headed for the showers and whirlpool spa. Then it started. Two muscle freaks grinding away against the glass walls, soaped up and acting out. Anyone in the bar could see them, which was the point. Open concept, designed for optimal viewing. I had to pass through the shower area to get to the spa and that was touch and go. Playful critters I must say. The staff had to tell them to behave. The whirlpool could seat about eight persons typically but I'm sure on some nights, it would exceed its limit. Two big-screen TVs hung on opposite walls with the Mr. Penis Show in full HD. I checked chemistry, doing a full compliance inspection and ensured the place was wired with ground fault circuits. No issues with the spa – final discussion was just review on safety and clean up, report left with staff, and out I go. *Now I know why the manager sent me.*

★ ★ ★

Thursday, while I was heading out of the office door, my lawyer phone rang.

I returned to my desk and scrolled to the email. *Ms. Stevens. We need you to attend High Park this Saturday. Target is female. Unknown time of arrival, but assume around 10:00 hours. Follow and shoot activity. Individual may attend area restaurant. Attached is name and photo. Unknown vehicle. Car booked at Dufferin Mall. Angela. Blakley, Delahunt & McCoy.*

Well, I could handle that. Finally, get to stakeout a place that I know like the back of my hand, and I could actually get some other photos too. Yippee!

I looked at the name and picture on the cell phone screen. "Oh, this is not good!" It was Ms. Boobs. It seemed I hadn't been following Dufner that previous time; the real target was the tartlet he was with.

I hazily recalled what Donny had said on our tenth anniversary night out, something like, "*...they build a case, just like the cops...*" I leaned back in my chair and looked up. I wondered why the ceiling tiles had little holes in them anyway.

★ ★ ★

Friday, after work, I checked my camera gear and had an early night. I thought I'd get to High Park around 07:30 hours, grab a spot for the car near the restaurant, and then wander about for a few hours shooting wildlife. If the target was walking around the park, then the best place to stake out would be the Garden Spot parking lot. Although there were other small areas around the green space to stop a vehicle, this would be most logical. *I have a plan.*

★ ★ ★

When I checked at 06:00 hours, the weather channel predicted sun with cloudy periods, calm winds and a high of twenty-six Celsius. After a quick shower, and dressing in moss green cargos and a muted-grey colour tee, I laced up my hikers and tied my hair back.

I took my vest, loaded with peanuts, along with my two cameras and a lightweight Slik tripod. I thought about taking two other lenses, a kit 18-55mm and a 100mm macro but the weight was already too heavy. Then I mumbled to myself, "Screw it,' and stuck them in my bag anyway. I could leave them in the trunk and use them as needed.

I grabbed the car at Dufferin Mall. I think it was the same red one I'd used the last time. It was still early, little traffic, so I drove west on Bloor Street. Grabbed a Tim's coffee and bagel at a drive through and cut into the park from the north end. Wound around the one-way lane towards the centre of the park. Not a lot of people walking around yet, but it would get busy by 11:00 hours or so. The Garden Spot restaurant was already buzzing with the breakfast crowd, but still lots of parking and I slid into a space at the far southeast end, near an exit.

I checked my watch, now 07:40 hours. I still had a couple of hours for myself and trundled off south towards Colborne Lodge. As I walked, making little 'tsk tsk' sounds calling the squirrels and chippies, my friends came bounding at me for a treat. I just love it when they put their little hands in mine and take a peanut.

A few birds buzzed my head, letting me know they were friendly. I held out broken bits of peanuts in my hand and had a chickadee, downy woodpecker and female blackbird land one after the other and take a bite. Quite a feeling, having the little birds come right to you. I spotted a red fox at the edge of some garden plots and blasted off a dozen shots with my big lens.

There are paths leading all through the woods and I cut south off the road and downhill towards a flat and another large pond. It always surprises me, the number of people living, or just sleeping, in the park throughout the summer. Sometimes you almost trip over them while walking on the trails. *Freaky man!*

I got some good shots of the wood ducks. One photo had the bland female nibbling at the neck of the showier male. That looked pretty cool. I snagged a few pictures of a snowy egret, replete with a nice mirror reflection in the water. Cut through another area, mindful of the poison ivy, and headed around to the south end of Grenadier Pond. A black-crowned night heron tried to hide from me in a tree but I got him showing his crest.

I couldn't see much on the pond, so I cut towards the restaurant and climbed the rise where a waterfall runs through tiered rock formations. After setting up my tripod and changing the camera lens, I slowed the shutter speed to one-third a second and shot the water flowing down to get it looking silky. Tried a few other speeds and was happy with the result.

Checked my watch, 09:10 hours, I still had about thirty minutes to check out the small zoo they had, so I scaled the rest of the incline and then humped back down another sloped road to the caged animals. They didn't have much worthy of photos but I got some shots of a peacock spreading his feathery tail. There was also a goat standing on a rock mound, looking quite proud, kinda like king of the castle and I got that pic too.

At 09:45 hours, I headed back up the road towards the restaurant and had maybe enough time to grab a drink and set up somewhere to wait for my target. As I walked, I looked at my cell phone and studied the woman's face I was supposed to find and follow.

As I looked up, she was five metres in front of me, coming straight at me, hand-in-hand with a rather smart-looking fellow. My heart bouncing, I stopped and just pretended to look at the phone. *What else can I do? Maybe poop my pants* came to mind. It was definitely her, Danielle Simons.

The guy, who looked like a professional golfer type, was tall and lean with a controlled swagger, not gangly or awkward. He was very well dressed in two-tone, brown-on-beige shoes, cream pants with the hem turned up, reminiscent of the fifties and wearing a white cotton shirt with the sleeves rolled slightly. He was damn near perfect, from tinted brown hair to toes, except for a goofy gold chain and medallion around his neck. *Schmuck!*

She was a real looker and had all the right curves. I hadn't really focused on this woman the last time when she was with Dufner. Ms. Boobs wore white cotton, high cut shorts and a pale-pink, short-sleeved top which went well with the light-blond streaked hair, nice low-heel canvas sandals, a Louis V. purse on one shoulder and a white cotton sweater draped over the arm. Short, manicured nails on both hands and feet, in a soft pastel pink. Big bust – I guess some guys like that. Definitely dressed in money, I thought.

They had to have come from the parking lot at the restaurant. It would look suspicious if I went back down after them, so I planted my butt on a bench and started shooting video.

Nice thing about digital cameras and video is that you can pull an individual frame out of the movie and it is like having a snapshot. I took thirty-second clips, adjusted for distance, and waited.

Ms. Boobs and escort could have exited at the bottom but it really only led to a small parking area and playground. They would have had a bit of a hike to get back around so I just waited some more, as I knew they would most likely come back this way.

Sure enough, they turned and started the trek back towards the restaurant at the top of the incline. Now for some full frontal shots if you please! My little puppets didn't disappoint. Not much kissing and groping behaviour, like when she was with Dufner, but definitely close and intimate touchy-feely stuff. They stopped at each cage, looking at the animals and pointing to various curiosities.

As they walked by me, the golf pro dude eyed me and said, "Nice day."

I had no problem agreeing with him, "Couldn't be better!" I chimed.

I followed them right to the restaurant. They sat by the windows and I took a seat about three metres away, perpendicular to theirs. I set the 75-200mm camera on the table and did my thing, catching all the sweet moments. No awkwardness here, as most of the other photographers who frequented the restaurant were checking their shots as well.

I inhaled a grilled cheese sandwich and fries and while they were still eating, paid the bill and hit the washroom. I grabbed a cold bottle of water before I left, making sure they were still there, then headed for my car and got into position.

About twenty minutes later, they came out and slowly wandered over to a beige colour, two-door Jaguar about forty meters away from my position. Luckily, I captured a long passionate kiss before they got in.

It was just after 12:00 hours. I thought I might as well give a bit more effort and practice my tailing skills, so I followed them.

They left the park from the south exit and headed east on Queen towards the city core, then cut south onto the Lakeshore and continued east. Golf pro's car was easy to spot and follow, no speed records, no hurry. They were east of the downtown and going towards Scarborough. Perhaps one of the yacht clubs, maybe a golf lesson?

I followed the Jag north to Kingston Road, and then eastbound for a fair whack, definitely Scarborough area now. They pulled left into a motel parking lot and I quickly cut right and backtracked through a strip mall.

"My little puppets are gonna practice afternoon putting, how nice!" I said to myself, grinning as I turned into a space facing towards the motel. I had the tiny car angled so I could shoot out the side window again. My vantage point was perfect, slightly elevated and looking downward towards the motel area. The distance was far, pretty much the end of my lens' capability, at least for anything really clear.

I watched through my 100-400mm lens as the golf pro guy went in and got the room key while Ms. Boobs waited in the car. Click, click. Coming out now, click. Backing in to a parking spot, click. Getting out of the car and at the room door, *Oh lucky number seven,* I thought to myself. Click, click. "What, no luggage?" I was having too much fun.

I could make out his licence plate, and copied it down and updated my log. 13:15 hours; I was going to be here for awhile no doubt. I shot the sign of the motel, the Twilight Inn. Probably should have called it Afternoon Delight. I hoped their little tryst would be short-lived.

I was baking in the sun. I checked out other parking places to see if I could get a better vantage point and not roast to death. Not much shade, since no trees were growing from the tarmac, so I eyed a spot to the east of the big sign showing all the businesses in the strip mall. The sun would arc down behind it soon and offer a respite but several cars were parked there. I ran the air for a while but it wasn't much help.

Now it was 15:00 hours. I ran into a small deli-style restaurant, used the washroom and grabbed another bottle of water. The place was air-conditioned and I spent twenty minutes watching from the window, cooling off and enjoying the short absence from the giant scorching orb in the sky.

I saw enough cars leave from below the big sign and jumped into a spot, again angling my two-door compact so I could shoot through the passenger side window. Took a test shot, adjusted for the change in light, and waited.

16:00 hours and counting, "What are these guys, rabbits!" I thought I should just blow, but it was feeling cooler now since I had blocked the sun with the statuesque sign. Besides, I didn't have much of a life to go home to anyways. "Screw it Lizzy girl, stay the course." *Always putting in a little extra*, I thought, *one of my better traits.*

As I was doing some stretches outside the car, to get the body moving and stem the aches of sitting so long, I saw a pizza delivery car pull up and go to their door of the motel. The golf pro dude answered in his shirt and boxers, and paid for the food and drinks. I missed the shot. No big deal but it meant that I was now here for dinner and I started to get hungry.

I went back to the little restaurant and ordered a roast beef sub, toasted, and another bottle of water. It was devoured in less than five minutes. Another bathroom break was needed too. *Geezez, I may need to start taking an anti-diuretic.*

17:00 hours and I was coming up on a ten-hour shift. The motel was getting a bit busier. Several cars had come in, a small RV camper unit, and a few more couples; some even with kids in tow.

18:00 hours went into my log sheet. I noticed a middle-aged man walking through the parking lot looking at the cars. Not a burglar type – he had black slacks and a fitted shirt with his greyish suit jacket over one arm; too well dressed for a hooligan.

He stopped at the Jag and looked at a piece of paper and then at the licence plate. Click, click. *This was interesting.*

He looked around at the rooms and then walked slowly back, towards the farthest east side of the motel, then slipped out of sight. *Now I was intrigued.*

Ten minutes later, two men came around the corner from the east side and went directly to the golf pro guy's Jag. Both were dressed in similar slacks and dress shirts with jackets over arms. The first guy I saw, taller, with longish black hair seemed to be doing all the talking. His shorter counterpart, buzz cut, not quite as slim, nodded frequently.

My first thought was, *Cops?* No, couldn't be, no guns. Click, click. I ran a video for a bit. They appeared to be unsure, briefly. One went to the motel office while the other sauntered back to the corner of the building but not quite out of sight. Click, click.

I shot video of the dude coming back from the office. As he walked by the room, he pointed then he held up fingers to his partner. He must have signed the room number with his digits. *Unlucky number seven more like.*

The distance was far for my lens. I tried zooming in with the internal feature and thank goodness I had image stabilization or it would have made the viewer sea sick. I shot more video of their little huddle up conference at the corner of the building and then they disappeared again.

This was fascinating. Not only was I following Ms. Boobs and the stylish golf pro guy, but so were other people. Very cool!

I tried to make out the two dudes scoping my target but I didn't recognize their faces. These guys were well built though. I hadn't really noticed while shooting, but on review of the pics, when I zoomed in, both really were 'no-neck gym jockeys' and it showed. I wouldn't want to tangle with these ruffians.

Changed batteries in both cameras to be sure they wouldn't conk out and then verified I had good shots and video. Switched out the memory card in the 100-400mm lens camera too, so I had lots of space.

Maybe Ms. Boobs, aka Danielle Simons, was being a very naughty girl and probably an old hubby was getting some dirt for future leverage. *Wait, that's what I'm most likely doing. So what are they doing?*

It was 18:45 hours. The sun's angle was getting low and shining directly against me again, messing up any chance of a clean shot. I had to move to a new location and quick. "Think!" I needed the sun behind me for the best light. "Screw it!"

I spun the car around and sped out the west exit of the strip mall, crossed the two lanes of Kingston Road and zipped into the motel parking lot. Creeping along slowly, I found the right opening and backed into a spot on the east side of the camper van, which blocked the sun and anyone in the office from seeing me.

However, I was only fifteen meters west from room seven. Awfully close to the action and I could be spotted easily.

I could shoot through the passenger side window and cracked it down about eight inches. I grabbed my vest, hung it on the window to block any view into the car, and threw up my camera bags on the dash to block that angle.

I was a bit too close for the 100-400mm so I switched to the 75-200mm and took some test shots. Excellent.

I changed the memory card in the 75-200mm lens camera and waited. The Jag was about ten metres east of my car; its definitive nose sticking out. The corner of the building was a good forty metres east. I had the angles covered.

Updating my log; 19:20 hours – about an hour of good light at best, I thought.

I bumped up the ISO to 400 and shot the room door, the Jag and the east corner of the motel. All okay.

Waiting, uncomfortable, and getting cranky. I played with setting the camera on the headrest and other positions. It was seriously uncomfortable and I decided to get into the back seat and try from there. Much better and I patted my back for the incredibly brilliant on-the-spot thinking. Now 19:40 hours and still waiting – I updated the log.

I saw a dude peek around the east corner of the motel. Three men appeared now, in plain view, two from before and a new guy discussing something at the corner of the building. Click, click.

One looked vaguely familiar. I had seen him before. He was putting up his hands and didn't seem to want to be with the other two. Click. Couldn't place his name or face but I met so many people it could just look like someone I knew. Click, click. I pulled the 100-400mm and shot some video as they stood far back at the corner of the motel. A phone call and the taller 'no-neck' took it; nodding only, no speaking on his part, phone back in his pocket now. I stopped the video and blasted a few photos only. Click, click. I was hoping to get focus spot-on. The third guy was always shying away, hunched, but I nailed his face. He was about the height and size of Buzz Cut Dude; suit jacket on, dark brown hair, kept neat and short.

The third guy left and the two from earlier talked between themselves. Click, click. They finally proceeded to room seven, all casual-like too. I rolled video with the 75-200mm and watched.

They straddled either side of the doorway and knocked. I could hear something being said but couldn't make it out.

The door opened and before one could blink, they burst into the room then slammed the door shut. *Wow! Somebody's gonna get an ass-kicking.*

I let the camera record. After a few minutes I stopped the video – didn't want to overheat the unit. Ten more minutes went by until the door opened. Roll camera. The two no-neck dudes leaving, the shorter guy with his jacket on now and buttoned up, kinda strange in this heat. They closed the door softly, looked about, and then calmly made their way back to the east corner of the motel and disappeared. Stop camera.

Was that too fast? I thought a beating would take longer. These guys looked like they would take pleasure in slamming the golf pro guy's head senseless to send the message.

20:15 hours and I was beat. No sense hanging around to see the poor schmuck come out, battered, and deflated. I folded up my tent and headed back to drop off the car and go directly to bed.

★ ★ ★

Slept late – my body was knotted up from sitting in that damn compact car. Coffee up the system and some toast first, then a scalding hot shower to get the kinks out. *I had a plan.*

I downloaded the pics and video, Sunday, around noon. Everything was sharp as a tack and well lit. I watched the video a few times and looked at the photos. That third guy, I knew him, definitely seen him before, somewhere. But for the life of me, couldn't place the face or come up with a name.

I copied the good files to an attachment, along with a scan of my log and wrote an email synopsis for Delahunt. Then I sent all my documents through the server with, luckily, no bounce-back file showing up on the computer. Sometimes that happens if the files are too big, they fail to go through, and this was definitely a lot of data.

I put the raw files on a memory stick, verified they were actually there and placed the stick with my work-work stuff for Monday morning. I sensed I would get a call from Angela to drop it off at Delahunt's office so I might as well have it with me. I blanked the computer and was going to blank my memory cards for the cameras but didn't. I wanted to show Donny that face I thought I recognized. The other two dudes might interest him too. The police usually want to know about guys that go around thumping the crap outta innocent people.

I fell asleep watching the golf and didn't get out of bed until 05:00 hours, Monday morning.

★ ★ ★

One week to go then I'd be free from work for a whole month. I couldn't keep the smile from my face. I was looking forward to the peace and quiet of Algonquin. The excitement was building. My area calls were up to date and no outstanding issues.

No call from Angela yet so I left the memory stick locked in my desk.

★ ★ ★

The next few nights were spent checking my equipment and getting some freeze-dried meals and other necessities ready. I booked a car at the rental place on College, for two weeks,

September 4th to the 18th. My credit card covered the insurance, which saved me a whack of cash, gotta like that.

Sure enough, Angela did call. She normally emails me. She wanted me to come in Wednesday, and I did, dropping the memory stick off at the office. Delahunt was out. She took charge of the evidence, assuring me it was okay. I didn't give it a second thought.

★ ★ ★

By Thursday night, I was all packed and ready, so I could enjoy the weekend with Donny and little Andy at the air show. I had called Janet but she was a no-go; work kept her away all weekend. I said I'd see her when I got back from Algonquin. She wanted to see me before that … apparently it was important. We agreed maybe Monday – I'd call.

Friday, I did no outside work, only admin stuff, didn't want to get caught up in any legal crap prior to going on holidays. I set my office email and phone to an 'away' notification and said 'see ya' to my work colleagues. I put a 'happy face' drawing on the inspector status board. Gone for a month – I earned it!

★ ★ ★

Donny had said that if Saturday was a bust weather-wise, we could go Sunday. I checked the weather channel in the morning but didn't really need to, since I could hear the thunder outside. It said rain for the better part of the day. I called Donny and he agreed to wait until Sunday but that would be the only other day he could attend. He had a whack of homicides on the go and had to get back Monday, stat holiday be damned.

Hyped up and bored, I shot my mini crossbow for a few hours then let the dogs in for a treat and scruggles. Turned on the golf, and the dogs and I watched in awe as the pros made magic on the course. We all fell asleep on the couch. I awoke sometime later, dog fur in my mouth, four eyes staring at me and two tails a-wagging. *Good grief!*

I charged up the batteries for the cameras and cleaned all the lenses. I was only taking one camera, along with the 75-200mm and 100-400mm lens, for the trip into Algonquin. It would cut down on the weight and bulk slightly, plus everything would fit into one camera bag. I could manage a full backpack that had a yellow cocoon tent, thermal sleeping bag and high-density mat strapped to the outside. My food and a pump water purifier would occupy about two thirds of the internal space. Then I would stuff in all the other little things, like water-proof matches, tarp, compass, utility knife, fishing line, thin nylon rope, metal tea cup, spork and a small high-lip pan for cooking. Rain poncho, mitts and a hat – it would pour a few days for sure. Had my hatchet, its hand-sharpened blade to a nice fine edge, ready for a workout. I would lose about ten pounds of body weight in just under two weeks time. *What fun!*

★ ★ ★

Sunday was gorgeous out; a few high clouds with a little breeze from the west and still warmish. The rainstorm had cleared that low pressure system through and Donny was a go for the air show at the CNE. We had agreed to meet at the foot of Bathurst Street, around 12:45 hours.

I left my apartment at 11:45 hours, and was crossing the Lakeshore, headed towards the Airport ferry crossing by 12:30 hours. Still had about fifteen minutes, so I watched all the boats motoring through the western gap headed out onto Lake Ontario to catch the show of planes. The volume of boats, all converging, heading through the constricted gap between the inner bay and Lake Ontario, created a violently sloshing waterway with waves getting to a metre high or better, kinda scary! I blasted off some shots of the mayhem.

I heard Andy call out, "Aunt Liz, Aunt Liz!" and turned just in time to catch him as he jumped up and gave me a big hug. Guess I was family after all and a tear welled up. *I'm such a softy.*

Donny gave me a hug and peck on the cheek and we made our way west, following the boats towards the end of the pier, which gives a great vantage point for watching the jets scream by. We were about forty-five minutes early, before the first plane would show, but the space was filling up quickly.

We staked out our area and Donny laid a small blanket on the ground and brought out treats. As we sipped beer and ate sandwiches that Peg had made, I brought out both cameras and pulled up the photos of my last assignment.

"Have a look at these guys, will ya."

Donny took the camera and examined the shot for a few moments. "I think I know them. They look mighty suspicious too."

I smiled at him and said, "Everyone looks suspicious to you, big guy." I scrolled through the photos, to that third guy; the one I thought looked familiar. "What about him?"

Donny's face did something really weird; scrunched up and not in a good way either.

"Can you zoom in on this guy?"

I showed him the button to push.

"Where did you get this?"

I was at odds with myself. The info I garnered was confidential. I'd been explicitly told not to share this with anyone, and repeatedly, not with police. I was already breaking a rule.

I started out with vague answers. "I tailed a couple – an assignment from the lawyers."

Donny looked at me with a hard stare. "This guy, here, this is Savoy. Do you remember?"

I shook my head.

"Remember our anniversary night at Cyrano's, when that cop came up to our table all drunk and rude?"

The light bulb went off. "Oh yeah, Junior! What was his first name again?"

"Freddy, Freddy Savoy – he's a detective, remember."

I nodded, thinking of the crude prick that Donny had pushed back to the bar.

Donny asked, "Where was this?"

I hesitated again, "Somewhere in Scarborough, at a motel on Kingston Road, the Starlite or something. Why?"

Donny's face lost colour. "The Twilight Inn?"

"Yeah, that's it."

"Shit!"

Andy looked at his dad and giggled.

Donny got up and dialled a number on his phone as he walked away from us.

A jet screamed by overhead but I really wasn't interested. I had known Donny for a long time and he didn't get too emotional, but this … this was clearly deeply distressing to him.

Twenty minutes rolled past and Donny was still on the phone. I couldn't hear any of the conversation as the crowd noise and other planes drowned out everything. Andy and I just watched the show.

Donny came back and handed me his cell. "Delahunt. He wants a word."

I took the phone and said, "Liz Stevens speaking."

"Ms. Stevens, this is Raymond Delahunt. You have authorization to share whatever info you got from that last assignment, or any other material, with Detective Jacobs. Do you understand?"

I said I did and as he hung up I asked, "What's going on, Donny?"

"Not here. Just watch the show and we'll discuss it after I get Andy home."

Once the Snowbirds started the final flyby, we left. Get ahead of the crowds. I took maybe ten pictures at best, what a bust.

Donny said he was taking Andy back to his house and he would come over to my apartment where we would talk. "Just go home and stay there. Don't answer the phone unless it's me. Don't talk to anyone, got it?"

I nodded. I felt a tad sick and a bunch more scared.

About an hour later, the phone rang and it was Donny. He was out front parking his car and coming around to the back door.

I opened the door for him and we went down the stairs and into my apartment.

"Wanna beer?"

"I think we should indulge in some Cardhu. You're going to need it," he said.

I poured and he gulped. What the fuck had I seen? My heart raced.

He laid it out for me. "There was a double homicide at that motel, the Twilight Inn."

I damn near shit myself. "Those thugs killed two people, right in front of me!"

"I want to see all the shots and video you have right now."

I grabbed my cameras and flash cards and used them to download the data again into the computer so we could have a real good look.

We sat at the desk and went through it.

"That rotten little prick!" Donny was fuming. "You see those two guys? They're muscle for Gregor Mutznig. They call him the 'Mutt' but not to his face. Not unless you wanna be dead or beaten in such a manner that you wish you were. Freddy has been under investigation for months now, suspected of ties to this animal. Special Investigations has his phones and computer tapped, but he has been logging in on other passwords, searching for data and giving intel to the Mutt. This time he is definitely tied to murder."

I was stunned. "Why would they go and kill the golf pro dude and Ms. Boobs?"

"Who?"

"Sorry, that's what I call them. I don't know his name but he reminded me of a golf pro sort so, well you know, that's how I labelled him. Anyway, the girl is Danielle Simons. That much I got from Delahunt."

Donny just shook his head. "Her name was Simons. She was married to the Mutt. And the guy is Derek Walters, he works, or did up until he was murdered, at a high-end women's clothing store in Yorkville."

"Well, you'll probably want to know, this wasn't the first time I saw her."

"Tell me."

I told Donny. "About a month ago, Delahunt gave me an assignment, late on a Friday night. The target wasn't her – it was a guy named Dufner."

"James Dufner?"

"Yeah, I think so, why?"

"He's dead, that's why. You still got those shots and such?"

"No. Sorry. It all went to Delahunt. All the raw data was put onto a memory stick and I dropped it off there at his office, weeks ago. I blanked the camera cards and dumped the info from the computer."

We sat in silence for a period of time, just running through the photos and video.

"His address, it was off Lawrence East, Humpfries or something, I can't remember the number."

Donny got up and had some more Cardhu. "He was murdered there."

I just stared at the computer then looked quizzically at Donny. "How do you know about all these killings? They're not in your area, not your jurisdiction."

He touched my shoulder, "Well my little investigator, I'm actually the detective in charge of Special Investigations."

We sat in the living room, sipping Cardhu. I had put some Doors on for background music and as Jim Morrison sang, Donny rocked to the beat, immersed in deep thought.

"Donny?"

"Yeah?"

"How did you end up in charge of these investigations?"

He reminded me of the dinner; the one with the lawyers when he had listened to their conversation. That was his inauguration. He was on a very short list. The Toronto Police Services was a nest of rats, leaking confidential info and supplying intel on busts and investigations. They needed new blood and someone beyond reproach. He got the job, his detective's shield and a hand-picked team, to go after and clean up the shit in the department. "I'm sorry I got you involved in this," he said.

Donny was leaving. He would see Delahunt in his office tomorrow. Raymond had agreed to come in on the holiday Monday and let him see the raw data, log sheets and anything else remotely linked to the cases. "I need your memory cards for your cameras and anything else you have."

"I'll put it all on a memory stick for you."

"No. That won't work. I need the shooting info from the camera, dates and such."

I gave Donny all my stuff; four flash cards – two different sets for each camera. "Who will be looking at this?"

"Don't worry. I won't let the forensic boys mess anything up. You'll get them back." He gave me a hug. "Listen, you need to keep a low profile. When are you heading up camping?"

"I leave this Wednesday, the fourth, and should be back in Toronto on the eighteenth or so."

"Alright, I'll keep you posted of anything relevant. Don't worry!"

"I'll not worry if you don't. Stay safe."

After Donny left, I took another slug of Cardhu and went for a nap. I was out cold in minutes. I really must have needed the rest.

★ ★ ★

Well past Kipling and south of Horner, close to the railway lines, sat a very dingy and vacant-looking industrial building. It was surrounded by more buildings, in various degrees of disrepair, all looking tired and worn out. Old equipment, trucks beaten down by years of neglect, and odd-looking pieces of what were somehow useful materials in some long-ago manufacturing process, littered the grounds. Very few people ever came down here, or even worked here. Not even crows or rats could find food here. No plants sprouted; the ground was dead and dry. The whole area was all brownish and yellowed, rusted and forgotten. The only things to stand out; some newer tractor trailers, parked by a line of bay doors and a few cars sat in waiting. A newer Park Avenue, mint condition, grey in colour, with tinted windows was neatly parked by the heavy metal entrance door to the building. Two other small compacts nestled close by, like babies, afraid to venture away.

Inside, this particular structure was way swankier than outside. No manufacturing went on here. The interior was spotless; perfectly clean cement floor, neatly stacked pallets of various wares, nothing out of place. The building was sectioned off into rooms at the back; washrooms, loading bay office and one specific office, palatial compared to the rest, hemmed in, solid, no windows to the outside. It was the office of Gregor Mutznig. The "Mutt" ruled from this location.

The phone rang and one of his goons picked it up.

"Yeah."

"Do you know who this is?"

"Yeah."

"I want to see him. Right now, not tomorrow. Tell him!"

The goon paused, "I'll call you in five."

★ ★ ★

Freddy Savoy picked up on the first ring.

"Is this a safe phone?"

"Yeah, it's a throwaway," Savoy answered.

"Okay. One hour, at the beach, usual place. Walk around and feed the ducks."

The line went dead. Freddy was pissed. "Feed the ducks. I'll feed the ducks all right ... your ass, fucking thugs!" Freddy already knew he was in a pickle. His source had said there were photos taken at the motel. Gregor Mutznig had snitches all through the police force and with half the lawyers too, probably. Everybody informed on everyone else. Juicy info flowed like Niagara Falls; traded as favours, debt repayment or even future leverage.

He shook his head while saying his name, "Freddy, Freddy, Freddy." Then he looked in the rear-view mirror of the car, talking to himself. "What a shit storm. This is not going to end well, buddy. I feel it in my bones." He had stayed out of sight and away from the room. He wasn't compromised just yet. He would to talk to Gregor and find out. He fired up his police vehicle and made his way west towards the Sunnyside area.

Freddy Savoy slid his Crown Vic in alongside a mass of other vehicles at the parking lot, between Lake Ontario and the Lake Shore Boulevard. He started walking east along the bike path and ended up near the Canadian Legion, which sat on the hill overlooking the water. He didn't feed the ducks, although by his demeanour he probably felt like shooting a few.

A newer four-door Park Avenue rolled by, Freddy didn't look at it but saw it nonetheless. About a hundred metres past, the car stopped and the driver opened the back passenger door. Gregor Mutznig stepped out. He was in his sixties; full head of greying hair, perfectly styled. Tinted glasses hid his eyes, designer label for sure. He was expensively dressed in a light-grey, two-piece suit, and black high-gloss shoes. Mutznig had stayed in shape, not fat yet, and had a confident manner about him.

The driver held a lighter, lit Gregor's cigar, and then handed him a plastic bag. Mutznig strolled over to the water's edge. He tossed some crusty bread and began feeding the ducks.

Freddy just shook his head and meandered casually up to the Mutt.

"Glorious day don't you think, Detective? Here, take some bread and feed our friends."

"Fuck you and your ducks!"

Gregor gave Freddy a stern look.

Savoy cowed. He knew right away he had overstepped that one, "Look. Sorry. This is getting out of hand. They have photos from the motel. Your Neanderthals were caught killing your wife and that other douche bag."

The Mutt just kept feeding the birds and looked out onto the water. "Yes, they have some photos but not of the actual killing … circumstantial at best. The real problem is a witness who may unfortunately get to testify … unless we do something about that…"

"No way!" Savoy wanted no part of it. "I give you info and that's it. I don't kill people."

Mutznig smiled. "You were at the scene. For a cop you're not so bright, Freddy. That is conspiracy to commit murder. You are in it up to your detective's shield."

"How the fuck was I to know your goons were going to kill those people? You said a little pay back; a beating at most. That's why I gave you the credit card track so quick."

"Nonsense, my boy, she had lots of opportunity to change her ways and I don't put up with a bitch that wrongs me and humiliates me, repeatedly."

Freddy was livid. "But why kill them there? Why not just take the bitch out and bury her somewhere?"

Gregor looked straight at Freddy, calm, and in an even voice said softly, "Because I wanted her to know that I knew, and that it was going to be her last breath. I had her precious boyfriend knifed in front of her very eyes. Then I had her face sliced up real nice before my boys slit her throat, all the while in front of a mirror so she could see it."

Freddy went white with fear at what this animal was capable of. "Take this paper."

"Why should I?" Freddy whined.

"It has the name of the person who took the photos. You get me all the info on this witness and that will be it for a while. You go back to work, relax, and when it's done, we'll both be in the clear."

"How do you know this is the person at the motel?"

Mutznig threw his cigar in the water and dumped the rest of the bread on the ground. "You'd be surprised at the information I have and the people I know who can get it, Detective. This little birdie called me last week, right out of the blue, can you imagine that. What are the odds? I had to bargain for the information but had it within a few days. Just get me what I want and I'll have the rest looked after. You can remain relatively removed from the whole situation still."

Savoy took the paper and walked away towards his car. He looked at it. Printed in Mutznig's perfect, block-style hand writing was the name – Elizabeth Anne Stevens.

★ ★ ★

Monday was a shitty day, even for a holiday. I wanted to stay inside, kinda afraid to go out now since all this weirdness had happened. My land barons were planning a BBQ later and invited me – steak as usual and I could not refuse. *It's steak for goodness sake!* Could I bring a guest? Surely, so I phoned Janet. I invited her over for a meal and the talk that she so desperately wanted.

★ ★ ★

Freddy was a sly guy. He was sneaky too and his plan went into play. He dropped in at 32 Division on the Labour Day holiday. He didn't even work out of there, no matter, flash the detective badge, scribble a name and in he goes. The place was a ghost town, skeleton crew at best. Plunking down at a computer terminal, he used one of several dodgy login names and pulled up info on multiple 'Stevens.' As Freddy scrolled through CPIC and other data bases, trying to find this bitch, he landed on something that disturbed him immensely.

"Mother fucker!" Freddy screamed it out loud. He glared at the photo that was staring right back at him. He quickly made copies of all the data he could glean. Then Freddy made a fast call to his sergeant. He asked for some emergency time off, hung up quick, raced out of the police station, and peeled away.

★ ★ ★

The dinner went well. We all ate in the land baron's expansive dining room. They loved Janet and were captivated with her stories of emergency room antics. Afterward, she and I headed downstairs to my apartment. I didn't exactly know what she wanted to discuss.

It got real soggy, real quick. She was torn. She had feelings for me. She was confused. Why hadn't I pursued her? What was it that I was supposedly waiting for?

I sat there in shock. I just wrapped my arms around her and apologized profusely. I had totally been under the impression she only wanted to date men. What could I say?

As I blotted her tears, I held her face and looked squarely at those beautiful green eyes. "If you only knew how much I want to be with you. At Pride, do you remember kissing me? I damn near fell over!"

"Then why didn't you continue? I was waiting all night you know. You should have asked me to come home with you."

"Believe me when I say this, I was up all night thinking of you … that kiss, all of it. But I just couldn't take it if I lost your friendship. I think my heart would actually break. Literally!"

We sat there, hugging each other, rocking a bit. She finally stopped blubbering. I broke away from the clench. "Why don't you go into the washroom and freshen up a smidge."

I was freaking out. How long had I ached for this moment? Now, here it was, but something was off kilter. Was I ready? Was she ready? It would be way tougher on her, was she strong enough? She was gone for about ten minutes. *Jeepers!* Janet was reassessing, I'm sure of it. Was this what she really wanted? It would be a huge leap for her. The dynamics of a relationship like this had all sorts of pit falls. I needed to put her off until I came back from Algonquin. But how do I do that without making her feel like I'm rejecting her? I got up and went to the kitchen, grabbed some paper towel and wiped the sweat from my brow. My heart beat felt like a jackhammer.

Janet came back out to the living room. She didn't sit and acted a tad sheepish. I knew it was too soon right then and there. Rushing forward into a relationship now could ruin everything. Going to her, my arms swallowed her up and I held her tight. I said the words. "I love you, more than you could possibly know. You are a best friend. I only want the best things for you, as you see it, on your terms." Giving her one last squeeze I grabbed her hand and said, "Let's go. I'll walk you back to the subway and we can talk a bit more on the way."

Janet didn't say a word in protest and followed me outside. We walked to the Ossington Station, mostly in silence. At the turnstile I looked deep into her gorgeous eyes and said, "You need to think on this for a spell. When I get back from camping we'll get together and really talk about what you want. Okay?"

We hugged one last time, and when she was turning to leave I could see the tears well up in her eyes. She wasn't ready for this emotionally. As I turned and walked away my own emotions gave way and a trickle streamed down my face. Maybe I wasn't ready for this either.

★ ★ ★

On Tuesday, I headed downtown to get some more memory cards for the camera since Donny had taken mine. I spent two hundred bucks on two, top-of-the-line eight gig flash cards for the camera I'd be taking with me. Unfortunately, each new generation of camera didn't take the same old cards, or batteries for that matter, so you had to keep buying new shit. *What a racket!* I grabbed another battery, on sale at least, so I had lots of juice and wouldn't run out. Ten days is a long time without power.

I looked through HMV for some movies and had lunch at a new burger place. Went over to Canadian Tire and bought some more camping stuff that was on sale, including a nice folding cross-cut saw; very compact, lightweight and sturdy.

I headed back home, thinking of my trip to come. By this time tomorrow, I'd be driving up Highway 11 and closing in on Algonquin Park for a much-needed rest.

I had checked my gear several times and repacked it twice, going over my list and verifying again. I had extra dry food. I wouldn't go hungry, that's for sure. I had all my coats, vests and other clothing ready to go in a neat canvas bag.

It was still early but I was beat and about to hit the hay when my cell phone rang. It was Donny and I picked up. "Hello Donny, what's the word?"

"We need to talk."

"Okay, what's up?"

He explained that somebody ... he was confirming right now through closed circuit video, had been into the computers and had pulled up my info on CPIC and other data bases. "They have your address, licence-info, everything, the works. I need you to come in so we can put you somewhere safe."

I laughed. "That's ridiculous. You think a cop is going to come over and kill me? Just go find that Freddy puke and arrest him."

"We can't find him. His sergeant said he called in yesterday and wanted two weeks off, then he hung up and now he's gone. I'm still waiting on a judge and warrant for his arrest. We are pretty sure he is in deep with Mutznig and probably others. I've got two more warrants pending for the dudes at the motel, an Olig Steig and Tony Molinara, but they're MIA. I don't think you're safe."

"Look Donny, I love you and trust you but it is starting to become apparent that we can't rely on anyone else. How could I depend on some cops I don't know to keep me safe? How can you trust anyone?" There was a silence.

"You could stay with Peg and me."

"No way! I'm not gonna let someone get close to your family because of me. No way will that happen." More silence.

"Yeah, you're right, bad idea, I'm grasping at straws here. Can we agree on any options that you'd be okay with?"

I thought about it. "How long before you catch Savoy and the others and get this cleaned up?"

By the pause, I sensed Donny didn't want to commit on a time line.

"I couldn't say, maybe a week or two. We're close to nailing a bunch of people."

I made up my mind. "Look, problem solved. I'll book the car for three weeks instead of two. I'll pick it up tomorrow at 07:00 hours, be packed and outta here by 08:00 at the latest, and then poof, baby! I'm gone into the bush for almost three weeks."

More silence.

"I don't like it."

I countered. "It's perfect. What fool would track me up there? They would never find me anyhow."

Donny couldn't argue. It was the best option.

"Alright, take the lawyer cell phone with you. They won't have that number and you may get a signal up there so if something does happen, we can communicate. Call me from up north, before you go all Dian Fossey on me."

"She was a zoologist and into apes."

"You know what I mean."

"Wrong continent too, big guy, not that it is overly important."

"Don't be a smart ass."

"She's dead too, Donny."

All I could hear was a dial tone. *We have a plan.*

★ ★ ★

After hanging up, Donny got busy, calling in to 14 Division and ordering a car to sit out front of a house on Rusholme Road. He wasn't about to take an unnecessary risk. He still had a flag on several people, inside the computer system, so if anyone accessed the right sequence of surnames or addresses, he would get notified.

★ ★ ★

"I've got some info. We need to set a meet." Freddy was terse.

"Call you in five minutes," was the response from the goon.

Freddy Savoy now knew he was a hunted man. His last good contact at the department, the only one to answer the phone, simply told him they were getting a warrant for his arrest, then, "Don't ever call me again." Savoy had no more access to the Toronto Police, he was friendless and homeless.

He had called his sergeant yesterday, after seeing that photo, told him he needed to leave for at least two weeks due to a family emergency, and hung up before there was an argument or more details given. It was a gut reaction, to buy space and time, which proved to be a good hunch. Knowing the connection to Jacobs, and what he did at headquarters, Freddy knew he was jammed up big time. It was 02:00 hours Wednesday morning and he had no place to run to. He had cleared some personal items over the last day, grabbed what he could of value, now hiding like a rat. The Mutt was his only way out and Freddy slammed his car hood with his fists, in rhythm with the words, "Fuck! Fuck! Fucking fucker!"

The phone rang. "Come to the office."

"No way! You're probably under surveillance right now. Give me a different location."

"Hang on."

Freddy was sweating like he had just run a marathon.

"Parking garage in North York, usual place on Yonge, level four. Make the meet in a couple of hours time from now." And the line went dead.

Savoy tossed the phone into the garbage. He got into the back seat of a borrowed car and napped.

* * *

I didn't sleep much. The clock said three and I knew that was a.m. because the little dot was by the numbers shown. *How could it be anything but? Geezez.*

I got up and made coffee. It was going to be a long drive and even longer trek to get to my site in Algonquin.

As soon as Donny had hung up last night, I got on the computer, reregistered at the park for another eleven days, and paid by credit card. The site didn't spit me out and confirmed the time change. I had printed the receipt and the park permit. I'd be there by sunset today – Kettle Lake, outback site-seven.

My gut hurt from stress. I rummaged around my dresser and found the most recent bottle of codeine pills – about twenty-five left. I popped two and stored the rest in my knapsack.

I sat in silence, drinking instant coffee. My mind raced. Am I in danger? Would they come up there and try and kill me? If they did, what would I do? If those apes from the motel came at me, I didn't have a chance. Or did I? A funny little voice in my head recited that old adage: *When there is any doubt, there is no doubt,* and I spent the next two hours getting my crossbows ready. My old Harrier had given out and I had bought a new compound crossbow about a year ago; a Vortex 'Vengeance' with a one-fifty-five-pound draw, carbon black and a 3X32 laser scope. I'd also replaced the mini over the years, twice, and now had a Vixen SX-80 pistol. *This way,* I thought, *I would have a chance.*

★ ★ ★

When Freddy pulled into the garage at 5100 Yonge Street and wound his way to level four, both dumb and dumber; Olig Steig and Tony Molinara, were standing there with Gregor, outside of the Mutt's car. The Mutt's driver, Angelo, was about ten feet away, angled slightly for cover. They chose this spot because it was close to Gregor's house.

Freddy parked a few spots down and checked his weapon. He looked at himself in the mirror and reaffirmed his position: "If you don't provide a solution Mutt, then fuck you, I'll shoot all of you pukes right here and now." He steeled himself for the ultimate outcome.

After a few moments, he walked up on the group of men, right hand in coat pocket holding his gun; ready to take them out.

Gregor smiled at Savoy. "Well, Detective, what have you got for me?"

Freddy shook his head. "I need to know that you are going to help me get out of here. I got a warrant out for my arrest and have to leave."

"Don't worry about that. My boys are going to find this woman and deal with her. Then everyone will take a little boat trip to the motherland and you can work for me there."

Christ. Freddy rolled his eyes, probably in anticipation of living in a heartless waste land and having to learn Russian. "I can't go home or anywhere. I need a place to stay."

"Not a problem. I have a house north of the city; Kleinburg as a matter of fact. Indoor pool, sauna, it'll be a vacation. I'll have someone drop off food and lots of those other little necessities; the ones I know you're fond of. Just say the word."

"Yeah?"

"Yes. Now what have you got on the woman?"

Freddy filled them in. He gave them the home address, licence info and pictures, work location, and phone numbers for office and cell. Then he paused, unsure of how much to give up. "There's something else you need to know."

"Go on." Mutznig loved getting juicy details on people; that's how he controls them, usually. The human puppets were like chess pieces to him. He liked positioning them and manipulating them for his benefit.

"She has an investigator's licence and works for some lawyer, I think, doing surveillance and such. And this I know too, she is in tight with another detective, Jacobs is his name. They are long-time friends. Plus, and this is a bit weird, she was a guy, like … before. She's now a girl; a sex change."

This brought a chuckle from the no-neck gym jockeys. "It'll be easy Boss, don't worry – one, two days max. Me and Tony will nail this fag."

"Alright Freddy, that is very good. Here is the address of my other house. Go there. Just wait. Don't do anything stupid and I'll call when we've got this thing sewn up."

Savoy did not look overjoyed. "You brought this on us all, Gregor. If it wasn't for your sick, twisted sense of retribution and inflated ego, we'd be in the clear right now. Remember that!" Then he left them.

Savoy floored the car and squealed around the curves on the levels, popped out onto Yonge Street and headed north out of the city to find his new home. Freddy had no idea where Kleinburg was.

After scanning the documents, Mutznig rallied his boys. "Now listen, Tony, you go down to the work address and wait to see if this Stevens bitch shows. Once you locate her, start a tail, call Olig for help and we'll pick our spot and take her out.

Olig countered: "But shouldn't we go to her house first and grab her early this morning?"

"No. It would be too obvious and mistakes have been made already. The police are probably there anticipating that move; they may be shadowing this witness. If they know about Detective Savoy, they will certainly have a hunch about others. We need to make this look like an accident and make sure it doesn't come back on us. We have time. Once it is done, then you two go home for a bit, see your families. Then in a few years, maybe, come back to Canada."

Tony asked, "What about the cop? He ain't coming with us is he?"

Gregor smiled. "No. I fear our friendly detective is under great stress and may accidentally shoot himself. But, for the time being, he is on ice since we may need him still. Nobody touches him until I say so."

The plan was set. Olig and Tony didn't dare argue with the Mutt. They watched Gregor leave, then Tony started their car and Olig hopped in.

Steig sat rigid, with a pensive look on his face, as the car moved out. Tony had glanced over several times and noticed his sidekick was not being very talkative and looked a tad pale. Something was up.

"Oli, what gives bro? You ain't said shit and you look like you've seen a ghost."

"Just thinking about what the cop said, Gregor bringing it all on us because of his ego and such." Steig let out an enormous sigh and spilled his guts. "It was my fault. It wasn't intentional. I just didn't want to spend time following those assholes around."

"You let that shit Madden talk you into using that service, didn't you?" Tony said, shaking his head. "Gregor told you to do it – follow his wife and eyeball the dude. Christ almighty Oli, that jerk-off lawyer wanted to look like a big shot, calling in for service … his friends, they're all creeps and you fell for his sell job."

"It sounded so easy and I had plans already. Then the second time, I didn't even think about it, I just made the call to Madden and it was sorted."

"Why did you tell Madden to have Gregor's wife tailed all day?"

"I didn't. Alls I said was go to the park – that's it. Why did that bitch have to follow them all the way to the motel? Who does that?"

"Well, you best keep your mouth shut on this one. The Mutt will have your balls on a plate if he gets wind. You best keep that schlock lawyer from blabbing too."

Olig was sweating a bit. Then he shivered violently. Tony said he'd put the heater on if he was cold.

★ ★ ★

I left the apartment at 06:00 hours. I noticed a cruiser was to the north, parked on the east side of the one way street, idling. Donny was obviously worried about me. I ignored the cop and walked away, down to College and over towards the Cracked restaurant for a big breakfast. My last real meal, then it would be dry goods for the better part of three weeks. I enjoyed every morsel.

I was at the car rental place just before 07:00 and changed my booking for three weeks. A good size Chevy Impala; four-door, large trunk and all fuelled up. It would be nice driving a car of size. *Better than all those shitty little compacts*, I thought with a pleasant sigh.

I was headed back home by 07:15 hours. In front of the house, as I pulled to the curb, the cruiser pull in behind me. I got out and approached the cop. "You could have come to breakfast with me instead of all this cloak and dagger shit."

The cop just smiled and said, "Orders!" and raised his palms up in defeat.

I ran from the street, to the apartment, and back to the car, twice. In just two trips, all my gear was loaded. I attached a note to the back door, letting my landlords know when I'd be home, to please feed the pups some biscuits, and to check the dehumidifier level. I told the cop not to follow, as I was heading out of town. By 07:45 hours, I was driving away, heading out of Toronto towards Algonquin. The cop followed me until Highway 400, then he peeled away.

★ ★ ★

Tony Molinara was a good-looking Italian man, who had grown up in Russia, spoke three languages, and could have been anything. But the life of crime had won out, due to its hours of work and many benefits. His whole family was bent, even the in-laws. This is what he'd grown up with – this was normal. How could he not be a crook? But this part of it sucked. The waiting and watching were not for him. He liked action.

He had been sitting in his blue, two-door Mazda coupe outside the public health office on Victoria Street since 06:00 hours Wednesday morning. Sipping a Tim's coffee and stuffing his face with donuts, he had a picture of the target in his lap and he was eyeing everyone that walked by. There were two other entrances to the building. He could only park here on Victoria and be comfortable so that was that. Decision made.

Tony was doing the stake-out because Gregor didn't really trust Olig, who was a blunt instrument in more ways than one. Tony had actually tried to teach Olig how to dress better, match clothes for the occasion, and act with a little more finesse around the ladies, but it didn't really take. One thing for sure though, if Olig was sent to kill you, you'd stay dead. He was good at it. He never hesitated, never missed.

★ ★ ★

Donny was now in the process of attaining warrants for seven more cops; three of them constables, three sergeants and another detective. Plus, he finally had the warrants for Savoy, Tony Molinara, and Olig Steig. His frustration over the delay in getting the warrants for Freddy and the other two was justified. But the game had to be played. You couldn't rush a judge. You had to be really nice and suck it up, especially for a warrant on a cop. Hopefully the next ones wouldn't take so damn long.

Forensics had retrieved all the data from the camera flash cards and he had more raw data from Delahunt. He also had about twenty taps going on various phones, and three surveillance teams watching people. He was close to busting it wide open and salivating at the prospect.

Donny scanned the board with all the photos of possible department rats and the criminal scum they most likely aided. The caseload was huge, the paper work outrageous. "I gotta get outta here for a bit, clear my head and shake off this headache."

His number two, Stan Cooper, the second-most trusted cop he knew, just waved at him and continued to work his sources.

★ ★ ★

I stayed ten kilometres over the speed limit on the 400 Highway, heading north. Cut onto Highway 11 just the other side of Barrie, fuelled up in Gasoline Alley just before Orillia, then worked my way north towards Huntsville. I had to grab a few coffees on the way, which led to a few snacks, the sugary kind, since I was feeling a bit drowsy. Lack of sleep the night before and driving this much was taking its toll.

A tad past 12:00 hours, I was pulling into Bob's Bait and Tackle to pick up a kayak.

"Hey Bill, how goes it?" There was no Bob, just Bill and his kid running the place.

"My perennial fall camper returns. How are you doing Liz?"

"Chipper as a jaybird and chomping at the bit, ready to get out into Mother Nature's country. Have you got a double kayak for me? I'll need it for maybe three weeks."

Bill checked his computer and asked what colour I preferred.

"Oh, maybe dark-green or something akin to that would do nicely."

"I've got a fairly new, two-tone camo unit."

I took it and gave Bill my credit card.

Bill had his kid strap the kayak to the roof, using foam blocks and tie-downs, throwing two double end paddles and life jackets into the back seat.

"What else can I do you for?"

"I might just grab some more food and such."

"No problem, take as much as you can. I'll even knock off ten percent since I want to unload it."

I browsed through the aisles of the food section, picking up some items I thought would be tasty. I would now need twice as much food. I calculated the number of meals; one for morning and one for night. Grabbed some hot chocolate packets, more granola bars, a one kilo re-sealable pack of black-oil sunflower seeds for me and the kids, and I could always fish for a meal or two.

I followed Highway 60 out of Huntsville. About fifty kilometres along, came to my designated parking area for outback permit holders, where I could launch the kayak onto Dawson Lake. Pretty good time, as it was only 13:10 hours.

I double bagged my camera and lenses in green garbage bags and would keep them with me in the back seat of the kayak, in easy reach. The backpack went into the second-person seat, then I loaded the rest of the gear into the two compartments, along with the crossbows.

The first leg would take about thirty minutes paddle-time or so, then a two-trip portage for just under a kilometre, then another forty minute paddle to my reserved outback site on Kettle Lake. I figured I would make it by 17:00 hours, allowing for dawdle time and pictures, and still have light to set up and gather wood.

I called Donny on the lawyer cell phone.

"Detective Jacobs," he answered so formally.

"Hey Serpico, it's Liz, I'm just about ready to head into the bush. What's the word on our felons?"

"No change. Still haven't caught anybody. Listen try not to use your credit cards since they can be traced. Use cash only okay."

"Well great. Now you tell me. I've used credit all the way up here!"

"Sorry, just came to mind. It probably won't matter anyway. But still, you keep a lookout and run if you see trouble. Call me immediately if you suspect someone is up there, especially either of those two goons from the motel. Got it!?"

"You can count on me, Detective Jacobs, sir."

"Don't be a smart ass and stay in touch. Bye."

I pushed off and felt the weight of the world lift from my shoulders. Three weeks living in Ontario's best-kept secret, this would be the ultimate trip.

★ ★ ★

Olig called Tony. "What's happening, pisano?'

"Nothing yet, no sign," a frustrated Tony responded.

"The boss said to stay put, keep watch, you want me to send out someone?" Olig relayed.

"No. I'm okay."

Tony was a patient guy. But by 13:25 hours, he lost his patience and entered the building. He looked at the directory and went to the fourth floor.

He gave the receptionist his best smile and said he had an appointment with Elizabeth Stevens.

Jenny Lynn was a sucker for a cute guy. "Oh I'm so sorry. She is away on holidays for the next several weeks. Could one of our other inspectors assist you?"

Tony gave his soft brown eyes a big ol' blink and pasted a wounded look on his face, one he'd practiced for years; his best rendition of a person put out and needing to speak to that particular individual. "Gee whiz, it's really important and only she can deal with this. Would you be able to call her and maybe I could talk with her?"

Jenny melted. "No, that wouldn't be possible. I really shouldn't say but she has gone camping way up north and won't be back until October."

Tony pressed. "Way north, wow, that's pretty brave of a group to go this time of year."

"Oh no, she just goes by herself. I couldn't do it, you know, being alone like that for weeks at a time. I must admit she does take some really nice photos up there."

Tony turned up the charm. "Wow, all alone. I didn't know she did that. But I guess it's pretty safe in those small parks and camp grounds."

"No she doesn't do that. She goes right into the bush, canoe and everything, and it's a huge park. I think it's the biggest one we have."

Tony wasn't about to blow it and push too far. "Okay, thanks so much. I guess I'll see her when she gets back. Bye." He gave her a wink and muted wolf whistle.

Tony started his car, got on the phone immediately and called Olig. "Coming back to the office right now – got news. Is the boss there?"

"Yeah. How long?"

"Less than thirty."

He made it in twenty-five minutes. They all knew they could be under surveillance and played everything very cool.

Tony came in and briefed Olig and Gregor. The Mutt made a phone call as soon as Tony finished his update.

★ ★ ★

Donny got a call from the surveillance team as soon as Tony Molinara drove in.

"They're both here right now."

"Okay, I'll notify SWAT and we'll be out in twenty-five minutes tops. Hold tight and keep eyes on. Got it?"

"Will do."

★ ★ ★

Gregor Mutznig got a call back in less than twenty minutes.

The voice was terse. "Two things. One; credit card used in Toronto last night for an Ontario park service booking and this morning for a rental car; four-door Impala, licence EAMF 599. Also, the credit card was used in Orillia for gas, then around Huntsville for a boat and gear. This one's a favour, for future consideration; warrants issued for both Tony Molinara and Olig Steig; first degree murder. Don't call again until you clean up your mess."

The phone went dead. Gregor was sweating slightly, a very rare anomaly indeed. "You two boys get out now. Take the passageway and use another car, head to the house in Kleinburg and burn the cop. I'll call you on the phone up there, give you directions. Quick now, go!"

★ ★ ★

Donny got up into the surveillance unit and coordinated the SWAT team raid on the building. He had the pricks now.

Fully-armed assault cops circled the building with speed and precision. No-knock warrant. They hit it hard, flash bangs and smoke tossed through the windows. A ram for the heavy main door, two attempts and a pry bar later, they were inside. "Police! Search Warrant! Police! Police! Everybody stay down! Police! Search Warrant! Police!"

Sitting in the van, Donny was pumped. "This will scare the shit right outta the pricks. This is it!"

Gregor just sat at his desk, smoking a cigar, not moving an inch. His office was fairly well insulated from the rest of the building. He could see all the smoke and heard the yelling. Police, looking more like combat soldiers, peered into his office, assault rifles trained right at him.

When the dust settled, Donny got the call.

"They're not here, only Mutznig. Clear to come in."

Donny couldn't believe it. How had they missed them? It had only been minutes.

He stormed into the building and plopped his ass down right beside the Mutt. "Where are they?"

"Why Detective, whom do you mean?"

"Fine, be that way!" Donny gave the order. "Tear the place apart. Find the hide!"

He and the Mutt just stared at each other.

★ ★ ★

The passageway led them south. Little grate-covered air holes allowed some light in to see. Near the tracks, the tunnel curved right and ran back along a ditch, putting them inside another building, about fifty metres west. Through that building and back to a parking spot, they picked up a clean car and headed north, out of the area. As they drove away, Olig and Tony had heard the bangs going off.

★ ★ ★

The water was like glass and the kayak cut a path with ease. The first lake was long and narrow, running mostly northeast, and I was basically going from tip to tip. *Perfect day*, I thought, as I glided along, *no wind, no waves*. I took my time. A cow moose calmly watched me, as I cautiously watched her, feeding in the bulrush. I stayed vigilant. They could get spooked and charge after you. I snagged a good shot of her munching on reeds while eyeballing me. Saw a few deer scamper along the shore's edge. I snapped off a few shots. It was tricky in a kayak, for sure, and I wasn't a fan of shooting from the water. The two person craft gave me a bit more stability but still, the fear of flipping and losing my camera equipment was very real.

There was some colour in the trees, not a full-blown change yet; still mostly green with splashes of red and yellow. Since I was going to be here for three weeks, I should luck out and really get some great shots of the autumn foliage. A kingfisher nattered at me, telling me in no uncertain terms that I was trespassing on his range. I saw another camper to the south and waved. He waved from his site. I was glad to see another lone soul, camping and braving the elements, happy to be in the forest. Further along, some campfire smoke swirled up at another site on the north side. I couldn't see anyone – maybe out fishing or birding, or just smoking dope and communing with nature.

The orange marker for the land route came into view. The portage used to be relatively short, ten years ago; maybe two-hundred metres long. But consecutive years of low water and increased reed growth had bogged the area – now it was way more difficult. The route had been moved to the south and stretched much farther, over rocks and through bush, instead of on the relative ease of the open flatlands.

I slipped in to shore sideways and got out with little fuss and no wet feet. Good start, 14:35 hours; not bad time.

I left the kayak, paddles and life jackets just up on land. The first run would be the back pack, camera gear, crossbows, and other stuff.

It took almost twenty minutes to make my way through all the gnarly bush and rocks. The path was not all that great. I felt like a pack mule and sweat poured off me. "Geezez, I'm outta shape!" I dumped my load at Kettle Lake, sat for a few moments, then headed back at a fast walking pace.

By the time I got the kayak back through, it was almost 16:00 hours. *Burning too much daylight,* I thought. I'd have to up the pace. My back was aching from the two portage runs, so I dry gulped a few codeine pills. I needed to cut the throbbing down before I did the next water leg. Finding a nice flat rock to perch upon, I allowed myself a longer break, absorbing the outstanding view and the pain meds.

★ ★ ★

"Detective! We found it."

Donny went over to the false wall and swing panel in the warehouse. "Slimy little prick must have been tipped again that we were coming. Okay, send a couple men through and see where it goes."

He went back to Mutznig, pulled up a chair and sat facing him. "You can be charged with obstruction."

"My dear Detective, all I have been doing today is paperwork. I haven't had a chance to get lunch, I'm so busy. If I had known you wanted to speak with me about something, I surely would assist you in any way possible."

"Yeah, right! Where are Tony Molinara and Olig Steig?"

Gregor grinned at Donny. "Again Detective, I've been so busy in my office I didn't see anyone today. Perhaps one of my foremen can assist you, as they look after the workers and day-to-day business. I don't have much contact with that aspect any more."

Donny began to smile. What you know and what you can prove are two very different things indeed. He had nothing on the Mutt at this point. He then gave Mutznig a hardened look. "I'm going to be on you, every day and night. I'll squeeze you and soon I'll pop you, like the throbbing infected zit you are!"

"My goodness, Detective, are you threatening me?"

Donny just shook his head and glared at the Mutt. Gregor was a seasoned criminal and didn't scare easily. Playing stupid was a good defence and the Mutt did it well, but stupid he was not.

The two SWAT guys came back through the passage and reported, "Goes out past the tracks and comes up inside another building, quite a ways over, to the west of here."

Donny decided to fuck with him, "How's you wife, Gregor?"

The Mutt picked up the phone and hit speed dial.

"Put the phone down!"

"I don't think so, Detective. Speak to my attorney – he'll be real pleased you came in here and ripped up my business, then berated me about my dead wife while I'm still grieving."

Gregor had Donny cold. He could do nothing, at least not yet. "Everyone clear out. We're done with this piece of shit!"

★ ★ ★

I snapped a photo before pushing off from shore; the last leg. What a scene in front of me. I got wet, a bit of a boot soaker getting into the kayak, but figured that will happen a few more times this trip – no big deal. I could see smoke rising in the north, along a narrow finger that ran out from the main lake. At least someone else was brave enough to come in deep. I had camped in that area for the last few years, only because the east end was always booked. This time I'd lucked out, I would return to the farthest part of the lake. The sunsets were better, so hopefully the photos would be too. The fishing had more potential, due to the islands and shallows. And finally, no other sites were down that way. More secluded, less possible chance of boaters coming that way, and hopefully, more animals wandering about, around me.

The sun was definitely on its downward angle. Fortunately, my site was sitting in the open with a northwest exposure, meaning I'd have lots of light even after sundown. I eased up on my stroke and enjoyed the calm and sereneness of the lake. No need to hurry.

Kettle Lake was really long and fairly wide at its middle. The south side was quite reedy, which is probably why there were no campsites located there. However, it was covered in a mixed forest beyond that, held every animal to be sure, and was where I would be hiking through, often. To the north, it was all rock and coniferous trees, jutting in and out, making a beautiful landscape. In the middle of the north side, a finger of water ran off and up – there were at least two other sites located that way and I had camped on them both. Then there was the east end and I was coming up on it now. The water level drop was noticeable on the shear-faced rock wall at the very farthest point, at least a meter from the last watermark. Reeds had filled in the area as well. Still, it was picture perfect. No wonder the Group of Seven had enjoyed painting the northern landscapes so much. The material; rock, trees, water, sky, all the shapes were so gritty, so basic. The scenes they drew must have spoken to them. It spoke to me, that I know for sure. This was my spot – I felt truly fulfilled. *How often in life can one say that?*

It was well past 17:00 hours when I neared my site. It looked exactly the same after all these years of coming up here. I remembered each tree and rock, every island, and the air was pure. Heaven, if such a place existed, was right here. Nothing better than arriving in good weather; I absolutely hate setting up in the rain, or tearing down in a foul spit for that matter. The kayak's nose touched land and I pushed sideways to close in on a shallow sandy area. I could skirt the water on my egress. First things first, needed to pee and have a stretch, then a walk around the site.

The fire pit looked used recently and a blessed camper had left some kindling. Good karma. I went to work unloading gear, setting up the tent first. I wanted a strip of earth that was slightly angled and higher up, so any rain would run away. Getting flooded in the middle of the night was not a fun experience. I picked my spot, towards the back of the site, swept in some old, soft debris and laid a third of the tarp down on top of my natural cushion. The tent went on top of that, then the rest of the tarp got folded around the exposed area of the tent. It would be virtually impossible to get wet now. I staked it down tight and secure – happy with my set up. Off to gather fire wood – the pickings would be slim close by so I headed west into the bush. The fatigue was setting in and I would find sleep easy tonight.

★ ★ ★

When he'd arrived at the house earlier that morning, he had crashed on the couch and slept for a bit, after a line of cocaine of course. Once up again, he had a swim. The pool wasn't exactly indoors. It was off a room through sliding doors and outside, covered in one of those plastic domes, complete with skylights. The sauna was in the room of the walkout and really helped him relax. A few more lines of powder, gaining energy and feeling better, he had another swim. Savoy choked down some cold chicken and a few spoonfuls of potato salad from containers in the refrigerator. Another nap and finally, Freddy made a drink and pondered his future. Swilling his scotch and water, he was lost in a chemical haze.

"Yeah, I can do this," he said aloud, trying to bolster his mood and looking towards the future. He was a survivor. He poured another shot into his glass and chugged it straight.

★ ★ ★

After grabbing some personal stuff in Toronto, a bit of a risky chance taken since the Mutt didn't authorize it, Tony and Olig headed north. Neither was about to leave empty-handed. They picked up money and personal effects, squaring away some outstanding items.

Making good time, nearing the house in Kleinburg, they had been discussing where they would go after all this was over – now the topic was how to do the cop.

"I say we walk him outside to look at something, then whack him on the head. Throw him in the trunk and we dump him or bury him somewhere, away from the house."

Tony countered. "You're right on one count, he has got to be out of the house, can't leave him there."

They drove in silence. Either way, they would figure out how to unburden Freddy of his life in about thirty minutes.

★ ★ ★

I had managed to amass a good stack of wood, mostly deadfall, in about half an hour. That would last for cooking a meal and some warmth tonight, along with a small cooking fire tomorrow morning. My tiny hatchet and new cross-cut saw would get a workout, as would I.

I threw my thermal sleeping bag, camera gear, and roll-up mat inside the tent. I'd make a pillow out of the few clean clothes I'd brought in the other canvas bag. I put my loose gear in the tent as well, cutting the weight of my knapsack.

Slinging a nylon rope line between two trees, I raised my pack up and down. That would work. Keep the animals away from the food; no scent near the ground. Just throw a garbage bag over it at night to keep the contents dry – perfect. My stomach grumbled, time for dinner. The cross-cut saw worked real nice. In minutes, I had enough small chunks of wood to keep a fire going and I gathered some fallen birch bark and twigs off the ground. I sparked the tiny mound of tinder using one match only. Goodness me I'm such a good Girl Guide!

★ ★ ★

Donny debriefed everyone and thanked them all for their good work. The surveillance team was pulled from Mutznig's building and given a rest.

He sat in his office. Donny already knew the Mutt owned many businesses, from shipping and warehousing, to buildings under so many layers of companies, that you'd never find them all. Molinara and Steig could be at any one of them. They could be on their way out of country for all Donny knew. Freddy Savoy would be with them – he had no other place to go. The phone taps had produced nothing other than brief, three or four word questions and answers. No names, no addresses.

Donny yawned and stretched – time to go home and sleep. The warrants for the cops would give him something in a few days. The judge should approve them by tomorrow. After the day's frustrating results, Donny grabbed his jacket and left the office, deflated.

★ ★ ★

I used my water purifier to fill some lake water into my deep pan. Brought it to a boil over the fire, threw in a red beans and rice packet of dried food, and in ten minutes had a meal fit for a queen.

I was starving – snarfed it down in about three minutes, burning my mouth in the process. Thought about eating another bagged meal but held off and didn't. I'd be here a long time and needed to ration food appropriately. Washed the pan and spork in the water with sand and shook them off. More water brought to boil for a few teas while I relaxed.

This was one of the best parts of being up here. Full stomach, fire for warmth, laid back on the kayak and watching the stars come out, and the creatures meander by. Thank goodness most people are too lazy to come this far in! Being totally alone is bliss. Staring up towards the northeast I saw that wonderful inky colour again; seems to only be present in early spring and fall. I grabbed my camera and set it up on a rock outcrop, framed the shot, set the timer and blasted off some early-evening landscape shots. I didn't check them on the screen; uses too much power and I had to save all the battery life I could. Just couldn't recharge anywhere up here. I tucked the gear back in the tent, under the sleeping bag for warmth, when done. The cold zaps the power in the batteries really fast. The other two power cells were in a zippered pocket, close to my chest, staying nice and toasty warm.

★ ★ ★

It was starting to darken by the time Tony pulled into the driveway. He had been here several times before. He and Olig still hadn't decided on what to do with Freddy. They sat in the car for a bit, discussing it more. Tony took the lead. "Look, let's just play it as it comes. Maybe we can get him drunk and then tease him outside and pop him. Either way, don't off him inside and get the place all messy."

They exited the car and went inside, finding Freddy splayed out on the couch. He was definitely hammered and they both smiled at each other.

★ ★ ★

Donny got home about 20:30 hours, kissed Peg, and went in to see Andy. He read a very short story to his kid then walked to the bedroom, stripped and passed out without any supper. Peg let him sleep.

★ ★ ★

Gregor was heading home and had his driver stop at a payphone. He had been busy on the computer after the police left and found Algonquin Park could be the only logical place this Stevens bitch could go. The credit card purchases were like breadcrumbs. He knew the right man for the job; someone who could go in fast and hard and clean this situation up once and for all.

He spoke in Russian for about five minutes, hung up the phone, and continued on to his real house on the Bridal Path. It was only 6,000 square feet, but comfortable.

★ ★ ★

Olig greeted his target with a hardy roar, "Freddy, my man! How you doing bro?"

"I'm okay. What's going on guys? Are we close to leaving?"

"Yeah, man. Just waiting on a call for the all-clear and then we're out of here," Olig said as he flopped down on the couch with Savoy.

Tony made a beeline straight for the kitchen; no chit chat for him, he started rooting around for plastic garbage bags; big ones.

"Hey Freddy, you know why women get their period?" Olig asked.

Savoy was stunned by the question. "Ah, no, why do women get their period, Olig?"

"So they get to know what it's like to live with an irritated cunt every month!" Olig howled at his joke and fell over laughing.

Freddy just looked at him, dumbfounded. "How did I ever end up so lucky?"

When he recovered, Olig asked, "Any food?"

"Yeah, help yourself."

Olig went to the kitchen, got Tony's attention, put his finger to his head, and pretended to blow his brains out. Tony had to stifle his giggle.

★ ★ ★

I was beat. The drive and the portage, no sleep the night before, I couldn't keep my eyes open. It was the perfect night to shoot star trails with the camera but I couldn't stay awake for the hours it would take to accomplish the shots. The fire was almost dead; no flames and the embers were covered in a soft white ash. I was tucked away by 21:00 hours and fell asleep as soon as my head was down.

* * *

After finding enough big bags to wrap up old Freddy, Tony and Olig had a bite to eat. They joined Freddy for a drink and turned on the TV, getting the sports channel as opposed to a news station. That would be bad … if there was a police warning on the tube about their good buddy here.

They toasted Freddy and his new life and freedom. Freddy toasted Freddy and both Tony and Olig smiled at each other. They all did a few lines of coke and acted like the best of friends. Any cop worth his salt would have known this was a situation going south – fast. Freddy, unfortunately, wasn't worth all that much.

The property was well away from other houses. No one would hear a small pop. Guns don't sound like they do in the movies. Olig and Tony looked at each other, watching as Freddy drank his booze. He was close to passing out. It was time.

Olig made the first move, going out the sliding doors that led to the backyard. "Wow, you guys! You should see the stars, man."

Tony nudged Freddy. "C'mon, let's have a look."

Freddy wasn't impressed. "Big deal – stars. You can see them every night, damn near."

Tony pushed. "Not like up here, Freddy. You can see more of them and they're clearer – c'mon."

Savoy didn't have a clue and that was probably best. He stumbled over to the sliding door and stepped out, bumping into Tony, who gave him a little nudge farther out towards Olig, who stood at the edge of the patio stones. Looking up, reeling slightly from the booze and drugs, Freddy started to say something.

It took only seconds to press the small, twenty-two calibre pistol to his head and pull the trigger. A faint pop and Savoy flopped onto the grass; no exit wound and virtually no mess. Olig added a second round into the cop's brain, just for good measure.

Tony grabbed some bags and cord. They put one bag over Freddy's head and tied it tight with rope. They stripped him of ID and everything else of value. Olig went to the car, popped the trunk and lined it with more plastic bags.

They both hefted what remained of Detective Freddy Savoy and unceremoniously dumped him in the trunk, slamming it shut.

"After you, Oli."

"No please, after you, Tony."

Quite the comedic pair – killing was a game; a joke; a minor inconvenience in their lives. They checked the house for any of Freddy's belongings and cleaned up the glasses and anything else he may have touched. Once the house was secured, they grabbed some beers and watched ESPN.

"That was my first cop," Olig stated, in a matter-of-fact voice.

"Yeah!" responded Tony. "I almost did one about ten years ago."

"Was he chasing you or what?"

"No. Downtown club that was popular back then, happened right in the shitter, when I was doing a deal. Put two in his chest. Thought it was a rip – thought I was set up and he was going to steal my dope. Didn't even know it was a cop until later, when I read it in the papers. He survived."

★ ★ ★

It was getting light out when I awoke. I could hardly move. My poor body was not used to this type of torture. I worked up some saliva and choked down three codeine pills.

I squeezed out of the tent and stretched. No clouds, little wind, and reasonably warm for the time of year. It was going to be another great day. *Nice.* Kettle Lake in front of me was cloaked in mist, I could see about halfway, if that, then a creamy white obscured everything else. I'd give it an hour or so, then shoot the view as the natural curtain lifted and burned off.

Gathering a few fallen pieces of birch bark and some twigs of various sizes, I lit the small clump and had the fire ablaze in no time. The tiny amount of warmth felt good on my bones. I got some water purified and heated it up. "Tea please." *Already talking to myself – no one would hear.* As the twigs caught and burned, I started to plunk a few larger pieces of wood on the tiny flame, building it up slowly, getting it ready to cook breakfast.

It didn't take long for them to arrive. A red squirrel chattered at me from a nearby pine tree, swinging its tail in a stuttered motion.

"Hello neighbour!"

A chipmunk ran right past my feet and tried to climb atop the kayak, but slid on the plastic, flopping to the ground and scurrying off. They were testing me. Was I friend or was I foe?

I pulled out a granola bar and broke a piece off, placing it on a small rock. I enjoyed the rest with my tea and watched the diurnal activity rev up. After a second tea, I boiled more water for breakfast. "Powdered eggs if you please!" *There I go again.*

★ ★ ★

Donny popped straight up from the bed, looking like a startled cat. He was absently rubbing the bullet wound scars on his right chest. He focused in on the clock; 08:00 hours. "Jesus, Peg!"

She came running in, "What? What is it?"

"Look at the time! Why did you let me sleep so late?"

"Honey, you needed it. Relax now, have a shower, and I'll make you something special for breakfast."

"I don't have time to eat. I have to get going."

She went over to the bed, wrapped her arms around him and held him close. "Listen, you have to slow down and look after yourself or you'll be no good to anybody."

Donny looked at this beautiful creature that actually loved him. "Sorry. I don't mean to take it out on you. There's just so much at stake."

Peg gripped his shoulders and looked him straight in the eyes. "Have a shower – you'll feel better. Then we eat and talk for five minutes ... end of."

He did as he was told and he felt better. What would he do without her in his grubby little life?

★ ★ ★

After breakfast, rummaging around in my gear, I finally found the phone. No signal though and it didn't seem to matter where I held it; high or low, east or west, nada. I'd give it whirl later, maybe out on the lake. I stashed the cell in an outer coat pocket.

If they came after me, how long would it take them? I had today at least ... most likely tomorrow. I pushed the notion out of my head. *No way they'd come here. No way.*

Using the rock formations to steady the camera, I delayed the shutter speed and used the internal timer. I blasted a few shots of the lake expanse, with mist rising so that it slightly obscured the far north side. It was a postcard photograph. The sun illuminated the whole northwest – few shadows. *Coming to Algonquin*, I thought. *Priceless!* I sprinkled a few sunflower seeds around the rocks and knew my friends would indulge at their leisure while I was gone. They can't resist the small black-oil seeds, a favourite, as opposed to the larger type ones.

I hopped into the kayak, camera in tow, and slipped around the small islands to see what was what. It was really quiet, save for the wildlife; no other campers could be heard or were even in view. *People should write books about this place.* I circled northeast, then headed west so as to have the sun on my back and give me a clear view. I could hear the weight of a bigger animal trashing the woods somewhere to the north. I waited for a few minutes but nothing popped out. A large blue heron fished in the shallows off a small island. I traded out the lens, opting for the 100-400mm, and shot the elongated fellow for a few minutes from a distance. The backdrop was perfect, and the ambient light gave me enough speed so I could keep the ISO low and maintain the hand held shot. This was why I came here.

★ ★ ★

Donny finished his plate of food in record time. Three eggs, four strips of bacon, two pieces of toast and he drained his second coffee. "I could eat that again!"

Peg smiled. "Can I ask what is happening?"

Donny shook his head.

"Can I ask how Liz is?"

That he could answer. "She's on vacation, camping at Algonquin."

"Is she in danger?"

"Why would you ask that?"

Peg sat down at the kitchen table and held his hand. "I overheard some of your conversation the other day. I'm sorry, I wasn't eavesdropping."

Donny gave her a kiss and got up. He grabbed his sport coat and keys. "It's possible that some pretty bad people identified who she is, along with where she was, and what she saw and photographed."

"Will they go after her up there?"

Donny just smiled. He knew the answer. "I doubt it. Listen, she has a ton of experience and knows that area really well. If trouble comes, she can hide from anyone up there. It would literally be like trying to find a needle in a haystack." He kissed the top of her head. "I'll try and be home at a decent time. Love you."

He was out the door before she could say, 'love you' back.

★ ★ ★

He could hear it. Faint at first but stronger now, definitely knocking. "Fuck me!" Tony got out of bed and went downstairs, sporting a T-shirt and tightie-whities. No doubt about it, someone was knocking at the front door.

He looked through the peephole. A man stood outside. Tony didn't recognize him.

"Yeah, whadda ya want?"

"Gregor sent me. Is this Olig or Tony?"

Tony opened the door a crack. "Who are you?"

★ ★ ★

I didn't move a muscle. The male loon had popped up right beside the kayak. My goodness, this was awesome. I could almost reach out and touch him. I enjoyed the gift; just watching. The loon's red eyes were aglow, looking so mischievous. In a blink, he disappeared; one swift movement, back down under the water to fish for breakfast.

I pulled my camera out, put on the 75-200 mm lens and checked the settings, keeping the strap around my neck; ready to shoot. If he came up again, I might just get him good. I scanned for the female as they are usually not far apart, and back paddled gently, trying to guess where he'd come up.

Bingo! But as soon as I moved with the camera, he dove under. "That's okay my friend," I muttered to no one. *Let him get used to me, I've got all the time in the world.*

I continued on and covered the east quadrant of the lake, doing a bit of slalom between the small islands that peppered the area. Came across a blue marker on the north side, indicating a campsite location, but not active; no one home. Didn't even remember there being one there before. I guessed they add a few sites here and there – progress. Or just more demand. That was okay; mostly die hard campers came in here, not the yahoos you get every year at the smaller provincial parks. I've had my fill of those people.

As I made my way west, to where the lake splits direction and a finger runs off to the north, I saw the blue markers for at least three other sites. Looking through my camera, I spotted a lone camper on one site and three dudes on another. That was it for Kettle Lake. I kept my distance from them, not wanting to disturb, and not really wanting to make friends either. The only company I wished for was the feral animal kind – and the wilder the better.

I started to circle Joe Island, going at a snail's pace, patient, and waiting for that moment when I'd spot a critter and move in for the shot.

★ ★ ★

Olig finally came downstairs and saw Tony and the other man drinking coffee in the kitchen. He had never seen this guy before. He was about the size of Tony; black hair too, thinning a bit at the front; older with hard eyes; almost black eyes and following Olig's every movement. Olig was immediately suspicious. "Hey."

The man nodded at Olig.

"Who are you?"

Tony spoke up. "This here is Jerry Tesla, a friend of Gregor's. He is going to help us out."

"Yeah?"

"That's right, you're Olig, I've heard of you."

"So?"

Tony rolled his eyes. His colleague was not a very bright bulb in the morning – monkeys had a wider vocabulary.

"Mr. Mutznig will be calling soon. He will explain at that time." Jerry stated.

Olig checked the water in the kettle, placing his hand on the metal side, "Is this hot still?"

Jerry Tesla smiled, obviously finding this quite amusing. "I would suggest you boys get dressed soon, we're going to have a long day. By the way, where is the cop?"

Olig was terse, "Outside, trunk of the car. Why?"

"Just wondering," Jerry responded. Then he asked, "Any problems there? Anything to be concerned about?"

"We handled it, thank you very much. We're not idiots, you know."

Tony shook his head and went upstairs to dress, leaving Tesla and Olig in a battle of wits, one of them unarmed.

★ ★ ★

The Special Investigation office was in full frenzied mode by the time Donny walked in. It was after 11:00 hours. He shook his head – half the day was already over. A few raised eyebrows shot his way. He was never late.

"Listen up, meeting in five. I want updates for everyone on the big board."

The big board was the flow chart of faces that connected the group of suspects. Each team member had a handful of identities to track. In turn, they used their underlings to bring in meaningful data, which in turn, was filtered up and given to Donny.

He poured a coffee and checked his email and voice mail … nothing from Liz. He grabbed a sticky note: 'Must get flowers today!'

"Okay, let's get to it." They huddled up in the conference room and ran down the faces and status of each. "Stan, you want to lead us off."

"Tony Molinara, Olig Steig and Freddy Savoy have dropped off the face of the earth – whereabouts unknown."

That much, Donny figured. He asked his second to continue.

"Warrants produced three constables, two sergeants, and one detective; an Arthur Buckles, now in holding cells waiting to be interviewed. One sergeant is still outstanding, unknown location. Mutznig is not wanted at this time."

There was an audible groan from some frustrated team members.

"Okay, forensics. Do we have a good line list of dates, times, and info scanned, along with the related criminal acts for our detainees?" Donny enquired.

"Got it boss – all chronological order and broken into cases. We're ready to press them at interview and see if we can break a few."

"Good. Let's pair up into teams and turn up the heat. Some won't talk, that's alright. Give it time. Let 'em think it through and know, that we know, everything. Feed them slowly, build the case and nail them down." Donny would watch them on the monitors. This was a good start.

★ ★ ★

The phone rang and Tesla picked it up before the second ring. "Yes."

It was Gregor. "Put me on speaker so you can all hear this."

Tesla did as instructed and Olig and Tony crowded in to get their directions.

Gregor was straight to the point – Tesla was in charge. He would lead them into the park since he had bush experience. Do what needed to be done, quick. Get back to the house and call, at which time he would have their out arranged.

The Mutt did not let Tony or Olig know that they both had first-degree murder warrants and were being actively sought in connection with his wife's murder and that other slug she'd been with. He also didn't let them know that Tesla was authorized to sacrifice either or both of them to get the job done. The call was all of two minutes.

Tesla had already narrowed the search last night, by going on the park website and looking at what was vacant, booked, or taken. He had printed a map of the areas off Highway 60. He had the make of car and licence plate, pictures of the Stevens bitch and pedigree info. He informed his two colleagues as they got ready to leave the house, "This will take two or three days max, shouldn't pose any problems."

Tesla, with Tony and Olig in tow, left the house a half hour later. Travelling in three cars, they would first dump the cop's car away from the house then continue with two cars. They would stop for what supplies they needed en route. He drove ahead of his two new colleagues, keeping the speed dead on the maximum and obeying the rules of the road. They would have to dump the body before their camping adventure. Tesla already knew the perfect spot.

★ ★ ★

From the small room, Donny watched the interviews on the monitor screens. Everything was being taped. He was looking for the weak link. Unblinking, he waited for that uncomfortable moment – that point in time when the sweating, squirming, twitching, and avoidance behaviour mannerisms began. He leaned in, hanging on every word. The language used by suspects can give quite a bit away, if you know what to listen for.

Two of the three constables had already given up that they gave out licence plate info and some personnel data. That was all-low level stuff. They would be fired at the very least. His team worked at getting signed statements from them and that would end the constables' part in his investigation, along with their careers in law enforcement. The other street cop was holding out and denying everything.

The two sergeants were hanging tough as well. "I want to speak to my union rep and have a lawyer. Do not ask me any more questions."

That basically ended their involvement until all the legal wrangling was done.

But the detective, Arthur Buckles, was still the best bet. Not only would he have had access to critical info and intel, he would have been able to manoeuvre other staff on the street, and within the department, to help him.

He was Donny's main player. Donny gathered up the reports and joined the interview team to exert some pressure – even if it was just by his presence.

★ ★ ★

It was after 12:00 hours and I tried the phone signal out in the middle of the lake. Nothing. "What did you expect dummy?" My tour around the island and back again had produced nothing. Not even a good landscape shot. Nothing! I was disappointed indeed. I thought maybe the campers on the other two sites along the finger might be a tad noisy and have scared off any bigger animals. That could work to my advantage, pushing them towards me on the other side. I decided to head back to my site, start wood detail for a bit, and make some other preparations. I cut southeast from the middle of Kettle Lake, lazily, admiring the view. The water was a mirror; hardly a ripple. The sun felt great, the tension and aches were finally leaving my body. My eyes wandered as I slowly paddled.

I had more company! My heart thumped so hard it damn near left my chest. Another kayak was coming at me from the southwest end of the lake. Right from the portage area, no doubt about it, headed right at me. "Shit!" I was in the open. "You are a dummy!" I looked around and slowly paddled back towards the bay where the other campers were. If I was closer to other people then maybe I'd be safer.

I exchanged the smaller lens and snapped in the 100-400mm. "Let's have a look-see." Still too far away to be identified so I floated for a few minutes. Tried again. "Ah, it's our friendly neighbourhood park ranger." I could make out some type of shoulder patch and the kayak had the Ontario Parks logo on it. I started to relax a bit. I bagged the camera and moved slowly towards the ranger.

★ ★ ★

They stopped in Barrie for some clothing. Boots, coats, and sweaters would be needed. Tesla had to baby sit Tony and Olig; they were like children. They had no clue as to what was needed in the bush. He got them each a vest and coat, gloves and hat, long johns and thermal socks, and waterproof boots. He let them pick out a T-shirt, flannel shirt, and sweater on their own. Next, they located a Canadian Tire where Tesla bought all the gear, including a tent, sleeping bags, some cooking utensils, matches, fire starter, flashlight, and a cooler. Once Tesla got farther up north, he would buy food and find a spot to grab a canoe. Everything was paid for in cash. No traces.

Tesla led the boys through Orillia and back over to the old Highway 11. Rarely used and rough, it was one lane each way. He had lived here as a teenager and remembered most of it. He wound his way through the back road, then onto dirt, and finally stopped at some woods.

Olig got out of the car and walked over to Jerry. "Why here? Christ we could have found woods anywhere."

"Just grab the body, Olig, and follow me."

Olig looked at Tony who came up to them. "Hey, you help too, man!"

Tesla glared at him. "Your mess, you clean it up. Let's go!"

Tony grabbed Olig's coat and pulled him back to their car trunk. As Freddy was fished out, they looked around then followed Tesla through the woods.

Five minutes later, they all stared off a cliff and into a quarry, half-full of water.

Tesla said, "Check him for any ID, papers, anything."

"We already did that," Olig rebuffed him.

Tony didn't argue and checked Freddy's pockets again.

"Okay, take some rocks and weigh him down – put them in his pockets. That's right. Good work. He's going into the quarry water. Put some holes in the bag that's around his head so he sinks. Good."

Olig and Tony did as they were told. Savoy's body made a hard slap sound as it splashed down, hovered for a bit in the water, then started a slow downward trajectory to his final resting place.

"Did you use a gun on him?"

All happy and smiling, Olig pulled out his small-calibre weapon and said, "Yeah, this here."

Tesla snatched the little pistol from his hand and tossed it over the edge.

"Hey, that's my favourite … that's mine, damn it!"

"Not any more. Let's go."

Olig just growled at Jerry. Tony had to restrain him and physically walk him back to their car.

★ ★ ★

I spoke with the ranger, as we both floated in the middle of the lake. Nice guy, friendly, early-twenties, his first year here at Algonquin. His name was Adam Milner. He was making a pass through the lakes checking permits and he verified mine. Thank goodness he didn't search my kayak and find the crossbows. We talked for about twenty minutes while bobbing side by side in the water. I told Adam of the times coming up here, starting with some smaller lakes and not going in too deep, but how after gaining more experience, I wanted more of a challenge.

I asked if he camped out overnight but he said no, it was easy to hump the lightweight kayak in and he usually did a few lakes each day. It depended on the permits taken out as to where he went. A few days doing this, then back to the station for a few nights – it was great. Once most of the park closed off in mid-October, leaving only the smaller area open for winter camping, that was the end of the season for him and he headed south for sun and fun.

"Nice life you got going. Maybe I should have become a ranger."

"It's not all fun. There is some pretty tough grunt work and the bugs in the summer are nasty."

"I hear that. One reason I come in the fall."

We ran out of small talk. He had to motor, still needed to check the guys on the north finger and wanted to make it back before dark. He headed up the slipper of water and out of sight.

I glided back to my camp at an easy, calm pace but inside, my stomach was churning. This little episode had put a jingle in my jangle and spooked me something fierce. I was determined to be more careful. That meant planning for the worst.

Once back on shore, I pulled the kayak up out of the water, kicked myself in the arse, and got to it. I was not going to be complacent.

I looked at my position in relation to the lake. I was slightly southwest of a point, at the east end of Kettle Lake. The ridge jutted up and out. There was maybe a hundred-plus metre span of water between that and my site. The lake was in front of me, to the north and stretching westward. I walked about a kilometre west and found a location that gave me a clear view of the farthest access point, where I had portaged in. This would be my lookout location and an emergency exit from my site. I looked around – lots of mixed woods, dense brush. It would be a hell of a hike to get back to civilization if I was forced this way. On the other hand, I could run in this direction indefinitely, with lots of hides and screwy terrain. I could out-manoeuvre someone with ease. My confidence grew.

I came back to my campsite, carrying a few pieces of dead wood and I dumped them near the fire pit. I walked directly south from there, following several paths, trying to remembering where they led.

If I had to flee on foot, and couldn't go west, this would lead me to a bog about a hundred metres back. I remembered pooping here through the years and actually made another deposit. I searched for a cross-through point. To the west of the bog was more bog, with mixed-in iron trees and swamp – no way through. It was too open anyway, little brush grew around the dead-looking trees and it would be impossible to outrun or even hide from someone.

To the east of the boggy area, I found a way to go further south. I curled back more left and humped over some rock formations, which led me to a stone wash below a high ridge. I climbed up the steep slope of rocks, picking my way through broken stumps and fallen trees. I found myself overlooking my site, which was directly to the west of my perch, across the water, about a hundred and fifty metres away. This was my next safety exit. If they came in close and I had no other escape, I'd scale this mother of a climb and hide. I walked it twice, picking up spare wood each time and dumping it closer to my site. I had the landmarks burned into my head. "Enough work for one day," I said to no one. It was closing in on 17:00 hours and time for supper.

★ ★ ★

Tesla made it to Huntsville with Tony and Olig in tow. He found a sporting goods outlet and rented a canoe, three paddles, and three life jackets. He had to show identification so he laid a fake drivers licence on the dude and paid in cash. Tesla growled at the young prick at the shop because he made him leave a hundred-dollar security deposit too.

"I'll be back in about an hour. Stay here and load the boat onto your car."

Going in search of a motel and a place to buy groceries, Telsa left them to figure out how to tie down the canoe to their car roof.

★ ★ ★

The interviews had not yielded the info Donny really wanted. The detective was a veteran and held out. Donny put him back in cells and went home.

Tomorrow he would have to press Buckles hard and play the accessory-to-murder card. He wanted the names of everyone, however remotely linked, so he could ferret out all the bad apples from the department. He had gotten news on the outstanding sergeant ... dead. Shot himself with his weapon, through the mouth and upwards into the brain, while at a cottage of a friend. Not the outcome Donny had hoped for.

Donny picked up a dozen roses for Peg. He'd take her out for a slap up meal and spend some time with her ... do something, be spontaneous. He had ignored her ever since he'd gotten this damn job. As he drove home, "Smarten up asshole!" squeaked out of his mouth.

★ ★ ★

Tesla had booked two rooms just outside of Huntsville, right on Highway 60. He bought ice and a bunch of food, leaving the grocery bags and fully packed cooler in the trunk. Found a liquor store and bought three twelve packs of canned beer and three pint bottles of whisky.

As he pulled back into the sporting goods store, he just shook his head, a large smile forming on his face. "Clueless bastards." Tony and Olig were still wrestling with the canoe.

★ ★ ★

After humming and hawing, I decided on Alfredo pasta with beans for dinner. Seemed every dried food meal had beans, or rice. I tasted it. "Good golly almighty! This is shit!" I forced about a third of it down my throat. Not able to stomach any more, I walked well back into the bog area and dumped the putrid slop. "Somebody is going to eat this meal tonight."

I went back to red beans and rice. I had five more packages of those, two more of the shitty Alfredo pasta, another five of pasta and tomato (with beans of course) and six 'Mexican Delight,' whatever that was. It contained rice though. There were nine powdered egg meals left and ten oatmeal packs for breakfast. I also had two cans of beans for emergency, life-saving, 'I can't eat this crap anymore,' usage; for when I tired of dry food. *A small luxury in an otherwise inhospitable place don't ya know.* I had granola bars stuffed everywhere, so I could last for days on those bad boys. The tea would last; a whole box. I had ten hot chocolate packets as well, for a bit of sweetness and energy on occasion.

Once the dishes were done, I sparked the fire with plenty more wood. It would last for tonight. The weather was turning. I could feel it cooling down quickly as the sun dropped in the west. *I'll pop up to that perch tomorrow morning if the weather is nice, and shoot from there, that will be a good location.* Snapped a few photos of the setting sun – not overly dramatic without clouds, I thought. It was looking like a great night to capture star trails, I'd have to stay up this time and work at it, might not get another chance at a clear sky.

★ ★ ★

The kid at the sporting goods store just watched from the window, not sure what to make of the two guys that couldn't tie down a canoe. Tesla faced him, gave a thug's glare, shot him the finger and he scurried off like a frightened bunny. Once Olig and Tony had been instructed on tying down the canoe, they followed Jerry Tesla along the highway.

At the motel, he gave them some beer and whisky. "If you're hungry, go find a place and eat. Get to bed early 'cause you're going to need a good rest. We leave at five in the morning." He threw a key at Olig. "That's you and Tony. I'm in here."

Olig looked at Tony as the door on Tesla's room slammed shut with a 'don't bother me' thud. "Why does he get a room to himself and we have'ta share?"

"Shut up Oli. Let's get a good meal in us while we still can."

★ ★ ★

After the fire died down, I called it a night. I noticed the clouds were rolling in from the east and it smelled like rain. Not going to shoot star trails tonight. Just in case, I put some wood inside a plastic garbage bag, using that to partially cover my meagre pile. Checked the pegs of the tarp over my tent, made sure any water would roll away and not into me during the night, then crawled inside.

I just lay quietly in the tent, listening to the nocturnal sounds and movement of critters. I thought of past times where raccoons and other mammals had come sniffing around. Once, a few years back, I had been awakened around 03:00 hours by loud grunts and moans. Then the heavy pawing at the sides of the tent, I'd realized a bear was right there. I had felt like a sausage in a bun, minutes from being gulped down. Would the bear kill me? As it happened, I was safe. Never take any food or scents into the tent. *Remember that, campers. Even gum or mints will bring them on top of you.* I started to think of death ... then, whether I had it in me to kill. I thought about this, trying to be rational. The stress crept into my head and wound its way through my body. Tomorrow they could come and I needed to be more prepared. Sleep did not come easy.

★ ★ ★

The knock came early, just as Jerry said it would. Tony had had a shower the night before but Olig hadn't, and now it was time to get up and move out. Olig would be a stinking slob this whole trip. He just wouldn't learn. This is why Tony didn't like hanging out with Olig at the bars. The women couldn't flee fast enough once they had a whiff of the stinky swine. He was crude too, women aren't like that and they really don't like that type of behaviour.

They followed Tesla to a breakfast place and ate big. Once they were done, the plan was laid out by Jerry. "This is the car we are looking for." Tesla gave the info to Tony. They would follow the highway through Algonquin, checking for the vehicle and once it was found, would enter the waterway at that point.

Olig was not impressed. "This could take days just to find the car. We should split up and look. Be twice as fast, right?"

Tesla would have no part of it. "No. Follow the plan and we'll find the bitch, then we waste her in the woods. Once we find the car, the rest will be easy, trust me."

They paid the bill with cash and started out, Tesla in the lead car, and Olig driving the other car with Tony riding shotgun. The rain came softly at first then pounded them with a vengeance. Olig didn't like this at all. "I can't see shit, pisano."

★ ★ ★

The rain thundered on the tarp, deafening to my ears. I was warm and dry and had no intention of getting up. I lit up my watch with the flashlight, 06:30 hours. Not enough light out there anyway so I rolled to one side and pondered my options. I would leave the tent, tarp and sleeping bag at the site and everything else would be stored in the kayak during the day. If I was on land and they came at me, I would grab the tarp, the knapsack, and the crossbows, taking my emergency exit to the south and then fleeing east into the woods. If I was on the water, no problem, I had everything I needed sans the tent, tarp, and sleeping bag. If I couldn't outrun them, then I would hit the south side of the lake, to the west of my site and scamper hard and fast on land. It would be tough, but if I stayed on a south-western track, eventually I'd hit the highway or someone's place.

I needed to scout the east end of the lake and find a spot through the reeds to make land, so I could hide and watch from my perch on the rock cliff. Hiding the kayak in the reeds would help too. I started to relax a bit. *I have a plan.* I floated, half asleep. This was my holiday and I wanted to enjoy myself, take some good photos, and get close to the wildlife. They wouldn't come. I'd be fine. How could they even know I was here?

★ ★ ★

Donny was in a great mood. Flowers for Peg had led to a long talk, which led to a meal ordered in, which led to a night of great sex. He gave Andy a soft tussle on the head, kissed Peg, and was out the door before 08:00 hours. He was on a mission and couldn't hold back the driving force inside. Today was the day he'd break that detective, come hell or high water.

★ ★ ★

Tesla had found two possible areas so far, but no Chevy Impala. There were signs for car parking and lake access – permit holders only. That was the clue he wanted. He looked at the map. Dawson Lake was ahead, another possible.

Olig and Tony were sitting in the car behind him, drinking beer. "Think we'll even find the car, Oli?"

"Not a chance. The bitch could be anywhere. We should have taken her in Toronto, at her house, like I said before."

"Yeah Oli, you may have been right on that one. Look, he's pulling out, let's go."

Olig spun the car tires and tail gated Tesla for shits and giggles. About twenty clicks up they saw him turn left.

Tesla pulled into the next parking area and his eyes were drawn right to the car. The rain had eased and he got out and motioned Tony and Olig to come over quick. They huddled up around the vehicle.

"See! Look at the licence plate – a match. Okay, park over there and get the canoe down. We could be done the job before the end of the day and back to civilization, no camping, no cold nights. Let's go boys!"

Tesla found the launch area and started bringing the equipment and food down as Tony and Olig hauled the canoe over.

Once all gear was at the water's edge, Tesla had them come back to his car, opened up a hidden vault in the trunk, and pulled out a heavy cotton bag.

"What guns do you have on you now?" he asked.

"You took mine, remember," Olig said with a hint of snarky attitude.

"I'm good," Tony said confidently as he pulled out his sparkling, silver-plated Sig 9mm.

Tesla gave a fully loaded, matte-black S&W 38-snub nose to Olig, along with a dozen bullets in a plastic bag. It had a taped handle to hide any fingerprints.

"Tony, you got ammo?"

"Two full clips."

Tesla pocketed a Glock 9 for himself with an extra clip. "Now guys, give me your ID, wallets, anything that could identify you."

"What for?" Olig griped, tired of all the rules being made up.

"Because I said so, give it, now!"

They obliged Tesla and he put all the wallets and such in the vault and sealed it up.

"Okay, let's lock up the cars and we'll get going."

Olig and Tony fiddle farted around their car for longer than was necessary then followed Jerry down to the canoe. They all stood at the boat, Olig and Tony with hands in pockets, unsure of what was next.

"Now, who is gonna be my bowsman?" Tesla inquired.

Tony and Olig stared at him, with big blank unblinking deer eyes.

Tesla groaned as the nightmare began. "Guys, which one of you is going in the front of the canoe?"

Tony volunteered. He stepped into the canoe. It flopped to one side and he almost did a face plant into the water. "Shit!"

"Look buckwheat, use the paddle to brace yourself on the gunnels, the sides of the canoe – like this," Tesla instructed.

Tony made it to the front, wobbling in the tiny craft, afraid to move in any direction.

"Now turn around, we're gonna hand you all the gear."

It was Keystone Cops on water, Tony refused to move in the slim vessel and Jerry kept getting more and more pissed. Finally, after using soft, gentle coaxing, Tesla had him facing backwards and they could start sending in the supplies.

Once they were loaded, Tesla stuffed Olig in the middle and pushed the canoe stern right to the edge of the water, ready to shove off. He just looked at Tony and Olig. Both men were facing him with vacuous looks.

"Ah, you guys want to do a one-eighty and face the other way, please." Tesla put on his life jacket. He advised his fellow travellers to do the same. With Tony and Olig finally in the proper position, paddles in hand, he pushed the canoe hard, and jumped into the stern position. As the boat skimmed the water, it almost tipped, striking primal fear into two of the three men. Excited little-girl noises could be heard for several moments.

★ ★ ★

The rain had petered out but it was still overcast. I could have tea or breakfast, but not both, since there wasn't enough dry wood.

I opted for tea and granola bars. Even wet, the birch bark lit easily and finally, twigs caught fire with some effort and blowing. As I boiled water, the day was planned out. I would devote the morning to wood detail and the afternoon to scouting the east side of the lake for my next emergency exit. I would have to hide the kayak deep, and the reeds were the perfect place. They were super-thick and high. The reeds themselves offered a good place for me to hide, if it came to that.

I walked to the bog, had a squat, and did my business. Picked up some dead wood and carried it back. *Never go anywhere and come back empty handed.*

It was spitting a bit so I donned my camouflaged rain poncho, walked to the western lookout, and had a peek. No one was coming from the portage area, not a soul on the lake. I gathered more wood and hauled it back.

My chippy was waiting for me and I threw him a piece of granola. I made the trip to the western lookout three more times, gathering wood along the way, making small stacks and I had it all back at the site before 13:00 hours.

I bagged some small pieces and set the bags on top of my woodpile. It would last a few days, no problem. No sense cutting up any big stuff now, I'd do that as needed and the activity would keep me warm at the same time.

The kayak got loaded with gear and I left the tent, tarp, and sleeping bag in place. I started to paddle towards the reed beds, going in search of an exit point, somewhere in there. This could prove daunting.

★ ★ ★

"We've got you, Detective." Donny showed him the print-outs of the computer log-ins, the info that was scanned, the dates and times. Then he laid out how each one fit into case after case of missed busts, missed warrants, and finally the licence plate search of the car Derek Walters owned and his credit card info.

"This guy was killed, on the same day you accessed the info. Look! Look at the phone calls out of your location, right to numbers associated with Gregor Mutznig and Detective Savoy, hours before this man and a woman were murdered!"

There was a knock at the door of the interview room. The forensic IT guy spoke to Donny, handed him some more papers, and left. "Well, well. You were here when my attempted bust went sideways. We missed two murder suspects because they were tipped off. You also made phone calls at the same time, logged into the computer system, and pulled out some very interesting data. Want to tell me about it?"

The detective was stoic. Donny could see the edges becoming frayed though and worked harder, "Look asshole, you are gonna go down for conspiracy to commit murder if you don't start talking right now!"

Nothing yet. He played another card, probably the one the detective was waiting for. "Look, help us now and the prosecutor and judge will know you aided in the investigation. You might even save a life here. We can talk about some consideration."

"I need to think about this for a while. I want to speak to an attorney before we go any further and I want some decent food."

Donny was on the money; this was the guy – the one that could give him names and connections. "Okay, no problem. But this has got to be soon, like a day, no more."

The detective nodded, "Agreed."

Donny left the room and had the detective taken back to cells. He got his team together and briefed them. "Make sure the puke gets whatever food he wants and contact his choice of lawyer right now, go!"

★ ★ ★

Larry, Curly, and Moe struggled in the canoe for the first half-hour. Tesla was losing his patience and kept looking at his gun.

Finally, after what seemed like an eternity, he had them both paddling at the same time, on the same side, allowing him to use a power stroke and steer. He looked to the sky, just overcast and not too cold either. Little blessings come at the oddest times.

Tesla was looking for the blue markers indicating a campsite, then at who was on those sites. By his estimation, there should be five campsites on this lake and three were supposedly occupied. Too bad the park's website wouldn't give out more personal info as that would've made it a whole lot easier.

At the midway point of this long narrow lake were some islands – they stayed to the north of them and circled the area. A couple were back in a small cove. As they neared the site Tesla could tell it was not the person he wanted. They waved and continued on.

On the northeast side nearing the end of Dawson Lake, was another camper. Nope, definitely not who he was hunting; this one was a large male and dark-skinned. He steered around the point and into a converging area and saw three more men huddled around a fire. Nope.

Tesla thought about doing another circuit of the lake but he had counted three sites; that's what the computer said should be occupied. It was getting past two and finding a camp for the night was more important anyway. He spun the canoe and headed for the orange marker that signified a portage point.

Tesla, using boil strokes, powered hard the last few metres. Tony was freaking out and telling him to stop. They hit shore and the canoe drove up onto the fine sand landing. Tony just sat at the front, looking kinda pasty.

Jerry just shook his head in wonderment. "You can get out now."

The two men took several minutes to disembark.

"Okay, unload the canoe. Wait here, I'll be back." Tesla took off at a swift trot. He would leave Huey and Dewy with the gear and run the length of the portage to see what it was like.

★ ★ ★

From my rounded concave cove, I started at the most northern part of the lake and worked my way backwards, cutting into shore every so often where I thought it looked accessible, looking for that passageway where I could get onto dry land from the kayak. So far, any place I tried would put me in waist-deep water, in order to exit the boat. The rock face was over eight feet high and totally vertical – no way to get onto the land. The lowering levels of the lake water over the years had made it impossible to scale.

There were multiple stretches of reeds; each huge clump interlocked and got closer to my campsite. I slid slowly into the thicket, not knowing what I'd run into. Bumping and scraping along, running into logs or rocks. Over and over, I kept at it, trial and error.

Then finally, I hit a nice little piece of sand that rolled away from a flat rock on shore where I could kinda roll out of the kayak, and hopefully scale up a fat vertical crevice to the top of the rock face. Perfect. I backed the kayak out the same way I came in and tried to line up some markers so I'd know exactly the point to enter.

If I was in a frenzied hurry, like being chased, I couldn't waste time dickin' around trying to find the spot. Unfortunately, nothing lined up that made any sense marker-wise. I tied a little strip of green plastic bag to a reed stalk, close to the water, barely visible.

I looked at the plastic marker. "What are you doing?" I said to myself, shaking my head and half laughing. *I'm an idiot! No one is coming up here to get me. This is ridiculous!* My thoughts brought me to a giddy state. *Look at yourself, sitting in a kayak, in the middle of a reed bed, in the middle of no where, planning for an attack! Geezez!*

I hovered in the water, rocking gently, as the small waves bumped against the kayak. I looked down the lake and up towards the sky, it was overcast, grey, dull, lonely. I thought, *Fuck it! I am all alone here and I feel an ache, a tinge of something, a possible threat. Go with your gut! When there is any doubt, then there is no doubt! Believe it!*

Okay, try something else. I went to the start of the reeds, closest to my site and counted the lengths of kayak to the entry point; twenty, give or take a kayak. I paddled back to the point farthest away, where this clump of reeds started and counted the lengths

203

coming the other way. Ten. Give or take a metre. Ten-twenty is the code for your location on the radio, easy as pie.

    I went back to the access point, pushed into the reeds, hit the sand and got out of the kayak. Presto! Now, scale the rock face and onto the flat. I used the crevice, jamming my foot into the wide fissure and hoisting myself up. Easier said than done but I made it. Where did it lead?

    I worked my way south, getting closer to the rise overlooking my camp that I'd found the other day. Not the hardest climb but fatigue was setting in. I came out at the top of the rock cliff and could see my campsite. This was a good nest. Great view too, I'd have to take more photos from here at different times of the day.

    I looked down the length of the lake … nothing coming. It just dawned on me why they'd named this body of water Kettle Lake. The finger going to the north looked like the handle and the rest of the lake like a kettle. *Fascinating stuff!*

    I made my way back to the kayak and this time tried walking north, going the other way. The brush was too thick to cut into the woods but I could scamper along the top of the rock face fairly well and I made my way to the furthermost part of the lake. It was a dead end; just swamp, bog, and dense bush in the distance – not a good way out. If I had to come this way, I'd be trapped with nowhere else to go. If I started running in this direction, I wouldn't hit anything for probably twenty kilometres – it just led deeper and deeper into Algonquin. This was not an option.

    I ran the route from the kayak to the cliff nest twice and then sat up there, thinking. It was getting on 16:00 hours. I blasted off a few shots of the lake and I wondered what Donny was doing. I wondered what Janet was doing. I could see the sky clearing. A good sign, even if it meant colder weather. If they came for me, it would definitely be in the next few days. I needed to eat, then work with the crossbows.

★ ★ ★

Tesla came back to find Tony and Olig drinking. "Okay guys, we're moving to the next lake. Olig take the canoe. Tony grab as much gear as you can and I'll take the rest. Let's go, now!" He would make them pay for that little breach in etiquette, the rotten little pricks.

Olig whined, "Ah, come on Jerry, let's just camp here. It's nice."

"Can't do that, look, it's only a couple hundred yards," he lied. Once they got going, they wouldn't turn back and he wanted his pound of flesh.

Tesla helped Olig get the canoe onto his shoulders, then put most of the other gear around Tony's neck and arms and led them into the forest. The bitching started almost immediately and Tesla grinned all the way.

It took Jerry about fifteen minutes to reach the next lake. He dumped what little he carried, went back to help Tony and got him through to Kettle Lake. Olig was still cursing, fighting with the terrain and getting snagged up, but he eventually made it.

"You fucking liar! That was no couple hundred yards, asshole! Christ I can't feel my arm!" Olig was pissed.

Tony didn't really care, he was tough and they were at the other lake now and it was beautiful. He just looked out in wonder, probably realizing for the first time this was why people come up here.

"We camp here tonight and in the morning, we'll find our target and do her." Tesla stated.

"How do you know this is the lake? What if there is another and another?" Olig bitched.

"There won't be." Tesla barked. "You can't go past this lake, not unless you want to carry all your shit twenty miles!" He gave orders for firewood detail and food detail, neither of which he would be partaking in. Olig and Tony flipped on who got what.

Tesla found a flat area to put up the tent and dumped the sleeping bags inside. He bounced an idea off his two partners in crime, "If we left the tent and gear here tomorrow, got an early start and found this bitch, maybe we could just leave it and book back to the city real quick. It would be less to pack up in the morning and less to carry back. Besides, I can't see us ever using this shit again."

His two underlings liked the thinking, especially since it meant less work for them.

After Olig brought back the first load of wood, Tony tried to get the fire going. Everything was soaked. He rummaged around the bags, found some fire-starter blocks, read the directions, and in minutes had a flame going. He broke out the cooking gear and pulled steaks from the cooler. Grabbed the plastic grocery bags and proudly yanked out two cans of baked beans. The menu for tonight's dining pleasure was set.

Tesla decided to scout the area. As he was walking away, he heard a branch crack and then Olig screamed out. He grinned. Finding a perch, he sat and watched, looking at nothing, seeing everything. Jerry took a few pulls on his own whiskey bottle, savouring the burn.

★ ★ ★

The 'Mexican Surprise' was indeed a pleasant one. Yummy! I wolfed down another. All that exercise had made me famished.

Once the dishes were done I had my tea and sat by the fire, toying with the crossbows. I had ten small arrows with field points for the mini SX-80, and ten twenty-two inch arrows for the big Vortex bow.

The larger arrows had three-sided serrated tips about five centimetres long that would dig deep into a target and cause serious damage. The field points were just that – points. They could go in pretty deep but it was just a stab wound. I couldn't run around carrying both so I thought about stashing the mini-bow up on the rock cliff. Act as a fall-back position, perfect.

Should I make some weapons? "What are you Rambo? Geezez Lizzy!" *Talking to myself again... maybe a spear?* Yeah right. *They will have guns, dummy.* My stress level went up. Would the Mutt send the two goons from the motel? More? Would it be a lone person, come up on me all friendly, then bam!? How would I know? I set my mind right.

Brushing my teeth, I wondered all sorts of things. They would come. Trust no one. I popped some codeine and went into the tent – time for rest. I had to think what day it was, Sunday, no Saturday. Friday? Funny how quickly you lost track of time up here. I was passed out in mere minutes.

★ ★ ★

It was a nippy morning to be sure and I got a fire going lickety-split. I needed tea and oatmeal to start my day, something that is hot and stick-to-your-ribs tasty. I threw the chippy some of a granola bar and he happily munched away a few feet from me. Nice to have company for breakfast; we ate together. The red squirrel was not so inclined, keeping his distance but obviously interested in what could be available to nosh on. I'd have to work on him, tease him in closer, gain the trust. I plunked a few seeds down in key spots, he'd find them eventually. I gave my chippy a mound of sunflower seeds, which he happily vacuumed up into his pouches before he took off. I never get tired of watching these critters; tail straight up, cheeks full, scampering back to their hide hole.

The water had a bit of a chop and small caps tipped the edges of the waves. No one in sight, yet. Most people, if they were fishing, would stick to coves and shallows today.

I hadn't really taken the quality pictures I had hoped for. What a trip. Later today I'd get out on land and do some shooting. I stayed by the fire drinking tea and feeding my new friend. No hurry to get anywhere. I might as well stay warm and watch the morning unfold right from here. I threw a granola piece at my red squirrel. He'd find it soon and then inch closer. It was a game I've played many a time.

★ ★ ★

The stooges had made a non-fatal but hazardous error last night and paid for it. Instead of being careful about food spillage and where they dumped leftover waste, Olig and Tony just tossed it a short ways away without a second thought.

All night and into the early morning hours, it was a non-stop barrage of wildlife being drawn to their camp, fighting over scraps and bone from the steaks. No one slept a wink. The obnoxious gas inside the tent was just about as bad, as someone's digestive system was not coping well.

Tesla was pissed and ordered them about as soon as they crawled out of the tent. Do this, do that, right now!

Tony and Olig kept looking at their guns, and each other, but Gregor would hit the roof and you didn't want to get the Mutt angry. They got a fire sparked, boiled water and then scrambled eggs, threw in cheese slices, more beans on the side, bread plain and coffee instant; to soak it up and wash it down.

It was a late start, but by nine in the morning, Tesla had the canoe moving out onto Kettle Lake. The tent and other camp gear just left, casually strewn about, abandoned. None of them gave a rat's ass about it.

Olig, still relegated to middleman, was paddling like a weak old lady. He was severely hung over and sleep deprived. Tony, in front, did better but looked worse.

Tesla shook his head. They just kept drinking last night, couple of fools. The air was fresh and clean and he breathed deep. Being the captain, and probably wanting them to suffer a tad, he allowed the ladies up front to propel the canoe, opting to only steer.

★ ★ ★

Nothing on the text or voice mail from Liz – Donny didn't like that. Not knowing is worse than knowing in his book, always had been.

He marched boldly toward the interview room, entered swiftly and sat facing his opponent. Now down to the business at hand. "Detective Buckles, you ready to speak to me now and tell me what I want to know?"

Buckles nodded. His lawyer, Bernie Madden, sat with him and spoke, "Just so you know and its clear from the start, my client was not involved in any activity with organized crime. All he will admit to is that he provided some occasional information to someone who called him."

"What the fuck is that supposed to mean? Look, I have this piece of shit cold, providing Gregor Mutznig with countless tips on raids, busts, confidential personnel info. The works! Don't fuck with me. You better smarten up Buckles, 'cause if you don't, I will nail you with conspiracy to commit murder, accessory to murder and a whack of other stuff. Do you hear me? You will go to prison for life!"

Buckles, already sweating, gave it up. "Look, I didn't know who called. I was told someone would phone, ask a question or request some info, and that was it."

Donny was stunned, "Why would you do that?"

His attorney started to say something but Buckles cut him off. "I owed money. Not a few thousand, but over three hundred Gs for gambling, and I had a way out. My bookie said he'd take a bit off the top each time; all I had to do was sit and wait for a specific call, get what info they asked for and that's it."

Donny asked, "Why didn't you get some help? Christ, the department would have people to get you counselling, get you back on track."

Madden spoke up. "That's the point, it was an addiction! My client can't be held responsible for an addiction. It's a sickness, right?"

"No way in hell! He doesn't walk because you say it's an addiction. That won't fly here and do not test my patience with that shit.

If you want any leniency at all, I need to know exactly what things you divulged."

Buckles held his hands up and rolled his eyes, "I can't remember all the stuff I gave out. It was going on for years and… "

Maddan cut him off. "No more!" He turned to Donny. "You give us some assurances that he gets consideration, both on time served and place to be served, or no deal today."

Donny thought for a bit. He'd be damned if this prick was gonna skate on his watch. "Alright, Detective Buckles, answer me this, since your memory seems to be fuzzy. What info did you give this mystery caller, say on last Tuesday or Wednesday?"

Eyes looking up towards the ceiling, Buckles searched his brain. It was just before he'd gotten picked up on a warrant. "It was a credit card track, licence plate from a rental car…I think that's it." He conveniently left out the First Degree murder warrants on Olig Steig and Tony Molinara.

"What was the name for the credit card?"

As soon as Donny heard the name, he told Madden to go fuck himself and said that Buckles would rot in prison.

He bolted out of the interview room, got to his office, and grabbed some of his team members. They tried to figure out who to call and how to get someone up into Algonquin Park immediately.

★ ★ ★

Tesla came to Joe Island in the middle of Kettle Lake and he pondered which side to take. "A bunch of wrongs don't make a right," he said to no one, so he opted for left. As he and his crew headed upstream to the northwest side of the island, the park ranger, Adam Milner was coming across the mess they left at the portage access point about an hour ago.

★ ★ ★

The day had warmed up considerably and I decided to let the fire die down. The wind had eased and you could see the water had calmed. I thought about going for a paddle but stuck with my earlier decision on taking some pictures on land, since I had not captured much of anything out on the kayak.

First though, stash one mini-bow up on the cliff, just in case. I trotted back to the bog and up the slope to the east. I hung the pistol in the tree and stashed the arrows in a quiver under some brush. Had a quick scout on top of my ridge – seemed all clear on the lake and I snapped a few photos. Done. Once back at camp, I made sure the kayak was loaded with my other gear for a speedy getaway. Had a quick look down the lake to see if it was still clear, attached the 100-400mm to my camera and off I went, toddling towards the dense forest.

I started walking, quiet-like and taking my time. I tracked southwest on an angle, going into deeper bush as I moved. There are a couple of rules I follow for good photography. Firstly, if you don't have the camera with you, you can't take the shot. *A no-brainer, right Sherlock?* Secondly, humans are one of the few mammals with no real predators and they often just trudge along, making way too much noise. Animals, on the other hand, have many jaw-snapping forest creatures just waiting to gobble them up. They move in short bursts, stopping, listening, and looking about before moving again. That is the next rule, patience and short movements, picking spots, picking hides and spending lots of time just waiting. Your eyes and ears will tell you everything.

It wasn't raining but I had my camo rain poncho on anyway. Cuts the cold and allows me to blend in, along with keeping the camera toasty and dry underneath. I eventually found a nice hide, surrounded by a good mix of deciduous trees and I waited.

★ ★ ★

Adam Milner was pissed. He had noticed two cars parked at the permit holders' area when he drove by. Neither had passes on the vehicles and neither were on the computer, meaning illegal. Milner mumbled to himself, "No good, cheap ass, city boys thinking they can come up here, doing whatever they please. Well I don't think so, mister!" He had scouted the Dawson Lake area; they were all fine. It had to be Kettle Lake.

Now, finding all this gear just left in a heap, not even on a pre-scribed site. "Assholes!" The fire was still warm; he wasn't too far behind. He'd be able to nail them on about five violations and have them banned from the park. He took pictures with his point and shoot digital camera, for evidence.

Milner couldn't see anyone out on the lake. This would be his first major bust of illegal campers, plus getting to issue a whack of tickets. He pushed off in his kayak with force and a smile on his face. He was fired up.

★ ★ ★

Tesla cruised by a group of campers located near the first part of the lake finger that ran northeast off the main body. "Tony, Olig, you guys stay quiet, let me talk."

He could tell it was three guys and steered a bit closer, "Hello!"

The fellas looked his way and waved. "How are you? Grey day, eh!"

Tesla responded, "Sure is. Listen, we're trying to find a friend who came up earlier, we had an accident and got delayed. Have you seen anybody else on the lake?"

"Well, I think there is another person down a ways from us and the park ranger comes out every few days. That's it."

"The park ranger, driving around here?"

"No, no, he's in a kayak. They make passes through the lake every so often, to check on campers."

"Oh, yeah right. Okay then, thanks. Have a good one."

Tesla waved. "Tony wave for God's sake."

Both Tony and Olig gave it their best Miss America gesture and smiled.

Tesla pointed the canoe to head farther along the north finger of the lake to check the next camper. "More people than I anticipated and now the park ranger could be around. We'll have to do this quiet, no guns if the next person is our target."

★ ★ ★

I captured a pileated woodpecker, rare at the best of times and felt quite pleased with myself. He was damn near sixty centimetres tall. I had the ISO bumped to 800 since it was dull out but even that wasn't giving me a fast enough shutter speed. I dared not go past that as the photo would end up grainy looking. I had to time my shot between breaks of the woodpecker hacking the tree bark with his massive beak. I could hear a few animals of substantial weight moving through the woods, in the distance, to the south of me. Must be large I thought, for the noise they were making; probably moose, maybe a bear. I waited to see if anything would pop out near me while I watched red squirrels scamper about, chasing one another over territory. I moved more west and then north towards Kettle Lake, figuring I'd follow the shore back east. Maybe see if I could nab a heron or other waterfowl at the water's edge, or some landscape shots at the very least.

Nearing the lake, I realized I was farther west than my estimate, well past my 'lookout' location, so I started moving back east towards my camp. I checked behind me frequently as I went along, no sense taking chances.

There was a faint outline on the water, coming east from the portage site. I moved back into the tree line and waited, keeping an eye on with my big lens for the person to come into range, so I'd know if it was friend or foe. I kept moving east.

In less than ten minutes I knew it was Adam, the park ranger. I stepped out into the clear and waved. He headed for me at some pace, perhaps something had happened or he needed help. I felt tense, again.

* * *

The canoe edged right up to the site, Tesla wanted to be close and move fast if this was the bitch after all – didn't want to go chasing through the woods neither. "Tony, you get ready to run after her as soon as we know for sure." The men sat in the canoe, waiting for a camper to show. They knew someone was there; the canoe was flipped on land and the tent was up, fire going strong.

The bushes stirred and an elderly gent walked out after doing his business. He was startled by the three thugs in a tug; all staring directly at him.

"Howdy fellas, everything okay?"

"Hey, how are ya? We got lost from a friend. Seen any other people on the lake the last few days?" Tesla had a cordial smile working.

"Well, there are a few lads back down a piece. The ranger was by a few days ago, that's about it. Oh, hey!" the old guy remembered. "I did see a kayak about two days ago. I think that person went east, up the other side of the lake."

"Great, thanks, have a good one." Tesla knew right away that was it. He was excited and drove the canoe in reverse with a surging backstroke that threw Tony and Olig off balance and almost tipped them. "Boys, move like the wind, we got her!"

"How can you be sure? Could be anybody up here," Tony questioned.

"No way, that's our girl. I'm sure, has to be. Paddle!" and Tesla rammed the canoe forward, completing the turn about.

Tony and Olig were sweating – Tesla drove them like cattle. They made the turn in ten minutes, now headed east on the main part of the lake and saw a boater way south in the distance, on the very far side. "That's the bitch, now we got her!" Tesla carved the canoe more south and was pouring it on, out-powering both Tony and Olig with his boil stroke and having to compensate for pushing them off line.

★ ★ ★

Adam came close to shore and yelled, "Have you seen anyone in the last while, probably a couple of men?"

"Nope, haven't, not a soul all day. Why?"

"Couple of illegal campers came in, no permits, leaving a mess all over. Their cars are parked near you and they camped at the portage access last night, not even on a campsite. They just left all their gear sitting there."

I felt the blood drain from my body, nausea and shakes set in immediately. They'd found me! This was it, no doubt in my mind. No doubt in my heart and gut. When all three agree like that you better believe. No other possible explanation. *Always trust your instincts, Liz!*

"Adam, you need to know something."

He steered closer, right up to the shore line. "What?"

"There are some really bad dudes after me and you need to take off right now and call the police to come up here."

"What have you been smoking?"

"I'm deadly serious! Leave right now and make the call or you could be killed!"

Adam just fobbed me off, laughing, apparently thinking I'd gone bonkers. "Look, I don't know what is going on here but some illegal shitheads are going to get their asses thrown out of here and eat some tickets on the way."

I saw a speck on the lake headed toward us, at the far north end. I couldn't tell how many in the canoe; at least two, maybe three. As I looked through the camera lens, I could tell … definitely coming right at us. With speed too! "Adam, these guys will kill you! They are coming up on us right now, look behind you!"

Adam turned and said, "Got you now fuckers!" He started to swing his kayak toward them.

"Don't! It's not safe! Adam you can outrun them, head away, now! Please!"

Adam just lined up his kayak to the north and stated to paddle hard.

"Adam you have to listen to me! They came from Toronto! They work as muscle for a criminal. They kill people!"

He didn't listen. I took to cover in the tree line again. I felt even worse; sicker, my legs were wobbly and I was sweating, bad. What could I do? If it was the goons from the motel, then Adam would be killed, no doubt in my mind. What's one more dead body to these murderous pukes? I looked through my lens, following Adam, the two boats on a collision course. The canoe looked like it was in a Dragon Boat race, the way it heaved with each paddle-stroke and sped through the water.

The canoe was slowing now. Adam was headed right for them. I had a really bad feeling as they neared. I could see them close the gap. A few minutes later, both canoe and kayak hovered beside each other. They seemed to be discussing something. I watched through my camera lens, snapping pictures without even thinking about it.

★ ★ ★

"Where you fellas headed?" Adam said all friendly and matter-of-fact like.

"Just in for a few days of camping," Tesla said.

"Can I see your permits please?" Adam already knew these were the guys. He'd been at the station this morning and no permits had come in.

Olig had his right hand inside his coat jacket pocket as he searched for the revolver and then gripped it tight.

Tesla was caught out. "Oh, you know what? I think I forgot them in the car."

"Where did you park?" Adam asked.

Tony piped in, "We're just at the far end of the lake."

Tesla just shook his head. There was no parking near this lake.

Adam had them cold. "Alright guys, you're bullshitting me. You are going to follow me back out of the park and pick up all the camp gear you left back there too. When we get to your cars, I'll want some ID and I think a fine is also warranted here."

Olig pulled the pistol out of his coat pocket and shot Adam point blank in the chest. The kayak flipped as the ranger slumped from the fatal bullet.

I saw it! I heard the shot a split second later. I blasted off a half dozen photos. *I should run, now!* I couldn't, I had to watch. I could see them pulling the kayak close and reaching under the water.

The guy in back was really animated. He was pointing to the shore. I just watched in disbelief, clicking more photos all the while.

"Olig grab him and hang on! Tony start paddling to the cove ahead. We'll dump him in there."

Tony flailed, hitting the ranger and his kayak a few times with his own paddle. Tesla was powering the canoe straight south, towards land.

They hauled Adam and his kayak south towards a cove about five hundred metres away. I watched as they moved towards the shore. They were out of my sight line in less than five minutes.

I ran, terrified. This was crazy insane. My knees kept buckling; the adrenaline had me giddy. I focused on each ten-metre spot in front of me, not wanting to falter, and I hit my campsite within ten minutes. Camera bouncing around my neck, I vaulted into the kayak, and took off. As I moved towards the reeds and my escape exit, I kept checking over my shoulder to see if they were coming … nothing. I counted off the lengths and when I hit twenty, I cut hard into the long grass and was out of sight.

In seconds, I rammed into the sand, pivoted sideways and sprung out, leaving the kayak. I scaled the crevice and up the wall of stone, scraping the sides with my camera. I scampered up the incline to my hide, up top of the rock cliff. Soaking wet with sweat, shaking, waiting … then it hit me – the big crossbow. I went all the way back down, grabbed the big Vortex bow along with the ten arrows, and scrambled right back up to my nest. I was spent. I couldn't calm down and gasped for air. The moisture poured off my face. I closed my eyes, breathing deep, trying to slow my panic.

When they hit the shallows, Olig let go of the ranger. The kayak skimmed along the water a bit until it grounded out, curling slightly and stopping. The left side of the kayak, and that of the upper body of the ranger, was half submerged in the water. Bobbing slightly, the ranger's face had a look of horror on it. One eye staring at the other men with a shocked-looking appearance.

Tony was visibly shaken up and couldn't believe what had just happened. "Christ Olig, that was stupid!"

Olig pleaded his case. "I had no choice! Right Jerry? I had to do it!"

Tesla agreed. "It's okay Olig. If you didn't do it I would have. Now, let's get moving. What's done is done and we still have one more to go."

Olig felt redeemed and they back paddled, spun the canoe, and headed back in their original direction with renewed vigour and resolve.

★ ★ ★

Donny was livid. "What the fuck are those assholes doing up there? Why can't they just get a helicopter and fly into the bush!?"

Mary Liscar, a detective he'd handpicked for the team, was on the phone with Ontario Park Services. "Donny, they don't have the resources, it's just occasional rangers that canoe in to the remote areas every few days, checking on permit holders."

"Well do they have anyone in there now?"

"They're checking with the Algonquin office now," she said.

"Screw it!" Donny called the chief. He'd get his help one way or another. As he waited on hold, his face showed the strain.

"Chief Anderson speaking."

Donny introduced himself again and the chief remembered, since he was the one who'd ultimately chosen Donny for the job. Donny explained the situation. He had reason to believe that at least two men were about to kill a witness any time now, up at Algonquin Park. Donny was hopeful. "What could you help us with?"

"I'll get an OPP chopper in there, could take an hour or so. Give me the best-guess location."

He gave the chief all he had; the possible start point where the car might be, and by looking at the map they had pulled up, four possible lakes.

"Mighty big place up there, Detective, may take some time to find a specific person," the chief pointed out.

"Yeah," Donny agreed.

"Hang in there, Jacobs. Call me if any other info comes in."

Donny was about to hang up when Mary yelled, "I got the site location!"

"Chief, chief, hold on! We got a location!"

Mary wrote it down and passed it to Donny. "Chief, tell them it's Kettle Lake and the site is number seven," he grabbed the map and searched frantically, "Which is to the farthest eastern part of the lake. Got it?"

Donny slumped in his chair, totally drained.

I thought they must be burying him or something. It seemed like a long time had passed. I looked through my camera to see. The canoe appeared, almost on cue and was coming hard again, straight at me. I figured I had ten minutes at best.

The phone! Maybe it'd work higher up. Why hadn't I tried that before? "Damn it!" I scrounged inside my coat, found it and held it up. Batteries dead! The cold had zapped the power. I should have turned it off to conserve the juice. "Dummy!"

I looked through the camera lens again. They had slowed and were looking around. I didn't recognize the guy at the stern but was confident about the other two. Donny and I had stared at those photos of them at the motel for a long time. Definitely the assholes from there … definitely killers!

I tried to steel myself. It was kill or be killed; no other option. I didn't think I could do it. I felt like I was going to die up here. I puked up my breakfast. The blob of oatmeal dripped off my pants and plunked to the ground. My heart pounded. My head pounded.

Tesla sported a look of victory – this was the spot. "Slow it down boys, relax, we're just some men out for a camping trip, remember. If we see her, just approach all friendly-like until I make the first move, understand?"

Tesla saw the tent and made for the shore. With the experience they had now, all three drove the canoe hard for the last few metres and rode the sand up onto shore. They all got out quickly and started walking around, checking the tent first, walking south a bit, then west.

Tesla touched the grate in the fire pit. "It's still warm. She is somewhere around, close by."

All three stood in a wide circle around the campsite, heads swivelling in all directions, waiting for Tesla to give a command.

"Okay, I don't see a kayak, so probably out on the water. Olig, you stay here and wait in the back, out of sight. If she shows, just kill her – we'll hear the shot and come back. Tony, you come with me, we'll cruise around the islands and smoke her out that way."

As Olig strolled farther back into the trees, Tony and Tesla made for the water.

Watching from my perch, I could easily see guns in their hands as they searched the grounds. One of the motel thugs headed south, deep, past the back of my site. The other two got back into the canoe and headed for the islands. I lay on my back and thought about my situation. I was being hunted, three against one; not good odds in anyone's book.

I rested my eyes. They felt blurry from staring through the camera lens for so long. My ears were picking up every sound, every little noise, I was super-sensitive to the environment around me.

I looked at my crossbow; the big Vortex 'Vengeance.' *How apropos*, I thought. I had to do it. There was no choice in the matter. I waited until the canoe had passed through some small outcrops on the lake and gathered up the bow. I cocked and locked, putting in a serrated twenty-two inch arrow, and loaded five more in a quiver looped to my belt. I left the other arrows and gear. It wouldn't matter, especially if I didn't make it back.

I had to psych myself up. I drove my fist into the tree bark; the sting a shock to my system. "Just do it!"

Moving down the south side of the cliff quietly but swiftly, I headed for the back of my campsite. I would take at least one prick out of the equation. I thought of how they'd taken Adam, shot him, and then dumped him like garbage. The rage in me started to build. I'd even that score, for sure.

Olig was cold and still a little wet from fucking around in the water with the ranger. He pulled out his bottle of booze and took a nip. Then he took another, shivering from the chill and the harsh liquid. He stuffed the gun in his jacket pocket and tried to keep his hands warm. Sitting on a log, he kept drinking.

Olig looked around. He stood up – nothing in sight; no Tony and Jerry on the water. He had a pee, almost falling over, the booze going straight to his head. He giggled and plopped down on the log again.

I moved like I was tracking an animal for a photo, quiet, smooth, stopping every few steps and assessing. I would have one shot and had to make it count. I was at the bog in minutes, moved to the western side of it, and cut north towards my campsite, using the trees and bushes as cover. I picked my hides ahead of me, every few metres or so, moving closer – patience and stealth. The camo poncho gave me a good edge. If I squatted down, I'd almost be invisible. Slow and easy, no mistakes could be made. My breathing had reduced to calm, equal respirations, heart rate back to normal.

I scanned the area, slowly, looking for the one thing out of place, any slight movement. There! I watched. I could see part of him now, sitting on something. What was he doing? ... Drinking? Drinking alcohol? Facing slightly away from my approach, about twenty-five to thirty metres away now, the goon had no idea I was at his door step. I moved a tad more west, getting in behind him, and continued to inch closer. Two or three more hides and I'd be on him.

It was almost painful, the care and control of each foot placement, careful not to snap a twig or stumble on loose ground. Closer, now directly behind him, his back to me, fifteen metres away, right in my wheelhouse. I wouldn't miss. I scoped his back, the laser dead centre. *This is for Adam, you rotten prick!* My heart began to race and sweat poured off my brow.

I couldn't pull the release. Shooting someone in the back seemed to be unfair – wrong. Could I take him prisoner? Tie him up? Then what? I knew the longer I waited, the worse it could get. The others could come back at any time, then I'd be screwed.

"Hey asshole, hands up!"

He turned as he got to his feet and looked, his eyes locked on mine. He smiled, saying, "Oh, hi! Can you help me? I'm lost from my friends."

"Bullshit! I know who you are! You killed those people in the motel. You just killed the ranger. I saw it!"

He threw the bottle of booze at me, missing by a mile, stumbled, and was reaching in his coat pocket.

"Don't do it!" I knew the gun was about to come out. Scoping his chest, centre-mass, I fired my crossbow. The slender bolt sizzled through the still air, over three hundred feet per second, straight and true. 'Thwack!' The arrow dug into his right chest area. He let out the wild groan of an animal wounded and dropped to his knees. He was stunned, giving me precious seconds to reload. I had another cocked and locked, scoped him, and drove the arrow deep into his gut. 'Oomph!' The sound was audible as the bolt hit his soft fleshy area. He slumped onto his right side, unable to raise his right arm. The gun discharged, bullet hitting a log with a dead thud. I moved right up on him now and slammed another arrow point blank into his exposed neck. Blood spurted wildly and I knew I'd hit the artery. Kill shot! His eyes rolled back, body pulsating with red wetness.

I kicked the gun out of his right hand and watched him gasp for air and start to spasm. He tried to speak as blood gurgled from his foamy scarlet mouth, but no words came. I looked straight into his eyes, watching the life literally drain from his body. Nothing in heaven or earth could save this man now. "That's for Adam, you sick bastard!" He was gone in seconds.

I grabbed the pistol and pocketed the weapon. Pulled, twisted, and finally yanked one arrow out of his neck. The other two were in so deep you'd have to cut them out. No time, his buddies would have heard the shot and be on their way. I checked his pockets, found a bag of bullets, and stuffed them into my coat. No ID, nothing else.

I fled south, back to the bog, cut east, and hustled towards the rise and my perch. My legs wobbled; too much adrenaline pumping through me. I felt giddy again, faint and sick.

"Did you hear that!" he said excitedly. Tony's ears had caught the reverberation of the gunshot around the lake.

"Quiet!" Tesla said and they froze like statues in the canoe, listening, nothing more, no other sounds came.

Tony was energized, "Olig got the bitch! Let's go!"

They started back at a furious pace.

I collapsed against a tree in my nest, soaked with sweat and breathing hard. I was shaking uncontrollably. *Now what?* I had just rung the dinner bell. The other two Pavlovian dogs would be salivating and hungry, even more so once they saw their friend!

I rolled over and grabbed the camera, crawled closer to the edge of the cliff, and scanned the area. They came into view from the top of the lake, coming up on the reeds where my kayak was hidden. No way could they spot my gear in there, they'd fly right by.

I was screwed now, it would only take them a few minutes to find their guy and seeing as he was dead, they would know I was on land. Maybe twenty or thirty minutes, then they would find the path and be on me like bloodhounds. I wouldn't be able to out run them in the kayak. I have to run into the bush and hope for the best.

"Think!" I reassessed my position. I had high ground over these pricks, impossible for them to get close to me without exposing themselves. I had a gun now too! I loaded another two rounds into the pistol; full chamber, ten bullets left in the bag. I cocked and locked arrows into the big bow and the mini, safeties on. I could cut the odds down by at least one more by staying right here. Then, at least it would be a fair fight. *I have a plan!*

Tony sprung out of the canoe as soon as they hit the shore, calling out, "Olig! Where are you, Oli!" He moved towards the tent and started looking about. No answer, nothing.

Tesla pulled the canoe up onto land, keeping a watchful eye on Tony's actions. He had his Glock pulled and ready. This wasn't right. Olig should be out from the back of the site.

They called several more times – nothing. No one answered.

"Find him!" Tesla directed. Tony went to one side and he took the other. They moved past the tent and back into the trees.

"Here! Over here!" Tony yelled at Tesla.

I watched as the goons started to search for their buddy. What did Donny say their names were? I heard the one shout, "Olig." *Okay,* I thought, *nailed the one named Olig.* Now who was the other? Timmy, Terry? Something with a T, that much I recalled. They came upon their friend – I watched through the camera lens.

"Jesus Christ! Look at Oli – he's all shot with arrows! What the fuck, man? Look at this, his neck is all chewed up! Is this bitch a fucking vampire!?" Tony broke down over Olig's body, shaking uncontrollably.

Tesla looked dispassionately at the dead carcass and the scene around him. "This is no ordinary bitch we're dealing with here." He bent down and checked for Olig's gun. It was gone, as were the bullets, "Fuck! She got his gun."

I could only hear sounds when they spoke, not the words really. I could see the one motel goon was troubled about the state of his fellow gangster. The other guy though, he was calm, detached, like it was no big deal. That sent a shiver through me, right down to my toes. I watched their movements through the camera lens, waiting for them to decide what action was next.

Tesla scanned the area. "This bitch was on land." He looked around at the lake. "We would have seen her leave if she had the boat. I think she snuck up on Olig, caught him with his pants down – total ambush!" Tesla looked around some more.

I could see them. The calm dude was thinking it through. He looked straight up to my perch and stared. "Son of a bitch!" He had me cold.

"Tony! Get up and listen. Look, the rise up there, the rocks. See them?"

Tony found the area and said, "Yeah, so?"

"She is up there watching us. When we left Olig here and went in the canoe, that's the only way someone could see. She came down behind him, shot him and killed him."

"Look Jerry, maybe we should leave. Look at Olig man, let's just head out and forget it."

Tesla wouldn't let this go now. "No way! You and me, we're going to kill this Stevens bitch today, right now!"

I could see the two men talking and the leader guy pointed right at me. This was it. They would make their push right now, straight up here. I knew it in my bones. I got ready; all my arrows laid out, the gun in my pocket with the extra bullets, both bows, one at either side of me.

Tesla told Tony to go around to the south and find the path that led up to the rise. "Start to move in and squeeze her from that area. I'm going by canoe to the other side. I'll come at her, we'll flank the position, and push her hard, she'll have to move and that will be it. Go, now!"

I could see the one goon head south from the campsite. He'd try and come up – I could handle that. But the other one, the guy calling the shots, he got into the canoe. "Okay asshole, what are you doing?" He moved out onto the lake, swung northeast and headed for the other side of me. "Shit!" The prick was smart. They would come at me from two sides.

I rolled onto my back and shut my eyes, trying to calm myself. Use arrows at a distance, I thought, save the gun for in close. I squirmed on my belly and spied over the cliff ledge, I could see the canoe was well past the reeds. It might take him a while to find a landing area, or he might just get into the water and heave himself out at any given point. Once on land, he could make it up here easy.

I looked at my cover in each direction. It was a good nest; several big trees, a bit of a dugout behind some large rock outcrops. I could bounce between each side and scan for attack. Fend them off, keep them pinned, but for how long? Until I was dead ... or they were. I could see only two possible outcomes.

★ ★ ★

Donny picked up the phone almost before it rang, "Detective Jacobs."

It was the Ontario Provincial Police. "Detective Jacobs, this is Staff Sergeant Bill Collins. We have a bird in the air now, armed and heading to Algonquin to the reference points you gave."

"Great! Good going. How long before your guys can find the area?"

"Maybe get to the lake in a half hour to forty-five minutes flying time from our helipad here."

"Okay, thanks so much! Could you keep me posted when they locate the area and see how my witness is?"

"Sure thing, Detective, as soon as I know, you will."

"Appreciate all your help on this one. Thanks again. Bye."

★ ★ ★

Tony easily found the cut-through at the bog. He could see the boot imprints in some muddy sections and followed the clues. Five minutes later, he was eyeing the climb up, his Sig 9 ready, picking a route of ascent.

He couldn't see any movement up ahead. His hard stare and the building fury inside were visible. He paused and watched, then made the first advance, quick and catlike, keeping cover as best he could. Nothing happened, no arrows came raining down. Tony relaxed a bit and started to move up the incline faster, gaining confidence.

I watched his progress. The goon was stupid, didn't plan his next steps – just a bull in a china shop. He was a good forty metres away still. I wasn't about to give up my location until I had a sure shot. I swivelled to look at the other approach, nothing yet; no movement but this guy was cagier, calmer, more sophisticated.

I went back to eyeing the goon, closer now, getting a bit cocky, standing half upright, no real use of cover. I brought my Vortex bow up slightly and scoped him, dead in my sights. "Just be patient," I told myself. A bit closer and I'd own him.

Tony was getting fatigued. Sweat poured off his face and his movements were getting awkward and heavy. The protruding ledge up ahead gave him perfect cover and the option to go in two directions from that point. "Fuck it!" He made a dash, did a half-assed zig and zag, slipped, and stood hunched and motionless for a split second.

With the laser on centre mass, I fired, just as he moved slightly upright. The arrow hit on his right leg below the groin. "Damn it!" Did I compensate for down angle, too much? Too little? I reefed with all my might, cocking the bow, then locked another arrow as the goon continued to scream out. I brought the Vortex back up quickly and scoped his last position, but he had rolled off to the right, behind some rocks and logs. The top of his head bobbed about.

"You cock sucker! I'm going to kill you!" Several shots rang out and bullets whizzed by, well away from me.

Not today shit head, I mused. What was that word in German that means taking pleasure in another's suffering…schadenfreude? Something like that. A smile crossed my face. I rolled back to spy the other approach and took more time to see if anything moved. I split my ammo; three serrated arrows in my quiver, had one in the Vortex 'Vengeance' bow, and dug the points of the last three into the ground. I would save those for my reserve. I'd start using the mini now, as an annoyance more than anything. Keep the prick guessing.

Tesla couldn't find an area to get out of the canoe. It was a sheer, eight-foot rock face and he couldn't grab anything to haul himself out and onto land. He backtracked and went into the reeds, pushing through, getting frustrated, and cursing. There had to be an access point. He kept trying.

Screaming obscenities under his breath, Tesla couldn't find a way in. He heard Tony yell, followed by gunshots, rapid fire. He pushed the canoe in as far as it could go. "Son of a bitch!" He didn't want to get into the water and climb up the stone face, the water depth was past his paddle's length. It wouldn't work. "Screw it!" He backed right out of the reeds and paddled back to the campsite at a frenzied pace. He'd have to attack the same way Tony went; no other option.

I couldn't see any movement. I heard a swishing sound and peeked over the cliff. The other guy was racing for shore. When he hit my campsite, he would come up the same way as his buddy here.

Excellent, I thought, now only one front door for me to watch! My spirits buoyed. I began to feel like I might just make it.

Tony was writhing in pain. The serrated arrow was dug into the soft meat of his inside right thigh, God-awful deep, and he couldn't pull it out without ripping the shit out of his leg. He bled for ten minutes before it eased off. He could go back down, or wait for Jerry. Two choices.

He heard a noise behind him and aimed his Sig pistol, then saw Tesla appear below, climbing up after him.

"Tony, you okay?"

"Uh, no Jerry, I'm not really. Look at this fucking arrow sticking in my leg!"

Tesla had a look. It was bad but not fatal – not much blood now. "Missed the artery – that was good. You're lucky."

"How do ya figure, Jerry? Look at this thing! What kind of fucking arrow is that and why has that bitch got them?"

"Remember what she did to Olig?"

"Yeah, but still, look at this. Can you cut the thing off so I can at least move?"

Tesla looked at it – carbon fibre. "Probably not right now, no. You'll have to suck it up until we finish her, then I'll get it fixed."

Tony laid back and rested, his face showing sheer exasperation and the disbelief of the shit they were in.

Tesla, stone-faced, was looking about, silently.

The slapping sound was faint at first, then hard and echoing through the lake expanse. I peered over the cliff and saw the helicopter swooping in from the northwest. It was an older, bubble-type bird; open at the sides, with two greyish pontoons sagging below its belly. "Police" clearly marked on the sides.

The loudspeaker boomed. "This is the police! Show yourselves now!"

I snaked around to the far side and tried to wave them in to my location from the ridge. The cops saw me and I pointed to the other side, holding up two fingers and pointing again. The helicopter looped right and swung around overhead, edging nearer to the slope the goon and other guy were on.

Shots zipped by and I dove back into my nest. "Fuck me!" Then I heard some shots being fired, probably by the two idiots shooting at the helicopter. I slipped back to the cliff edge and used my scope to watch.

"This is the police! Put your weapons down! Stand away with your hands up!"

Tesla was having no part of it. He pounded a few more shots at the helicopter to get them off his back and the noisy bird swooped back over the lake. Tesla pointed his gun at Tony. "Give me your pistol and extra clips, now!"

"Jerry, what are you doing man? Just give up!"

"Give me your gun or I'll shoot you in the face, asshole. Now!"

With the only option open to him, Tony complied. Tesla scampered down the slope and back into the bog area, leaving Tony alone and unarmed.

I watched as the lead guy took off. The helicopter was landing on the water, pontoons flopping with the updraft of the rotors. I yelled out, "Hey asshole, how does it feel?" No response. "I'm gonna stick another arrow in your ass – better talk to me!"

Tony didn't want to die and certainly didn't want another fucking arrow like this sticking out of him, "Yeah, what?" he yelled back.

"Let me help you. Stand up and show yourself. We'll get you to a hospital."

Tesla was back down the rock slope, moving west, heading past the bog and aiming for the trees in behind the campsite. He moved up

231

swiftly, bushes for cover, closing in on the helicopter. Two police officers stood in his way, for now.

Tony struggled but eventually stood up, and raised his hands, "Okay!"

I rose from my nest and had the Vortex trained dead on his chest. "Where's your gun?"

"The other guy took it and left me."

"Start moving down the hill, slow, and keep your hands up. No sudden movements or I'll sink this mother fucker right into your ass, got it?"

Tony could only move slowly. He cursed under his breath, shaking his head, totally stunned that he'd been bested by this bitch.

The helicopter pilot eased the bird closer to the shore, gliding on the pontoons, and then cut the engine. The co-pilot just finished sending a radio message, letting the dispatcher know they were under fire and require assistance.

I heard the first volley of shots and ducked down. *Must be coming from the campsite*, I thought. I yelled at my prisoner, "Hey, asshole! Get down on the ground, spread eagle! Hands out! Do it now!"

Tony gingerly made it down to his left side and flopped over, lying on his back, arms out like an airplane. "Christ," he wailed, "what a fucking mess."

I laid the bow down and took out the revolver, safety off, then approached the goon and searched him. "Where is your gun?"

"I told you, Jerry took it!"

He didn't have a thing on him. "Okay, stay right here. Don't you fucking move!"

I heard more shots; different sounds, must be different guns. Ol' Jerry must be in a fight to get away. I pocketed the gun, picked up my compound bow, and headed for the war zone. I still held on to a little vengeance of my own.

Tesla had missed his opportunity and was now engaged in back-and-forth exchanges with the cops. He had them pinned down but he couldn't move either; he needed the canoe to get out of here. He had to let them move forward then he'd move, swing slightly on a northwest flank, and trap them in the open.

Each of my movements was planned, controlled, and executed in a swift, calculated motion from hide to hide. I watched for the slightest variation of the scene in front of me, looking for any odd colour, shape or shudder in the landscape. I had him in less than ten minutes. Hunkered down, sixty metres to the northwest of my position. I moved in.

"Give it up! We have more police coming! You will not get away!" The two cops were separated by ten metres; no place to go in the mostly open flat of the camp site.

No answer. They had to press forward. They made hand signals, indicating which way, agreed and moved cautiously.

Tesla watched. They were going to come. He moved slightly to his left, slowly, wanting to position himself for the flank, to take them out.

I moved farther west, parallel to the bog and then up into the trees. He was in front of me now; thirty metres at best. I closed the distance and watched him as he moved slightly to the west. He was trying to get around them, to catch them in a more open area.

Tree by tree, hide by hide, slow and easy; twenty metres now, the first one had to count. I scoped in on his back, no hesitation this time. No unfair feelings crept into my soul. Laser on target, I slammed the arrow dead centre. 'Thwack!'

Tesla didn't know what hit him and turned towards my direction as he felt the stabbing pain in his back. He fired wildly, emptying his clip – didn't have a clue. Then he saw a movement but it was too late.

I had cocked and locked already. Popping upright from my squat, scoping him dead centre, I fired another bolt directly into his chest. 'Thwack!' He let out a low guttural wail, staggering in place – the beast fighting until the end. I dropped back down, reefed with all my might and reset the bow, locked in another bolt and popped back up. I fired a third arrow and sunk it directly into his gut. The 'Oomph!' was sickly thick. In slow motion, he drifted down into a ball on the ground.

I stood still, waiting, watching him for any movement. Nothing. Was he playing possum? "Fuck it!" I reset the bow, primed my last arrow left in the quiver, and drove the final bolt into his front chest area. 'Thwack!' No sound or movement from my prey. I moved up and stood over this man who had tried to kill me, handgun trained directly at his head, and I felt nothing. No grief, no joy, no liberation. I was dispassionate; ice cold and heartless. I was changed forever. I wanted to spit on his body but my mouth was dry as a bone.

"Coming out! Don't shoot, coming out!" I left the bow on the ground, pocketed the revolver, raised my hands, and slowly walked forward towards the campsite. "Coming out, don't shoot!" *I really don't want to get shot after all this!*

"Keep your hands up!" The police officers huddled for cover, firearms trained on me. "Are you Elizabeth Stevens?"

"You're damn right I am!"

They stepped from cover, lowered their weapons, and came up to me. "You okay?"

"Yeah I am actually, not a scratch."

"Where are the other guys, the ones sent to kill you?"

"Two are back a bit. Both are dead. One is still in the bush with an arrow in his leg. I think he just wants to get to a hospital."

The two cops just looked at one another, flabbergasted. The pilot said, "You did this? You took three guys out single-handed?"

"I guess I got lucky. My crossbow kinda evened things out. Plus, I had a feeling someone might come at me up here and I planned for it." I was grinning ear to ear.

They just laughed, and told me to stay put. Both cops headed back into the woods to check on the bodies and the other guy.

"You'll hav'ta go back a ways to the southeast to find the one guy still alive." I yelled to them as I collapsed on the ground. "They killed a park ranger too!"

I just laid there like a slug, completely exhausted. The cops buzzed back and forth, finally putting the handcuffed goon about five metres away from me. They radioed for extra personnel and transport for wounded, took pictures of the scene and did other cop stuff. Nothing seemed real.

"Your name is Tony something, isn't it?"

He looked at me with complete contempt. "So?"

"The guys with you, that Olig fellow and the other one … Jerry, what were you thinking coming up here, killing people like that? What the fuck is wrong with you?"

"Fuck you!"

"I don't think so, asshole."

Tony's eyes watered, he was getting mad. He made a half-assed attempt to come at me, growling and then let out a high-pitched scream as his leg buckled. He couldn't get to me even if he wanted to, and he surely wanted to.

I laughed at him, "Big fucking killer dude, eh?"

The cops came back in a hurry, wondering what the fuss was all about. "Everything okay here?"

"Yeah," I said, "Just getting acquainted with the tough guy here."

The cops checked his cuffs. They went back to work, photographing the scene and making notes.

Tony let out another subdued wail, wetness forming in his eyes. I just smiled at the prick.

★ ★ ★

Donny had stayed in his office, right by the phone, waiting on any word. He grabbed it on the first ring. "Jacobs."

He listened for a bit. In a weak voice he said, "Thanks. Appreciate everything you did. Can you give me a few minutes? I'll call back in just a bit, thanks." He hung up the phone and laid his head down on the desk, tears making little plopping sounds as they fell and hit the wood veneer top.

★ ★ ★

The cops pulled out the photos of Olig Steig and Tony Molinara but didn't know who the other dead guy was. "You know this one?" They showed me his picture on the camera screen.

"No, don't recognize his face. But I think his first name is Jerry," I said.

"Okay, some other float planes are coming in. We'll air lift out the bodies and transport this asshole back to medical care."

I asked how they'd found me.

"You know a detective named Jacobs?"

"Yeah."

"He figured it all out and sent us."

Well, well, good ol' Donny to the rescue.

I got questioned about the multiple arrows in the bodies, which was a bit awkward. Overkill maybe, but they seemed satisfied. It was justified homicide, no real question. Even if the one guy had an arrow in his back, he was shooting at cops, for goodness sake.

I led them through it, what happened as best I could. Told them how they shot the park ranger out on the lake, where they would find Adam Milner's body.

We started from the first guy I killed and worked our way back to my perch, showing them where I'd holed up. I found the two shell casings up in my nest and gave those to the cops, along with the other bullets and gun, then gathered up my gear and brought the kayak back over to the site.

Within an hour, two float planes made a pass on the lake, one after the other, gliding atop the water – noisy buggers. Two canoes hovered out on the water; my fellow campers drawn to the excitement, having a great story to share around the campfire tonight.

It was getting darker; not much daylight. I was starving and cold.

"Listen, you need to ride with the first float plane. Toronto Police Services wants you back there, pronto. Detective Jacobs says, and I quote, 'No argument, just get on the fucking plane Liz,' end quote." He was smiling at me. "Nice guy is he?"

"None better!"

I had my camera and two lenses with me, along with my canvas tote, holding the few clothes I'd brought. All the other gear was left, including the knapsack – figured they may need the food and utensils, as it looked like some police were staying late. They made Tony hobble to the plane and climb up into the cabin – no way are the cops about to carry this rat bastard. They did trim the arrow a smidge, using bolt cutters, just to make it easier for him to walk and to fit inside the plane. Tony was heading to a northern hospital, probably relieved as hell to get out alive.

They took my bows away from me. I had had my fill of shooting, at least for a while anyhow. I hopped in the other float plane. Two body bags were in back storage; Olig and Jerry laid quietly, no longer a threat. They would have to come back for Adam, and that just didn't seem right.

The single-engine bush plane roared down Kettle Lake, lifted gently and was off, banking north into the breeze as it gained altitude, then cut around to the south, heading towards Toronto. I hate flying. The western sky was ablaze with a gorgeous sunset, but I didn't even bother with the camera as I was sleeping soundly in minutes.

★ ★ ★

I awoke with the jolt of the plane hitting the runway at the Island Airport in downtown Toronto. I must have had a look of shock on my face. The pilot just said, "Don't worry. There are wheels below the pontoons." I kinda wished the guy had nudged me beforehand so I could shoot some photos of the skyline and lights. Probably never get a better chance for that.

Donny was there to meet me. He wouldn't let go of me, just squished me tight and rocked me back and forth. What a big softy.

"Thanks for not giving up on me big guy," I whispered to him.

I was hustled to a downtown hotel in his police car, ushered into a room by Donny and two other cops, and told not to leave. Room service was available – order what you want.

"I'll be by in the morning. You have to be debriefed. Don't go outside, you are still not safe!" He hugged me again and left. One cop remained outside the door, armed and stern looking.

I jumped in the shower and soaked under the hot water, scrubbed myself clean and afterwards, dressed in a robe from the hotel. Fancy! Looked like the King Edward logo.

I ordered enough for two meals; BLT, chicken with pasta, two carafes of coffee and some dessert. Then I had something sent up for my guard outside.

When the food came, I scarfed it down; everything, every last bit, and all the coffee too. I watched the news channel. Nothing mentioned on today's events up north. It was well after midnight when I hit the sack. Golly the bed felt great!

★ ★ ★

Somebody was poking me.

"Get up lazy ass."

"What time is it?"

"Daytime, now get up!"

Donny was standing over the bed, grinning ear to ear. "I went by your place, got your landlord to pack some clothes. Here." And he tossed a large paper bag at me. "Get dressed. We got a lot of work to do."

"What? No breakfast?"

"We'll go to a drive-thru, get a breakfast of champions."

I dragged my butt into the bathroom and changed into clean underwear, socks, cargos, and a sweater. Brushed my teeth and swished some mouthwash from a little hotel bottle. Ready. Grabbed my camera gear and we left with another cop as security.

★ ★ ★

We entered the police headquarters on College Street through the underground access. I followed Donny through the maze with my egg and sausage sandwich, hash browns, and coffee. *It truly is the breakfast of champions.*

I was ushered into a large boardroom. Donny introduced his colleagues, along with the crown prosecutor and court recorder. We sat, I ate and they peppered me with questions for two straight hours. I gave up my last two camera flash cards which included the one that showed Adam getting killed. They seemed to like that evidence very much.

Donny got a call and left for a few minutes. When he came back, he suggested everyone take a break, leaving us alone in the room.

"We got Tony Molinara here," Donny said in a matter-of-fact voice.

I was a bit shocked. "That was fast. Doesn't he need surgery or something to fix his leg?"

"Well, not if you tell the doctor treating him what he did to people. Sign-off was lightning quick; fit for travel, and away he went." He smiled. He was truly happy. "I had a couple of detectives drive up there late last night and they had him down here about the time you were waking up this morning."

"Did he talk?"

"Oh yeah! Once we got him a lawyer and laid it out, he rolled on everybody, including Gregor Mutznig. We have a warrant and are actively searching for that shit bag right now."

"I'm surprised he gave it up so easily."

Donny just beamed. "He had a choice; life with no parole, or life with a faint-hope clause."

"What's that?" I asked.

"It means after twenty-five years in prison, he could apply for parole. Unfortunately for old Tony, he will either be killed in prison or rot there, because I will ensure he never leaves."

"What about that cop, Savoy? Do we need to find him?"

"That is a non-issue now. Apparently, at least according to Tony, Freddy Savoy is sleeping with the fishes, literally, somewhere up near Orillia. Molinara said Olig killed him, on Gregor's order, and that Jerry Tesla fellow had them dump the body in a quarry."

Donny couldn't keep the smile from his face.

"You're having too much fun Detective Jacobs!"

We had a small lunch catered in as we continued the debriefing. I stuffed my face, pounded back copious amounts of brewed coffee, and indulged in a few sweets.

Donny got some info and shared – turns out that our recently deceased thug, Jerry Tesla, was really known as Jelnik Tesculovic. He was a hitter for hire, bouncing between Toronto and Montreal. One nasty piece of work and everyone was sure glad he was no longer with us.

★ ★ ★

By the time I got out of there, it was 15:00 hours. Since Gregor Mutznig was still on the loose, Donny kept me in the hotel, under lock and key. Armed cop at the door.

He left me there. He said the tab would be picked up by the prosecutor's office so I should abuse the shit out of the room service and mini-bar. Since you must always follow a police officer's direction, I did exactly that. I made sure my cop outside was looked after too! I'm just generous that way.

I was having fun, watching TV and eating extravagant menu items, but after the second day, I was starting to get squirrelly. I was just about to hop in the shower when the knock came – probably the cop wanting to use the bathroom again. I peeked through the hole. It was Donny.

"Hey buddy, c'mon in." I was dying for company, someone to talk to, or anything to relieve the boredom.

He had brought me more clothes and some toiletries from my apartment.

"How are you making out? Is life tough living in a hotel, or what?"

"Truth be told, my friend, I've kinda had enough. What's the word on the Mutt?"

Donny shook his head, "Nothing so far. Its early days, be patient, we'll get him."

My confidence was not bolstered. "Really? Is this necessary, staying here?"

"Yes! No more chances like up north. You stay put! I'll cuff you to the toilet if need be."

He wasn't joking.

"Hey! I brought you a present." Donny pulled out a bottle of Cardhu.

We cracked it open and had a snort.

"Great, this will last me a few days then what?"

Donny just smiled and finished his drink. "Listen, gotta go, I will check in later. Call me if you need anything." He just stared at me for a few moments with that silly grin of his.

"What?" I was getting annoyed with him, company or not.

He shrugged and left.

That was strange. I got into the shower and scalded myself for about fifteen minutes. Changed into clean track pants and a T and came out of the bathroom. The lights were off? My heart stopped. There was someone in my bed.

"Hello?" It squeaked out of me like a mouse.

"I missed you."

"Janet! Christ you almost gave me a heart attack! What are you doing here?"

"I'm lying naked in your bed. Do you want me to draw pictures?"

"I thought we … ah, screw it!" I hopped into bed and snuggled up to her. She was naked too!

"Donny said you were getting bored so I thought I might come over and entertain you."

"He did, did he? That sly dog!"

I planted a kiss on her that made my toes curl. Then we did things that I could only dream of.

★ ★ ★

The next morning, the phone rang and I crawled over Janet and yanked the annoying sucker off the hook. "Hello!"

"Hey, it's me, Donny. Are you guys decent?"

"No and I don't plan to be for quite some time, thank you."

"Well too bad. Wrap a sheet around her because I'm coming up. Got big news. Bye."

Donny didn't even bother to knock, just let himself in with the pass card. He was bouncing off the walls, all excited. "We got him!"

I looked at him, bleary eyed, "Who?"

"Mutznig! Who else dummy."

"When? How?"

"He was trying to cross the border at Niagara Falls. Got into a shoot-out with the border cops and they took him out. He's dead!"

"You seemed pleased with that outcome, Detective."

"Damn straight! A couple of bucks in bullets compared to millions in a trial – I'll take that trade-off for that puke, any day!"

"Hi Donny." Janet's eyes were peering just over the covers.

"Oh, hey Janet. How's it going?"

We all just broke into uncontrolled laughter and couldn't stop for several minutes.

★ ★ ★

We couldn't stay in the room any longer. Vacate by noon. "Not really justified since the threat is gone," Donny said.

Janet had a shower as I packed up. Donny said the cop stationed at the door would drive us home.

"I'll see what I can do about getting you back up north, if you still want to go."

I thought for a bit. I still had two weeks of holidays…paid. It didn't seem right somehow, all of what had happened in just one week. Felt a lot longer. "Yup, anything you can do. I'll go for at least another week since I still have to get my gear, the kayak, and car."

"Okay, I'll call when I've got something arranged. See you later."

With that, Donny was gone. Janet was still in the shower. I decided to go see if I could extend bath time.

★ ★ ★

The cop dropped off Janet first, swung around to my digs, and I was standing in my apartment at 13:30 hours on Wednesday September 11th. *Too weird*, I thought. What a week.

The dogs came scrambling across the floor overhead and bounded down to my side. I dropped down onto the ground and played with them, cookies given in between tussles and scruggles. I needed this normality in an awful way, after what had happened. This is the best therapy ever.

I started a wash load of clothes. If Donny was going to get me back up north, then I had to start planning what I'd need, so that was next on my agenda. Then it hit me. "Those pricks have all my flash cards for the cameras!" I called Donny – no way was I going to buy yet more memory cards! Donny said he would get them all back and call me first thing in the morning, as he would have a ride sorted. I charged my camera batteries and cleaned the lenses.

Laundry dried and folded. I was beat. It is one of the best feelings ever, when you've been away sleeping rough or in an odd bed, to come home to your own mattress. Bliss! I was out like a light.

★ ★ ★

Wide awake at 06:00 hours, I checked the cell phone but no messages. I had coffee, no milk though and thought of roughing it, then heard my land barons scurrying around above me and decided to beg for some whitener.

Donny called at 08:00 hours. "I'm out front, let me in. I've got a ride for you."

He came in with a few bags in tow. "Your flash cards madam." And he handed over all of them, the four from before I left on holidays and the two new ones.

I stashed the two that fit the other camera and loaded one for the camera I'd take back with me. It was blank, so I formatted the card and was set. The others went inside a plastic box and then a zippered pocket of the camera bag. I guessed I would never see the photos I'd taken from this trip. *Spilt milk.*

"Now listen, I'm only giving your bows and shit back if you promise not to pull another Rambo. Promise me? The cops that brought Tony back had scooped up everything else, jurisdiction be damned."

After I placed them in the office, I held up my three fingers, "I give you my solemn oath Occifer Jacobs," and giggled.

"Smart ass! You ready to go?"

I was and we took off, hopped in his car, and started driving south.

"Ah big guy, the park is north. Kinda going the wrong way aren't ya?"

"You don't honestly believe that I would drive all the way up there, do you?"

We arrived at the Island Airport at the foot of Bathurst. Donny carried my stuff to the ferry crossing, dropped the gear at my feet and gave me a hug.

"Call me when you get back."

"What, I'm getting Porter to fly me there?"

"No, the pilot that brought you down has agreed to take you back up. I thought you would be a bit more gracious about it."

I gave him a big bear hug. "You are the best!" I grabbed my gear and headed to the gate for the ferry. Turning back quickly, I shouted, "Hey Donny, thanks again for saving my life!"

"Now you owe me dinner at Cyrano's," he said, pointing at me with a finger waggle.

The pilot met me at the terminal, took my belongings and walked me out to the bush plane. "I'll have you there before noon," he said.

★ ★ ★

We flew over Kettle Lake to make sure it was clear for landing and I could see my site; tent still there as was the kayak. It was a scary landing for me but the pilot, John, didn't seem at all phased.

The float plane idled towards shore and I was able to hop out on the front of the pontoon and avoid the water. John handed me my gear and a few other bags.

"What's in here?"

"Just a few odds and ends," he said. "Have a great trip."

He pushed off from the shore, making it look easy, and the sturdy plane drifted backwards out onto the lake. The engine fired up and he circled, pointing west towards the mild wind and hammered the throttle. The blow-back from the propeller could knock you over. He was gone in mere seconds.

Everything looked as it should, sans the dead bodies, and I started to get organized. The sleeping bag was in the tent, along with the mat – tent seemed secure. I noticed a nice pile of wood by the fire pit and wandered over. It was all cut real nice and stacked up. My knapsack was hanging in the trees like I would normally have it, even a plastic bag over it. I brought it down and checked all the food and supplies, just as I left them. *Excellent!*

I rummaged around one of the bags John had left me and found a selection of canned food and a note. 'Rambo. How do you eat that other shit? Serpico.' I broke out laughing and just about fell over. Who else but Donny? What a gem. Then, more – the other bag was crammed with tissue paper and I eventually yanked out a bottle of Cardhu. This note simply read 'Enjoy!'

Coming Soon

Deadly Selection

As stated in the beginning, this book mirrors my actual life. Consequently, you may have surmised that the author is transgender, having had sex re-assignment surgery some fifteen odd years ago.

Jeepers!

CPSIA information can be obtained at www.ICGtesting.com
Printed in the USA
LVOW11s0859110914

403468LV00004B/11/P